They Dream
in
DARKNESS

ROBIN L. TURNER

PAGE PUBLISHING, INC.
New York, NY

First originally published by Page Publishing, Inc. 2015

ISBN 978-1-63417-962-1 (pbk)
ISBN 978-1-63417-963-8 (digital)

Printed in the United States of America

Contents

To Mekia Mouse. Remember, we all have choices.
Row, row, row your boat,
Gently down the stream.
Merrily, merrily, merrily, merrily,
Life is but a dream.

PART 1

---⚜---

The Insomnia

The worst thing in the world is to try to sleep
and not to.

—F. Scott Fitzgerald

Chapter 1

The Kidnapping and Mom

> There is no greater agony than bearing an untold story inside you.
>
> —Maya Angelou

The Kidnapping—Age 5

Anna's spiritless existence on earth remained bleak at best. Audrey had lost two before her, so Anna's chances of survival were dismal. Audrey's thoughts were echoes from a postpartum dream. *Please let my baby live,* Audrey prayed. One pound two ounces marked Anna's weight at birth. The ruler used to measure her length had room to spare. A glass box protected Anna from the outside world. "How long will my baby be in the incubator?" Audrey asked the doctor through the hospital face mask. She slipped her hands through the cut-out round holes and into the protective gloves. Audrey rubbed Anna's pencil-thin arm ever so lightly. "I'm not sure," the doctor stated. "Depends on how fast she gains weight. She needs to be at least four pounds." The doctor checked Anna's vitals before he left the neonatal ICU room.

"I hate you have all these tubes coming out of your body. You look like a science fair project," Audrey said to Anna, who had yet to open her eyes to the world. "How can you sleep with all these noisy machines beeping around you?" Audrey questioned her baby. She looked around the room and noticed three other mothers dressed like her in blue isolation gowns.

"These things are so hot," Audrey mentioned to one mother whose eyes were bloodshot red.

"Yeah, they are." The mother's words barely squeaked out.

"She probably won't live past the age of three." The doctor's warning suggested that Audrey not get too attached to Anna. "And if for some reason she does live, she won't have the mental capacity to complete school." The doctor's prognosis didn't deter Audrey. Her other two children stayed at the house while she held a prayer vigil at the hospital. Audrey prayed to God to spare her daughter.

Anna celebrated her fifth birthday at the hospital. There were no balloons or streamers. The only celebratory whistles came from her mom's breathing machine, monitoring her stability. Anna's sister Virginia found their mom slumped over the kitchen table and called for the paramedics.

"Your cancer is back again," the doctors openly revealed in front of her kids. *That's not a good birthday present,* Anna thought. Anna's siblings began to cry, so Anna cried too, not fully understand the severity of the statement.

"Don't talk about my health while my babies are in the room," her mom demanded. The doctor turned on his heels and abruptly walked away, without a mere apology.

"Everything is going to be OK. Come give Mommy a hug." Audrey gathered her kids around her in the hospital bed. Anna climbed on the bed, since she was the smallest, and snuggled in her arms.

"Don't cry, Mommy," Anna pleaded as her small hands wiped the tears from mom's face.

"Mr. Doug can take care of us like he did before," Virginia suggested as she squeezed Anna's hand. She was sixteen and more independent than her siblings.

"Sorry you had to spend your birthday in the hospital," Audrey said as tears filled her eyes again.

"It's OK, Mommy," Anna lied. She didn't want to hurt her mommy's feelings.

Her live-in boyfriend, Doug, watched the children during her previous cancer treatments. "Doug. Come visit me please," Audrey called him on the hospital phone. The nurses propped her up in the hospital bed while awaiting Doug's visit.

"My cancer is back," she blurted out as soon as he sat down. *No need for pleasantries,* she thought. Audrey and Doug had a falling out weeks before, and he threatened to move out for good this time. Their on-again, off-again relationship had ended four months earlier, but they wanted to work on getting back together.

"I didn't sign up for this. You keep dragging me back into your sickness. I took care of your kids before because you begged me. I'm not doing it again," he lamented as he abruptly headed toward the door, never once looking back.

"I want your stuff out of my house when I get home," she said to the back of Doug's head. Audrey lay in the bed too feeble to fight or cry. *I can't waste my tears on him,* she convinced herself. *Someone has to take my children.*

Stage 4 cancer confined her to a hospital bed. Audrey was weak and needed someone she trusted to tend to her children. Her best friend, June Calloway, verbally agreed to take her daughters until the doctors deemed her strong enough to be back on her feet. Her son Michael was whisked away to live with Audrey's brother, who resided in a different state.

At age five, Anna lacked the capacity to grasp why she needed to move with these strangers. Her mom put it in simple terms for Anna to understand.

"Mommy can't take care of you right now, and Mr. Doug has something else to do. The Calloways are my friends. They will take good care of you until I get better," Audrey convinced herself and Anna. Anna was reminded that Virginia would be staying there as well.

"OK, Mommy. I love you." Anna gave her mom a bear hug. Her mom started to cry, which made Anna cry. Anna told her to get well quick because she was going to miss her. Her mom wept for hours after Anna left.

—⊗⊗⊗—

Reverend and Mrs. Calloway took in other kids before. The Calloways tried unsuccessfully for years to have children of their own and used foster kids to fill the noticeable void in their life. Reverend Calloway mandated everyone who resided in the house to attend church on Sundays and participate in Bible study every Wednesday without excuse. Reverend Calloway strutted around the house quoting Bible passages about sin and obedience. He had an unchallenged supremacy. These self-proclaimed Christians added Bible reading as a daily chore for all who lived there as well. Bibles littered the house. Pocket-size New Testaments Bibles lay in the bathroom in case the Lord called at the exact same time as Mother Nature. The walls donned iconic pictures of Jesus.

Greeting guests as they opened the front door was a hanging Jesus in all white with a red sash draped over his left shoulder. His right hand held up the two fingers showing peace, while his left hand pointed to his heart asking for love. A velvet painting of Jesus holding a lamb stared at anyone who used the bathroom. A record player kept the gospel music blasting from sunrise to sunset. Religious ornaments and relics overpowered the house and squeezed out all the love. The wooded tabletop crosses displayed in the house were devoid of Jesus, as if he knew something eerie roamed the house and he vacated the premises. The pictures of Jesus remained stuck on the wall, unable to escape. The Calloways were so religious, they forgot their religion.

Anna cried every night for weeks, using her thumb as a makeshift pacifier. She longed for her mommy. Her mind drifted to her own bed where Audrey would tuck her in and gently kiss her forehead. The sight of Reverend Calloway's face made her quiver like a mouse in a snake pit. She asked several times to talk to her mommy, but they outright refused.

"Your mother is too busy to talk to you," they convinced her.

"But I miss her," Anna replied in a whinny voice that irritated Mrs. Calloway.

"Stop all that baby talk. Ain't no babies in this house," June shut Anna down.

Anna and her sister shared a small room upstairs. Anna slept in the twin-size bed, while her sister was subjected to the rollaway bed.

"This bed hurts my back," her sister complained. Most nights, Anna noticed a shadow lurking behind their bedroom door.

"Daddy's at the door," Anna informed her sister several nights a week.

"Don't call him that. He ain't our daddy."

The Calloways insisted all the children who lived there call them Mom and Daddy. "Well, he always says," Anna mimicked Reverend Calloway's throaty voice, "Children, obey your parents in the Lord, for this is right. Honor your father and mother." Her sister laughed at Anna's impression, but remained determined not to address him as daddy.

"I know who my daddy is, and it ain't him," her sister said as she turned away from Anna and mentally plotted her escape. Anna pulled the covers over her face in a failed attempt to hide from Reverend Calloway. She never knew who her real daddy was and feared the one forced on her.

Virginia ran away after a month. She claimed she was running an errand after Wednesday's Bible study and never returned. Anna didn't get a chance to say good-bye or to beg to go with her. The

Sunday night after Anna's sister abandoned her was when Reverend Calloway made his move.

Anna flinched when a heavy presence weighed her bed down. She froze. She started to scream, but he clamped his meaty hand down over her mouth. The pointer finger on his free hand motioned *shhh*. He slowly inched close to her, never removing his hand from her mouth. Her tears wet his hand. He pushed her tiny hand down his pin-striped pajama pants to grab his flaccid penis. He put his free hand over hers to show how to fondle it. He was erect immediately. His lips, wet with saliva, whispered in her ear that if she tattled, he was going to hurt her mom. She tried to look away, but his hand forced her to watch. It was like exchanging stares with a statue. Together their hands stroked his penis until he came in his pajama bottoms. Anna was sure it was pee, even though it didn't smell like pee. He left the room as quietly as he entered. Anna cried herself to sleep, unaware she gave her daddy a hand job. Whatever it was, Anna didn't like the sticky residue he left on her hand. She crept out of bed to wash her hands.

Every night, Reverend Calloway's desire for Anna grew, and he became more aggressive. By the middle of the week, oral sex replaced the hand jobs. He shoved it in her mouth while it was soft. He grabbed the back of her tiny head with both hands covering her ears. His thrusting penis stabbed the back of her throat while he moaned with unabated pleasure. Tears slid down her cheeks. He stopped when Anna's gagging sounded as if she were going to throw up. "Next time I'ma cum in there," he promised her as he lightly tapped her cheek. Reverend Calloway fingered her private parts before he left. Afterward she cried herself to sleep, half-suffocated by his triumph. She was scared he would hurt her mom if she told.

Friday night, he snuck into Anna's room. Anna noticed it was already standing at attention. *Maybe I won't have to put it in my mouth,* she sighed with comfort. Reverend Calloway pinned Anna down on the bed. He used one hand to reach inside her private parts. She was a squirming fly caught in his web.

"Keep still," he demanded. He lay his heavy body on top of her and stuck it in her private area, clamping his hand down on her mouth because he knew she would scream. Anna was hurt and couldn't breathe. He grunted and moaned while his penis probed her private area. After what seemed like forever, her daddy let out an "Ahhhh" before he collapsed on top of her already fragile body. He rolled over and Anna noticed a wet spot intermingled with blood on her sheets. She knew she needed to say something to his wife.

Early that next morning, Anna walked to the kitchen and stared at Mrs. Calloway for an eternity before she spoke. "Mom. I gotta tell you something." Mrs. Calloway sat the kitchen table drinking her coffee. She shook the open newspaper to remind Anna she was not to be bothered at this time. Anna called her name three times before she looked up from her paper.

"Mom, I gotta tell you something very important," she continued. "Daddy did something to me I didn't like." She paused. She forced the next words out of her mouth. "He made me touch his stuff and put it in my mouth. He put it in me and it hurt." The blood on her bedsheets confirmed her story.

June dropped the newspaper on the table. She leaned in so close that Anna smelled the coffee on her breath. "If you don't stop telling lies about my husband," she snarled through her gritted teeth. "This man is a pastor. A man of God. We take you in our home and you tell lies. You know what happens to little girls that lie, don't you?" Anna stood with a look of confusion. She was sure she wasn't lying. It did happen. Her sore private areas ached in agreement. She repeated the story in case she left something out.

She watched as June left the kitchen and returned with the iron. She plugged it in next to the coffeemaker. After a few minutes, she held in the iron in her hand and tested the temperature on her finger. She grabbed Anna by the arm to reprimand her. There's a punishment when you lie.

"Take off your gown," she demanded. Mrs. Calloway grabbed the collar of Anna's nightgown and pulled it off her as Anna attempted to flee. She pulled Anna, now in just her underwear, toward the hot iron.

"I'm not lying!" Anna hollered the first time the hot iron met her back. The smell of cooked flesh nauseated her.

"I'm not lying. I'm not lying. I'm no—" The iron burned her back again. The screams echoed in the kitchen. "I promise I won't say it again," she pleaded. "I promise. I promise. I'm sorry. I'm sorry."

As Anna tried to get up from the floor, she glanced over and noticed her daddy at the doorway. He witnessed everything. The smirk on his face solidified the green light to continue raping a five-year-old child. She begged Mrs. Calloway to give her something for the pain. June refused to give Anna ointment to treat her burns. Anna wore loose shirts for weeks.

She learned to become a light sleeper at an early age. He would come into her room at any hour of the night. Anna stayed awake until he came in to rape her, then she would continue to weep until she fell asleep. She lay facing the door with eyes wide open, so he wouldn't scare her. When she noticed his shadow against the wall, she started trembling. She knew it was only a matter of moments before his heavy body would be lying on her, grunting and moaning. Her body drew into itself every time it crossed her mind. The nights he didn't come to the room, she was exhausted and fatigued after staying up waiting for him.

By the second grade, Anna started getting her period. Her initial conclusion was her daddy did it too hard and it made her bleed again. She stopped bleeding after a week of sex with her daddy. She cringed as she recalled the first time he did it and she did bleed. However, this time it was different. June never talked to Anna about a period. She didn't talk to Anna about anything. Anna's teacher eventually called Mrs. Calloway when Anna came to school on the third day with no pads or a change of clothes. The teacher insisted she get Anna checked out because she noticed Anna scratching her privates.

A checkup at the doctor's office revealed Anna contracted a sexually transmitted disease. Mrs. Calloway's face lowered when she heard the news. She darted her eyes at Anna with a glare so scary that Anna bowed her head in shame and silently sobbed.

"Anna is fast," June informed the doctor without missing a beat. Anna sat, too terrified to tell the doctor that she was not fast enough to get away from her daddy.

"An eight-year-old should not have an STD." The doctor looked concerned. Mrs. Calloway told artful and animated lies about Anna's indiscretions until the doctor believed her.

"I told her if she didn't stop, this was going to happen," June concluded. The doctor saw the signs of sexual abuse, and yet he didn't report it. "I'll take care of her when she gets home." Anna knew what that meant.

That evening after dinner, Mrs. Calloway plugged up the iron. "This is because you embarrassed me at the doctor's office," she claimed as she burned Anna's leg. "Stop drawing attention to yourself," June said as she waved the iron threatening to burn Anna's face. "Now stop all that crying and wash these dishes." June demanded as she unplugged the iron and put it away.

Anna desperately prayed for God to get her back to her real mom. She rubbed baby oil on her burns that night before bed. For years, the smell of baby oil made her gag.

Birth Mom

"First thing I'm going to do when I get out of here is get my children," a beaming Audrey stated to her nurse. Audrey's doctor said her cancer was in remission.

"You can go home tomorrow," the doctor announced. Three days later, she had all her children back except for Anna.

"Well, where she is?" Audrey questioned Reverend Calloway on the phone. He claimed he hadn't seen his wife in a few days. "I need my daughter back."

"I don't know what to tell you," Reverend Calloway expressed before he abruptly hung up the phone.

June was unwilling to relinquish Anna to Audrey. June changed her phone number after Reginald said Audrey had phoned several times. June's mother hid Anna at her house for months. Audrey stopped by the house several times, but Reginald insisted June was not home.

"I know she's there. I just want Anna back. After that, I will leave you alone. I promise," Audrey begged with tears rolling down her cheeks. Reginald refused to provide Audrey with any information on Anna or June.

"I can't help you," Reginald said as she slammed the door in her face. A dejected June collapsed on the front steps of the Calloways' house and wailed.

"I just want my daughter back!" she howled like a wounded animal, hoping someone would rescue her. Her son jumped out of the waiting car and raced toward his mom. His preteen arms engulfed her frail, shaking body. Audrey's head nuzzled in his chest as tears saturated his T-shirt.

"We'll find her, Mom," he claimed as he rocked his mom back and forth to console her. The role of comforter and child now reversed. They sat on the steps for what seemed like an eternity. June tried for years to reclaim her daughter, to no avail. Anna was as intangible as a pipe dream.

Mrs. Calloway changed Anna's birth certificate to Anna Calloway. The Calloways threatened Anna with violence and rape if she mentioned what happened in their home. They managed to brainwash Anna into believing that all the bad things done to her were her own fault.

"Think for a moment. Why did your mom get your brother and sister, but not you?" June questioned Anna. Anna didn't know what to think, at nine years old. She knew she missed her mom and her family and wanted desperately to be with them. This unwelcome thought made Anna cry even harder.

———∞———

The doctors diagnosed Anna's birth mom with cancer for a third time in late August. Audrey grew weary of fighting and arranged to die in the hospital alone. Leave this earth quieter than when she came in. She checked on her kid's progress. Not knowing how Anna was doing ate away at her more than the cancer did. Audrey hadn't seen Anna in four years. Mrs. Calloway called twice and convinced her that Anna was fine.

"I'm dying, June. I need to see my Anna. Don't take this away from me," Audrey pleaded.

"I'll call you later." Mrs. Calloway hung up the phone before Audrey could ask any questions.

Her birth mom's oldest sister was the only one allowed at the hospital. *She looks so helpless lying there,* Cora thought every time she stood outside her sister's door. *Don't cry in front of her,* Cora told herself before she entered the room.

"Hey, sis." Cora masked her sadness as she bounced toward her sister's makeshift coffin. Audrey lay in her hospital bed, weighing less than a hundred pounds. Cora brought Bible scriptures and daily news about her kids to help lighten the mood.

Cora needed to tell her younger sister something and didn't know how. Cora grabbed Audrey's weak hand from the hospital bed and rubbed it. "Something bad has been going on with Anna." Cora's words wept out. Her sister, too weak to move, sat straight up in the bed. Cora told her about Anna's birth certificate. She reluctantly told her all she knew about Reverend Calloway and a few uncles molesting Anna.

"I heard this at church." Cora overheard this babbling gossip a few Sundays ago. "I didn't want to tell you, but I thought you needed to know."

Audrey turned her face away from Cora and never said a word. Cora stayed and rubbed her hand and tried to talk, but Audrey refused to make eye contact. As Cora leaned in to kiss her good-bye, she noticed her pillowcase baptized with tears. Cora instantly regretted sharing this news with Audrey. She buzzed the nurse to bring her a new pillowcase.

"I'll be back later on this evening to check on you."

"Uh huh," Audrey faintly replied.

She died later that afternoon. Her death certificate listed the cause of death as cardiac arrest. "We expected her to live two to three more months with her cancer," The doctors told Cora when they called her to let her know Audrey had died. They were stunned she died from a heart attack. Cora knew the news of Anna is what broke her heart.

The Calloways didn't want Anna to attend her mom's funeral. They feared her birth family would try to take Anna back. They never feared Anna would talk. They beat the desire out of her. She was passively obedient. Anna overheard June on the phone when she received the news that Audrey passed away. Anna pleaded with Mrs. Calloway to let her go to the funeral.

"I need to see my mommy one last time," Anna cried out. June now had a baby of her own, Mallory.

"I am not taking my own child to someone else's funeral." June scoffed at the idea.

Cora stopped by the house a few days before the funeral. She convinced June that Anna needed to see her mother. "You took Anna away from her mother. Don't deny her this. That is not the Christian way to do things," Cora said.

"I'll think about it," June said as she opened the front door, letting Cora know she needed to leave.

The funeral was over, and Audrey's body was at the cemetery by the time the Calloways arrived at the church. They made no rush to get to the funeral. Once the car stopped, Anna jumped out and ran toward the grave site. Her mom's casket was sealed, and the service was almost over. She had an obstructed view of the casket because of the many family members there to bid her a final good-bye. Anna gave her mom a wordless farewell.

June grabbed Anna by the arm before she got any closer. "You better stop acting like this, or we will take you home," June scolded. Reverend Calloway stood at the car, holding Mallory.

"I didn't even get a chance to say good-bye to her. I don't know how she looked." Anna wailed. "What was she wearing?" Anna asked out loud.

"I don't know," June said. "A dress, I guess." Anna fell to the ground and wept. She cried a river, with streams flowing down her reddened cheeks onto the sagging collar of her white shirt.

Anna hated the last memory she had of her mom. She visited her two weeks before she died. The Calloways brought Anna to the hospital after being threatened. Audrey was weak. She lay in the hospital bed with tubes coming out of various parts of her body and machines buzzing all around her. Anna was unaware that her mom mirrored Anna when she was born.

Anna needed to ask her family why her mom never came back for her. Why did her mom rescue others but not her? The Calloways refused Anna access to her siblings after the funeral. Family members who attempted to speak to Anna were shooed away. Between tears, Anna begged to speak to her aunts and uncles.

"They are my family. Why can't I talk to them?" Anna cried out. The Calloways whisked Anna away to the car before she got any answers. Anna's eyes were swollen shut by the time she made it home.

"You look ugly. Go wash your face," June demanded. Anna lumbered up the steps, almost falling twice. Tears blocked her view.

She took a shower, attempting to wash the anger off, but it didn't work. Anna cried herself to sleep again. *God please help me*, Anna prayed. *God please help me. I said it again 'cause I don't think you're listening to me.* Anna felt more alone than she had in years. Her birth mom died knowing only part of the endless abuse Anna would suffer.

Chapter 2

High School Hell

Childhood should be carefree, playing in the sun; not living a nightmare in the darkness of the soul.

—Dave Pelzer

Anna memorized the only poster hanging on the yellow concrete walls in the guidance counselor's office. A tiny gray kitten managed to get itself stuck in a tree. Its little paws gripped the upper branch for dear life. The tail wrapped around the lower branch, and those helpless blue eyes made Anna want to climb into the poster to save the kitten. "Hang in there" is all it said. "I'm trying," she mumbled, frowning at the poster. College was a mere two years away. Too long for Anna to continue to suffer, she feared. "Hang in there," the kitten reminded her. The tears wanted to slide down her face, but crying would lead to questions, so she refused to allow them to fall.

"So what brings you in today Anna?" Her deep, heavy voice forced Anna back in her chair unintentionally. She was lost in the kitten's eyes when Ms. Beachum spoke. She sipped from her white 1982 World's Fair coffee cup and waited for a response. Her woodsy smell overpowered the coffee. She smelled as if a cigar was her lunchtime dessert.

"I need a job," Anna replied with desperation. Ms. Beachum's manly demeanor didn't diminish her compassion for children. Her words, although forceful in tone, were comforting and supportive. Ms. Beachum was every student's cheerleader. She attended all their after-school activities. She chaperoned on the buses for away games.

"You're already on the basketball team, you sing in the chorus, and you're on the flag team. Where are you going to fit a job into all of this?" she asked with concern. Anna didn't remind her she also ran cross-country and participated in any after school activity she could. Anna went skydiving one weekend with her JROTC program so she wouldn't be home.

"I wanna go to college," Anna blurted out. "I am going to need money for school," she continued.

"So what are you interested in doing, what type of job?"

Anna glanced over at the poster and responded, "I wanna work with animals." Anna grinned at the kitten.

A few weeks later, an animal shelter informed her of her new job. Her summer vacation job would be working as a junior veterinarian assistant. Anna called her best friend, Vickie, with the news. She kept her excitement to a minimum because worshipping money was a sin in her house. In addition, if her family knew she was in possession of money, they would steal it from her again.

Anna and Vickie met in first grade. The teacher called roll and said "Victoria Johnson." "It's Vickie," Vickie replied giving the teacher the business. Anna was impressed. Vickie sat down next to her on the bus, and an instant friendship developed. Anna was slow to share some of her secret with Vickie. In the past, people Anna thought she could trust betrayed her. Vickie lived in the land of no secrets. She grew up with three sisters and four brothers. She knew that if no one fessed up, they all got in trouble. Vickie longed to be more reserved like Anna. Vickie's bluntness often kept her in trouble.

Anna wanted Vickie's boldness. If Vickie didn't like something, the whole world knew. This symbiotic friendship would last for years.

She hustled and bustled even quieter in the house, catching the five-thirty bus to work. Anna tiptoed around the house unnecessarily. The Calloways' snoring traveled through two closed doors. She neatly packed her McDonald's uniform in her book bag the night before. Four hours a night, she took orders and made fries. She grabbed her lunch before she locked the door from the inside and raced toward the bus stop. She slept for an hour straight on the bus that took her directly to the train station. On the train, she slept another hour most mornings. From the train she caught a ten-minute bus to the animal shelter.

The odor of the animals became the smell of freedom. These days Anna dared to dream. The seemly small building housed thirty to forty animals weekly. Everyone who came to the shelter marveled at the largeness of the facility. Anna claimed this as a second home. She smiled at no one in particular as she clocked in and started her daily routine. The animals' names were nicely labeled on each cage, but Anna knew every animal's name by heart and talked to them as she cleaned out their kennels.

On her second week, she witnessed a cat being put to sleep. Max contracted feline cancer and writhed in immense pain.

"Doc, she fainted." An assistant helped Anna up from the floor. Anna didn't remember fainting.

"Is he gone?" she asked about Max as smelling salt was waved under her nose. Anna fantasized about how much easier her life would be if someone put her out of her misery too. She remembered admiring how peaceful Max's expression was after it was over. It was an odd but understandable jealously. She ached for freedom, like walking a mile in tight shoes.

Anna's coworkers treated her like family. Every Friday, they convened in the break room and had a potluck lunch. Everyone sat as a family and laughed as they discussed some of the crazy antics the animals did during the week. She managed to let her guard down a little. Her coworkers kept the conversations going, which kept Anna off the hook for any major talking. Nobody ever pressured her. Her coworkers accepted her shyness. Feeling accepted gave Anna more motivation to work.

Anna had been working a month when her boss pulled her to the side. He noticed her youthful ambition. "I admire your work ethic. You come to work on time, and you are good at what you do. I want to promote you to senior vet assistant." He also said the promotion included a small raise. Anna politely accepted the complement as well as the promotion. He also asked her to work there once high school started back in the fall.

"That will be fine. I can only work a few days a week because of my school schedule," Anna told him.

After her shifts, Anna used the bathroom sink to erase the smell of animal from her body. She brushed her teeth and threw on her street clothes. She made the mistake once of wearing her uniform on the bus. Some passengers recognized the golden arches on her solid red front shirt with red pinstripes on the sleeves. A few insisted Anna provide free food for them, so she stopped wearing it. She stuffed the smelly work clothes in her book bag, grabbed her lunch kit, and quickly left. If she didn't leave the shelter on time, she would have to wait thirty minutes for the next bus. She couldn't afford to lose money by being late for work.

Anna kept track of every dime she made and spent. She knew the Calloways refused to support her financially. Mallory went shopping almost every weekend. Mrs. Calloway bought Mallory the newest designer clothes and expensive snacks for Mallory's lunch. She only cooked the food Mallory liked and sometimes didn't make enough for Anna. Anna had sleep for dinner the nights the family went to fancy restaurants. They left Anna home alone because Mallory insisted that Anna didn't deserve to eat with them.

She kept nonperishable food in her room for the nights she grew tired of McDonald's food. Anna depended on her work money for clothes, school supplies, and transportation. Her bus pass allowed unlimited travel for a small monthly fee. It boggled her mind to understand that if the Calloways had money, then why would someone steal money from her bedroom? Hurt by another betrayal, Anna moved her money to her granny's house. Although it took an hour to get there, she knew for sure her money was safe.

Anna's teammates called her half-pint. Without wearing pumps, she stood a measly five feet and three inches. Sexual abuse from Reverend Calloway allowed her eight-year-old body to resemble a teenager. Her breasts and curves made uncles and cousins forget she was a child. Her slow mental capacity didn't deter them from molesting and raping her. Playing sports kept her away from her dad at night. Anna's determination to stay away from the house was mistaken for loyalty. She remained the only player who never missed a day of practice or a game, one of the reasons for her award.

Anna stopped by her granny's house with the news. She took two buses and walked two blocks to get there. She was winning two awards in basketball and one in chorus. Granny enjoyed Anna reliving her basketball games. Granny didn't drive and worked most nights Anna played. She replayed the moments in the games when she scored her points. She didn't played very often, but always gave it her all.

"One day I am going to come watch my baby play."

"You don't have to, Granny, I know you work." Anna secretly wanted someone from her family to see her play.

"Vickie and I are dressing alike," she told her granny. Her best friend came up with the idea of them both wearing pink and white. "We can go to the mall later this week and pick out the dresses," Vickie said with glee when she called Anna. Anna walked to back room where she hid her money. She counted out one hundred dollars in twenties. When she walked back to the front of the house, she noticed her granny's purse on the sofa.

"This will help you buy a nice dress for the banquet," Granny said as she shoved fifty dollars into Anna's hand.

"Granny, I can't take this," Anna insisted. Her granny guided Anna to the front door and closed it on Anna before she could give the money back to her. Anna strutted to the bus stop, clutching her purse.

The awards banquet continued to be the talk of the locker room. All sports activities and the school year was quickly ending. Anna's teammates were excited about their parents coming to the banquet. "Coach said there was going to be tables in the front with name tags for our parents to sit," one of her teammates said. Coaches and fine arts teachers went all out to honor the students for their hard work and to thank the parents for the sacrifices they made as well. Everyone getting an award received a letter to give to their parents, so they could share in this special occasion.

"I ain't got no money for nothing you wanna do," June huffed. Anna tried to hand the letter to Mrs. Calloway who didn't even glance at it.

"It's no money. They are having a banquet and I am getting an award," Anna stated. "They want the parents to show up. You get free food."

"I'll try to make it."

Anna's heart skipped a beat. June never said she would try to do anything when it came to Anna. Anna remained determined to get her family to love and support her.

"You didn't even ask when it was," Anna questioned her. June shot her a look, and Anna retreated upstairs to her room.

Anna spent a little longer in the shower than usual the night of the banquet. She wanted to look her best and not embarrass June. Two hours before the banquet started gave enough time for them to drive to the high school and get a good parking spot. Anna came downstairs wearing her new pink skirt and pressed white blouse. Her granny brought her a new pair of black pumps. She frantically searched each room, but the house was empty. In the time it took her to get ready, the entire family left her home alone again. She frowned at the clock as she ran back upstairs to grab her sweater and bus pass. If she didn't catch the next bus, she would be late.

The aroma of garlic roasted chicken and baked sugar cookies led her to the cafeteria where the banquet was taking place. Family members congregated in the hallway with talks of being proud of their child's accomplishments. Anna's eyes darted across each face in hopes of spotting her family there. She sighed, knowing they probably weren't. She made her way through the crowd to get a glimpse of the cafeteria.

Red and white streamers dangled helpless around the white walls of the cafeteria. The saturation of the reds and whites reminded Anna of her blood-soaked panties after anal sex with her daddy. She quickly diverted her eyes as she tried to shift her focus. The long cafeteria tables were rotated ninety degrees, so everyone could observe the stage. Plastic white tablecloths concealed the areas where students picked the particleboard laminate off. Red and white helium balloons, tethered to the tables, were unable to make their escape as they swayed when the air conditioner hummed.

Handwritten calligraphy name cards rested on the tables closest to the stage. Anna's eyes welled up as she searched for her parents' names. She ran her fingers over the cards, reminding her of the Bible verse of honoring your parents. Anna longingly wanted the Calloways' approval and love. She made her way to the pay phone and called home. With each unanswered ring, more tears fell from her eyes. The phone rang several more times before the answering machine greeted her.

She explained to the answering machine there were seats for them and reiterated the party was at the high school cafeteria. She reminded them that they said they would be there. She hung up the phone, hung her head down, and trudged back to the cafeteria. She mastered the art of maneuvering through crowds with her head down. Vickie spotted her and instantly felt her disappointment. She pushed through the crowd and gave Anna a big hug. She pinched her arm and complimented her on how pretty she looked. "You look good, girl," Vickie said in a manly voice and giggled. Vickie tried with no success to get Anna out of her funk.

They found seats with the other basketball members who were already discussing boys, clothing, and music. They didn't notice Anna's face. Most of the time, she presented a pitiful presence, so it was nothing new to them. One teammate started to ask about Anna's parents attending, but Vickie shot down the question with a stare she learned from her own mother. Anna called home again when the coach announced the banquet was starting in five minutes. When she left, Vickie explained to her teammates that they needed to support Anna because her parents weren't going to show up.

"It's about to start," Anna said when June picked up the phone. Mrs. Calloway explained that she refused to drive way out there for some stupid banquet. Anna's shoulders slumped. She knew begging was pointless. "It's gonna be late when it's done. Can you pick me up, please?" she asked, already knowing the answer.

"You better get home the way you got there."

"Don't lock the do—" June slammed the phone down before Anna could finish. She quickly wiped the tears away and dashed back to the gym when she heard the coach welcoming everyone to the event.

Anna walked back in and noticed almost every seat filled with family members. Parents sat behind every name card except for hers. She wanted to rip up the cards so no one knew that her family didn't show up. She plopped down like a discarded rag doll next to Vickie. Vickie held her hand and rubbed her arm in comfort.

Anna won the award for most improved player. Her teammates rallied around her and clapped like maniacs, so she didn't feel neglected when the coach announced her name. The coach handed her the gold-painted trophy with her name engraved on it. Her coach was not oblivious to the Calloways' absence either. Coach asked Anna in the past about her parents coming to watch her play. Anna mumbled some excuse, hoping the coach would believe why they didn't show up. Coach wrapped her arms around Anna and whispered in her ear that she was proud of her. Anna received two more awards.

During dinner, the room continued buzzing after the ceremony. Anna picked at her chicken and mashed potatoes. She knew she must leave to get home before the 10:00 p.m. curfew. In some ways, she felt relieved to leave early. It broke her heart to stand around and observe her friends have loving interactions with their parents. She dreamed of having someone to love her as she observed the love happening all around her. She missed her birth mom so much that her body ached for her loving arms to protect her. In other ways, she knew leaving early would result in her daddy being awake when she arrived home. By the time she stepped off the bus stop, her eyes were puffy and swollen, and the tears that fell bathed her trophy.

She met a locked door when she arrived home. She hesitated before she knocked. *Lord, please let him be asleep,* she prayed as she tapped lightly on the door. Reverend Calloway came downstairs and greeted her with an erection. "No!" Anna snapped. She pushed past him and ran upstairs. She locked her door and balled herself up under her covers.

Reverend Calloway unlocked her door using a paper clip makeshift key. Once the door was open, he descended on Anna who tried to kick him. She attempted to impale him with her trophy, but he snatched it out of her hands. "What is this?" he snorted. The trophy grew wings and flew across the room. Anna hear it hit the dresser. He pinned her arms straight up as if she was being arrested on the bed. His knees dug into her chest. "Don't ever tell me no," he snapped as he smacked her swollen face several times. Anna tried but was too feeble to fight his advances. He grabbed her thighs and forced her legs open.

When she woke up from the seizure, he was long gone. Sometimes the seizures can last up to an hour. Anna did a body check once she came to. Six buttons on her shirt popped off in the struggle. Her pink skirt sustained two rips. When she took it off, she noticed the blood. His anal-sex hiatus lasted only weeks. Her privates and butt were sore and pulsated in time with her tears.

Her weary eyes searched the room and stopped when she saw her trophy on the floor in pieces. The white marble base rested miles away from the golden basketball figure it used to hold. The arm that held the basketball was severed from its body. It lay on the floor, crippled. Anna was that trophy. Loved at one time, but now broken, away from her family base and damaged.

High School Graduation

No one but her granny knew she premeditated her escape. Anna maintained her determination to leave the Calloway household for good. For weeks, Anna filled out the college application with Ms. Beachum's assistance. Ms. Beachum didn't question Anna when she put her granny's address as her own. She applied for a few nonacademic scholarships. Anna was a solid "C" student but needed an edge to get her in. Her chorus teacher wrote to a few colleges and obtained two music scholarships for Anna.

Anna sang in diapers. The Calloways muted her true feelings. Singing allowed her to express herself. All Anna's shyness left once she started singing. She performed several solos at the chorus concerts. Anna and Vickie sang in the hallways, drawing a few students around to listen. Those were the times she didn't mind the attention. While in her daddy's church choir, she belted out solos for Christmas and Easter.

Anna and Vickie applied to the same small college Anna's boyfriend attended. She met Keith her junior year while trying out for the girls' basketball team. The boys' basketball team sat in the bleachers after their practice and ogled the girls' breasts as they jiggled up and down the court. Keith lusted after Anna's figure. "She got it going on," Keith said as he pointed at Anna and nudged a teammate. They laughed.

Anna and Vickie left the locker room, exhausted from practice. They noticed Keith still sitting on the bleachers. Keith pointed at Anna and patted the bleacher for her to come and sit with him. Anna's thumb instinctively tried to hide in her mouth, but Vickie grabbed Anna's wrist and yanked it down. "Remember, thumb sucking is for bedtime only," Vickie reminded her.

Anna knew Keith as a senior and the biggest flirt in school. "Why do you think he wants to talk to me?" Anna whispered to Vickie. Vickie cupped her nonexistent breasts, and then expanded her hands out to mimic Anna's large ones. Anna covered her mouth to keep from giggling.

"Sit down and talk to me," Keith demanded. Anna complied. They talked while Vickie stood with her mouth open in awe. They exchanged phone numbers. "I'll call you," Keith said as he winked at Anna. He grabbed his duffel bag and jogged out the gym. Vickie knew he was a dog and kept her distrust about Keith to herself. The two giggled about the incident as Anna floated to the bus stop.

Two weeks later, Keith and Anna were dating. They held hands in the hallways and snuck kisses behind the teachers' backs. They dated her last two years in high school. Her sexual encounters with Keith were rare. He was a gentler lover than her daddy and her uncles, but she still didn't enjoy it.

"Why do you cry every time we do it? Are you a virgin?" Keith asked the third time they had sex.

Anna looked away. "I have to go," she mumbled. Anna tucked her shirt back into her skirt as she slammed Keith's car door. Months passed before they had sex again. The fourth time they met up in his car to be intimate, she shared with him her forced incest. Keith wrapped his arms around her. "I will always protect you," he whispered in her ear. Those words melted Anna like butter. She was a virgin when it came to being in love. His pinky promised his faithfulness to her when he went off to college.

⁓

A month before graduation, Anna convinced her brother to take her and Vickie to visit the school. Her brother kept tabs on Anna throughout the years. They met up at her granny's house once a month once Anna turned fifteen.

"You are nice to let me visit my sister." Her brother brought flowers to Anna's granny on each visit.

"It's not a problem, baby. She needs you in her life," her granny stated. The Calloways went through great lengths to keep him away from her, so their mini reunions took place in secret.

The college drive lasted a short two hours from her home. Vickie was asked to babysit her baby brother at the last minute so she couldn't go. "Write down everything," Vickie insisted.

It had been years since Anna and her brother were alone together. They piled in his beat-up Chevy and drove toward the campus. He attempted to make small talk. Anna replied with one word answers then turned her body away from him to stare out the window. Her brother asked about life at the Calloways. "I remember it being very religious and very creepy." He shuddered. He apologized for not keeping in touch when she was growing up.

She wanted to tell him she was a sex slave, tortured and abused her entire life. She opened her mouth several times, but the words refused to come out. Anna turned away and gazed out the window again, blinking back tears. She harbored her misgivings in silence. Her brother, very oblivious to her pain, turned the music up to break the awkward silence.

Anna was young when she witnessed her brother beat up a person in the mall who called their mom out of her name. Her brother would kill Reverend Calloway if he caught wind of what happened to her after they were separated.

Although she wanted pain inflicted on her daddy, she couldn't risk it. She kept her secret locked up like Pandora's box. Opening it may possibly ruin her escape. She wanted freedom more than revenge.

She breathed profound relief when she saw the layout of the small campus. Crowds made her anxious and jittery. As she toured the campus grounds, Anna saw groups of people talking and laughing. She saw Keith in one of those groups. She recognized his basketball windbreaker with his last name and jersey number on the back. He wore it the last time he came to visit her. He intently hugged and kissed on some girl. *Probably his campus girlfriend*, Anna deduced. She was thankful Vickie didn't come. She would have called his name and busted him out in front of everybody. Once Anna settled in on campus, she planned on breaking up with him. Nothing would deter her escape.

"Don't forget graduation is tonight. Everybody's parents are going to be there," she said to Mrs. Calloway. Anna checked herself out in the mirror after coming home from the hair salon. June gave her the same tired line about how she would think about going.

"You never attended anything I participated in, but you always go to Mallory's activities," Anna reminded her.

"Well, Mallory is my real daughter." The words slapped Anna in the face.

"Be home by ten," she said as a dejected Anna ran upstairs to take a nap.

She wore her graduation gown but not the cap until it was time to march in. Several people on the bus congratulated her and asked what her plans were after graduation. Her family didn't acknowledge the fact that she was graduating. She heard June on the phone a few weeks before saying not to buy Anna anything for graduation because "She was an ungrateful slut." Anna held back tears, and she came to grips with the reality that there would be no celebration of her graduation. While her friends would get graduation gifts and have cake and ice cream, she would come home to nothing.

No one clapped as she shuffled across the stage, not trusting her feet. She grabbed her diploma and forced a faint, quivering smile for her picture. Anna was visibly embarrassed. She was disappointed but not surprised that her family didn't show up. The Calloway clan called her a dummy and reiterated daily how slow and stupid she was. She accomplished a milestone with no one there to help her celebrate. Anna was proud of herself for graduating. She pulled her diploma close to her body and squeezed it. She looked up to heaven and whispered, "I did it, Mommy."

The graduation ceremony ended in time for her to catch the bus to be home by ten. She made up an excuse why she needed to leave early, but her friends and Vickie knew. Her family stipulated she be home at ten o'clock for prom as well. Vickie gave her a big hug and told her to cheer up because they would be in college soon and out of the haunted house.

Her daddy's erection peeked out though his pajamas when he opened the door. She pushed him out of the way and tried to run up the stairs. He grabbed her and smacked her so hard she fell down where she stood. He took it from her right at the bottom of the stairs.

Before she blanked out, she stared at the picture of Jesus on the wall by the kitchen. He sat on a rock with smiling children gathered by his side. His arm engulfed them with loving protection. She wished she were child in the picture. Anna prayed to the picture to end her misery, and then she started convulsing.

She woke up from her seizure with her graduation robe over her head and her privates hurting and bleeding. His musky smell of rotten cheese, sweat, and cheap cologne made her want to vomit. She rushed upstairs to scrub her skin. No matter how hard she tried, her attempts were in vain to rid his smell of sin off her body. It seeped into her pores and overtook all other senses. She scanned her face in the mirror and envisioned the kitten on the poster telling her to "Hang in there." Her release date was on the horizon. She was determined to survive. She survived for this long. *A few more months,* she told herself as she curled her feet close to her body, hugged herself tightly, and rocked herself to sleep. Again.

Chapter 3 ———

Birth of Her Children

> May the love hidden deep inside your heart
> find the love waiting in your dreams. May the
> laughter that you find in your tomorrow wipe
> away the pain you find in your yesterdays.
>
> **—Unknown**

Natalie

On her last day of work, Anna sauntered into the animal shelter, sad to say good-bye to the animals. A store-bought lemon cake with white icing and black uneven cursive writing greeted her in the break room. "Good Luck Anna" announced the cake. Her coworkers were going to miss her after almost three years of working at the shelter. They marveled at her stellar attendance and quiet nature. Her boss slid Anna a money card containing fifty dollars. Anna stood speechless when her boss informed her that if she wanted to come back to work during the summer, her job would always be there. She stiffened up when he attempted to give her a good-bye hug. Her boss was unaware of Anna's disdain of older men touching her. Before she left for the day, Anna visited each cage and gave every animal a tearful good-bye. She would miss the animals the most.

Every week Anna stashed clothes and other small items in her book bag and transported them to her granny's house. The college handed her a list of dorm-room supplies and everything checked off laid packed up in her granny's back bedroom. She used the money her boss gave her to purchase the matching comforter set and pillows she and Vickie picked out for their dorm room.

The morning of her departure, Anna gathered what was left of her belongings and bounced down the steps with new dreams of her future. For weeks, she prayed to God for forgiveness for lying. Anna justified her lying by telling herself if she didn't, she would never get away from the torture she endure for thirteen unlucky years.

Those commandments were ingrained in her memory. Her mind was permanently scarred from the severe punishments of her supposed lying about the rapes and molestations. Anna still never comprehended how she was the only family member punished for breaking the commandments. She knew four commandments her daddy broke weekly. She left her broken most-improved player trophy on her shelf. The dreadful memories attached were something she didn't want to take. Her emotional baggage was already too full and weighed her down.

She informed Mrs. Calloway of her intentions to go to college. "What college gonna take a dummy," Mallory said laughing as she continued to ridicule Anna's decision to better herself. Anna's demeanor changed. She dropped her head with apprehension about her decision. Mallory relished in berating Anna, making her feel worthless. Mallory eyes lit up when she saw Anna's body language.

June laughed, which only encouraged Mallory to continue with the abuse. "Look at your ugly self," Mallory resumed with her insults. "Those college girls are going to beat you up for being so stupid. I hope you get raped so you will stop being so fast." Anna held back her tears as she closed the door without saying good-bye. She needed to hurry and meet her brother at her granny's house. Anna walked halfway to the bus stop when she heard Mallory yelling from the house. "I'm 'bout to come to the bus stop and kick your ass so everyone at school can see you with two black eyes." Anna froze but didn't acknowledge Mallory's threat. The bus came before Mallory could make good on her promise.

Anna arrived at the college an hour after Vickie. Her brother made a few stops on the way, so Anna could purchase the rest of the items on her checklist. He helped her move her suitcases, bags, and locker full of items into her room. He embraced Anna a little too tightly for her liking, but she didn't mind. He expressed how proud of her he was as tears rolled down his cheeks. He left so Anna and Vickie could organize the room. Anna sat on her unmade bed and let out a long sigh.

The dorm room they shared marked her new safe haven. The first thing she noticed was the deadbolt lock on the door. *No worries of someone using a paper clip to get in.* She smiled as she flipped the lock a few times to ensure it worked. Each room contained two small twin-size beds with storage space underneath each one. The dark brown wood reminded Anna of her bedroom at her granny's house. The stand-alone closets provided ample space for her clothes and shoes. The matching yellow comforters with big red roses complimented the yellow concrete walls in the room. Anna desperately clung to the hope of a new life.

Anna contemplated what she wanted her major her to be. Vickie knew right away that she wanted to be a business major. She wanted to own a chain of shoe stores. Anna soon chose the nursing profession. Her desire to help others stemmed from witnessing her birth mom lying sick in the hospital. Anna knew no one could save her, but she desperately wanted to. She remembered the Bible lessons about helping those who were less fortunate.

Anna walked in the registrar's office the next morning to get her schedule. Keith happened to be there and had his back to the door. His arm was high on the wall as he was leaned in talking to a coed. Anna thought the girl looked trapped in the corner, but her smiling eyes told a different story. Anna signed in and sat down. She coughed a few times in an attempt to get Keith's attention. Keith was in a deep conversation with a coed and didn't notice Anna.

Anna didn't tell Keith she applied for any college. She coughed again and Keith turned around. He immediately released his prey and moseyed over to Anna. Before he could say anything, Anna shut him down. "I knew for months you had been cheating on me. So this relationship is over," she informed him. Anna words came out strong and forceful. She looked around to see if anyone else heard her. The registrar called her name to come into the office before Keith was able to respond with some sorry excuse. Anna stood up and felt empowered for the first time in her life. She grabbed her book bag and strutted into the office. She could not wait to tell Vickie what happened.

Anna searched around for Keith when she finished registering, but he had disappeared. Anna secretly wanted him to fight for her. She met Vickie for dinner in the dining hall and confessed what she saw Keith doing when she visited the campus. Vickie didn't bat an eyelash. Anna continued to tell her what transpired in the registrar's office. Anna needed Vickie to be proud of her. Vickie needed Anna to understand her inability to fight off his unique and overwhelming charm. Anna's weakness was anyone who showed her love. They walked back to the dorm in silence.

Keith was hanging out on the bench outside her dorm. Anna assumed he was waiting for her. She covered her smile with her hands and struggled to hide her happiness. Vickie glanced at Anna and determined she didn't notice the girl sitting next to him. "That's not the same girl from the registrar's office, is it?" Vickie pointed to the girl who abruptly got up and walked away once Keith spotted Anna. "Nope." Anna dropped her head, looking directly at the ground when she walked up to Keith.

"Hey, Keith," Vickie said, giving him the fakest smile she could muster up. She hugged Anna and said she was going to the room and for Anna not to be out all night. "You have class in the morning." Vickie's eyes shot poison darts at Keith as the big metal door closed behind her.

Keith motioned for Anna to sit with him on the bench. Anna sat on the far end of bench. Her body was as stiff as a corpse. She felt dead inside. Keith scooted closer to her, "Don't be like that baby," he cooed. He put his arm around her and rubbed her shoulders, trying to resurrect the relationship. Keith insisted they get back together and things would different this time. He promised she was the only girl for him and reminisced about all the fun times back in high school. "You know you the only girl for me." Keith's words emitted a decomposition Anna had smelled before. The last time he said that, a mental salve stopped the smell from penetrating her.

In the boys' locker room, Keith was caught with a female student his senior year in high school. The coach and principal dismissed it because he was the star basketball player. It was rumored they were having sex in the shower stall. When Anna questioned him, he gave some story about how the girl lost her way and couldn't find the girls' locker room. Her love for him embalmed all rational thinking. Anna believed that Keith saved her from her family's attempt to annihilate her spirit, and he deserved another chance. Anna mentally rubbed more salve under her nose and eventually took Keith back. He continued to be the biggest player on campus.

"I don't feel right," Anna whimpered when she came back from the bathroom. Anna flopped on her bed and clutched her stomach. Vickie noticed her flushed face and asked if she threw up. "How did you know?" Anna inquired. Vickie's oldest sister was pregnant, and she knew the signs.

"I think you should go to the clinic and get checked out."

"But it's Valentine's Day and Keith planned a romantic evening in his room later," Anna pleaded.

"Just go," Vickie ordered, pointing at the door.

Anna struggled to get the key in the door when she came back from the clinic. Vickie opened the door and found Anna slumped down next to the door, crying uncontrollably. Vickie pulled Anna in the room to keep the other students from gossiping. Anna curled up in a ball on her bed, shaking and crying. Vickie attempted to get Anna to tell her what was going on. "Stop blabbering and tell me what's going on," Vickie demanded.

She sat up and peered into Vickie's eyes for comfort. "I'm three months pregnant," she wailed. Anna collapsed into Vickie's arms. Her hopes of a better life exploded like a dream deferred.

"Dummy can't stop being a slut even in college," Mallory taunted. Her hatred and aggression for Anna resumed once she moved back home. Reverend Calloway forced Anna to drop out of school when she told him about the pregnancy. Mallory snickered when she found out. "You are always going to be a loser," Mallory stated daily. "Keith don't want you. That's why he knocked you up. That's all you good for." Mallory laughed.

When Anna could no longer hide her pregnancy from the church, her daddy demanded she confess her "sin" to the congregation. "Anna, stand up and explain why you sinned against God and brought shame to this family," Reverend Calloway announced in a tone of pious satisfaction. As Anna started her walk of shame to the front of the church, her aunt grabbed her arm and told her to sit back down. Anna sat back in her pew and let out an exhale of deliverance.

"He who is without sin, cast the first stone," she said, glaring directly at her brother-in-law. June's sister knew all about his sexual escapades. He'd fathered a child outside of his marriage to Mrs. Calloway. She didn't mince her words.

"How dare you or anyone else in this church shame and berate someone for being human. People make mistakes. And if God forgives, then you should as well," she added. "The blind cannot lead the blind." She wanted to continue, but he asked her to sit down so they could continue with the service. After the congregation settled down, Anna glanced over at her aunt who winked at her. He never shamed Anna in the church again.

The reverend remained adamant that Anna not have her baby out of wedlock. One evening after Bible study, Reverend Calloway proceeded to Keith's house donned in his clergy robe with collar turned backward for extra emphasis. With Bible in hand, his goal was to intimate and bully Keith into marrying Anna. "You are going to marry Anna," he informed Keith when he opened the door to let the reverend in. Keith stopped him from coming all the way in the house. "You laid down to have sex with her, so you will do right by her," Reverend Calloway declared.

Reverend Calloway stood on the porch and opened the King James Bible to Exodus 22:16. "And if a man entice a maid that is not betrothed, and lie with her, he shall surely endow her to be his wife." He read 1 Corinthians 7:2: "Nevertheless, to avoid fornication, let every man have his own wife, and let every woman have her own husband." Keith shifted his body weight back and forth on each leg and checked his watch as the reverend quoted other Bible verses about premarital sex.

Keith bit his bottom lip when the reverend read Ephesians 5:11: "And have no fellowship with the unfruitful works of darkness, but rather expose them." He wanted to expose the reverend for raping Anna, but Anna had made him promise not to tell anyone. By this time, Keith's mom had come to the door. She listened as the reverend stood on his hypocritical soapbox quoting all the fornication and adultery passages from 1 Corinthians. He quoted so many Bible passages and scriptures, he eventually wore Keith's mom down and she reluctantly agreed to let them get married.

It was a no-frills wedding at the courthouse. Anna wore a black skirt and found an oversized white shirt to hide her belly. Keith walked in wearing black slacks that fit like a mitten. He didn't bother to iron nor tuck into his pants the dingy white button-down shirt. Reverend Calloway scrutinized Keith for not wearing a tie and frowned when they made eye contact. Vickie attended along with Keith's mom. "This is not a good idea," they both whispered to each other as they sat down.

Keith purchased a ring at the pawnshop, but it didn't fit Anna's swollen fingers. Keith scanned the reverend's face when the justice of the peace exclaimed, "You may now kiss the bride." He pecked Anna on the cheek. Anna stood like a pregnant bride wedding-cake topper. After the wedding ceremony, there was no reception. Keith retreated to his mom's house until school started again, and Anna stayed with the Calloways until the baby was born.

Anna worked two jobs most of her pregnancy. She wanted to go back to the animal shelter to work, but the smell of the animals made her constantly nauseous. In fact, most smells made her so sick, any fast food-job was out of the question as well. She landed a job working as a hotel house cleaner at nights and the secretary for her granny's church during the day.

She knew not to expect a baby shower, so she bought everything she needed not only for herself, but also for this new baby. She cut down her work hours when her swollen feet limited her shoe choices to slippers. Her entire body remained swollen the last two months of her pregnancy.

"The doctor recommended you come over and give me massages. It will help with the pregnancy," she begged Keith every other day on the phone.

"I'm busy," he argued and rushed off the phone. Keith did find time to stop by when he wanted to have sex.

"What about the massage you promised if I had sex with you?"

"I don't have time for that," Keith said as he pulled up his pants. He wanted to leave before her family came home.

Anna went in for her seventh-month checkup. The doctor informed her she had an STD. "This is not good for the baby or you," the doctor cautioned. Reverend Calloway stopped messing with Anna once he found out she was pregnant, so it wasn't from him. Keith was back to his infidelity ways, and she was too pregnant to fight.

Anna loathed sitting in the family room. The condom-looking slipcovers made noise whenever she sat down. She was sitting on the couch when her water broke.

"Keith, I am about to have your baby," Anna gasped, holding the phone in one hand, clutching her stomach with the other. His voice was stern. He wanted to know what he was supposed to do about it.

"This is your baby."

His mother picked up the other line. "That ain't Keith's baby," she denounced. "Keith told me about your uncles and daddy having sex with you," she argued. She told Anna the baby was one of theirs and not her son's responsibility. "He is not helping you with anything." She made Keith hang the phone up. Anna hung her head and cried.

Mallory offered to go with her to the hospital. Anna told her she didn't want her there. Mallory pushed Anna down the stairs while six months pregnant. She told Anna she didn't want her or the baby to live. "I was only being nice," Mallory snapped. "Don't nobody wanna see a dummy have a baby," Mallory barked some more hurtful things to Anna before the ambulance arrived.

"She's an ugly baby," Mrs. Calloway observed as she held the baby at arm's length.

"She's not ugly," Anna said as she reached for her baby from the hospital bed. The baby name was picked once she found out she was having a girl. She remembered a story she read as a child about a little brave girl named Natalie who unafraid to speak her mind. Natalie Renee is what she wrote on the birth certificate. Keith was not there to sign his name as father. When she called him from the hospital room, his mother informed her that he was out playing basketball.

"He don't think that baby is his?" the nurse queried.

"I ain't been with nobody else."

"Well, you gonna have to prove it." The nurse suggested she get a paternity test to prove Keith was the father. Keith's mother didn't permit him to sign the birth certificate until she saw the DNA paperwork stating there was a 99.9 percent chance Keith was the father of Natalie. He reluctantly signed the birth certificate two weeks later.

Roger

Without warning, Reverend Calloway evicted his wife of twenty-some years. Reverend Calloway upgraded to a newer younger Mrs. Calloway, so the old wife went out with yesterday's garbage. Janice was a member of his church and had been having an affair with him for years. The entire church gossiped about it to everyone but June.

As a child, Mallory relentlessly blamed her mom for not being a good enough wife to her daddy. Her bitter rage often left June with black eyes and bruises covering most of her body. Mallory found a kindred spirit with her new mother. Anna and Natalie were included in the forced eviction. Collateral damage. Anna reveled in the move away from her rapist. When Natalie turned one, Anna slept clutching Natalie, fearful Reverend Calloway would take her virginity as well. June found a two-bedroom apartment and a new church home across town. Though she hated Anna, she loved her granddaughter and didn't want Natalie to be homeless, so she took Anna in as well.

Anna and Natalie transitioned into their new home with ease. June worked at her day-care center all day and most evenings, giving Anna free reign of the apartment. She spent her mornings teaching Natalie how to bathe and dress herself. Singing the "Itsy Bitsy Spider" and "Old MacDonald" replaced her silent cries for help in the middle of the night. Natalie's laughter filled a room, and Anna exhaled with every giggle. Anna's seizures appeared to be under control with medication, and for the first time since she left college, she slept without fear.

Anna's life was seemingly wonderful, but she was missing something. Anna's desire to get into the health-care profession wasn't deterred by her first failed attempt at college. She needed another path. Natalie was taking her afternoon nap when Anna stumbled upon a TV commercial saying she could get her CNA licenses in as few as five months. All she needed was a high school diploma, and this license would propel her in the right direction of eventually becoming a nurse. She called the community college and enrolled in classes, which started in two weeks. Mrs. Calloway let Natalie stay at the day-care center free while Anna attended school.

Anna finished her classes and had her licenses when her Uncle Chuck started crashing at the apartment a few nights a week. His girlfriend grew weary of his antics and drunken stupors, so she kicked him out. His sister was the only one who took him in. Most nights he spent sobering up on June's couch. The white couch cringed at his heavy 275-pound frame. He was Papa Bear sleeping in Goldilocks's bed.

Anna locked her room door every night but still didn't feel safe. She knew from childhood that he could break down any locked door to take what he wanted. His aggressive nature often meant that sex with Anna would turn violent and brutal, just the way Chuck liked it.

"Please don't leave me alone with him," Anna begged most nights.

"He is my brother, and he is always welcomed here," her unsympathetic eyeballs dared Anna to question her again.

One evening, Anna came home from dropping Natalie off and observed Chuck slumped on the couch with a beer in one hand. A fifth of an empty bottle of brown liquor collapsed on the coffee table. "Girrrrl." His glossy eyes lusted at Anna's body. "I ain't seentcha in a loooooong time. Getcher shelf ova heeeere and chit down on ma lap," Chuck beckoned, slapping his thighs twice, motioning for Anna to sit on him. Mrs. Calloway was in the kitchen cooking dinner.

"I am too old to be sitting on somebody's lap," Anna snapped. At a distance, she could smell the alcohol on his breath. He smelled like beer and a terrible reoccurring dream.

She went to her room, thankful this was Natalie's week with Keith. A few moments later, June yelled, "Anna, I fixed dinner for you and Chuck. I'm going back to work for a few. Make sure those dishes are washed before I get back." Anna trembled at the thought of leaving the security of her bedroom to venture to drunk Uncle Chuck's territory. She prayed Chuck would pass out on the sofa, so she could sneak into the kitchen to wash the dishes.

An hour after June left, she heard Chuck knock over some things before he staggered out to get more alcohol. The door slammed so hard, she peeked out to see if it was still on its hinges. She advanced out to the kitchen. Her eyes watching the front door like a hawk. She rinsed the dishes off and shoved them in the dishwasher haphazardly. She made it halfway back to her bedroom when the front door opened. "I forgot my damn wallet," Chuck mumbled to himself when he spotted Anna halfway between the kitchen and safety.

Anna tried to run, but Chuck grabbed her waist from behind, nearly knocking her on the ground. "I beeen waitin fer dissssss." His slurred sloppy words crept past her ears and slid down the back of her neck. "Nufink can shomp me." She screamed, but he covered her mouth. Her feet dangled in the air as he led her by her neck to the bedroom, choking her the entire time. She tried to fight him off while gasping for air. He used so much force to throw her on the bed, the bedpost left a hole in the wall. The repeated banging of her head on the headboard during the rape caused her seizures to resume.

A neighbor overheard the commotion and came over to check it out. Chuck forgot to close the door, so the neighbor came in and used their cordless phone to call the police, but it was too late. He finished and looked down at Anna still having a seizure. He turned to the neighbor and tilted his head back. "You wanna ride on that bronco? Watch it doe, she feisty," he said with a chuckle as she showed the neighbor the scratches on his arms from Anna. He bragged about what a good lay she was. "I'm tired now," he commented as he flopped on the couch and drank the corner of beer left in one of the almost empty cans. The neighbor backed out of the apartment and waited for the police to arrive.

Anna filed a rape charge against her uncle after the hospital released her. "We need to keep you here overnight for observation," the doctors demanded.

The police went to arrest Chuck at his girlfriend's house the next morning. Chuck denied doing anything. His girlfriend tried to convince the police to let him go. "That slut is lying on me." Chuck promised they had the wrong person.

"We have an eyewitness who saw the entire thing, sir." The police officer cuffed his wrists and escorted him to the station. They released him after two nights in jail.

"Thanks for bailing me out, baby." Chuck pecked his girlfriend on the cheek as he got into the car.

"Yeah, you owe me two grand."

"You'll get your money." Chuck grabbed his crotch and shook it at her. "It's all right here." He smirked as she turned her lip up, rolled her eyes, and drove off.

Anna's family called her a slut and a whore when they found out she was pregnant again. Vickie wanted her to get an abortion. "Who has their uncle's baby?" she questioned Anna's logic and mental capacity.

Anna would never have an abortion. The Bible had a commandment about not killing. *If you disobey any parts of the Bible, there was place in hell for you.* These words haunted Anna. In addition, any act against the Bible's teachings would result in a whooping by Reverend and Mrs. Calloway.

"Well, how about giving the baby up for adoption?" Vickie suggested.

Anna flashed back to her childhood misery and torment. "No." She ended the conversation. She didn't want anyone to grow up as she had with no protection. Adoption was not an option either.

Nobody believed her unborn baby belonged to her uncle. June was insistent it belonged to Keith. Anna hadn't been with Keith in over a year, so she knew it wasn't his baby. Chuck's girlfriend called her on the phone when Anna was six months pregnant. "Ain't no way that baby is Chuck's 'cause I shot off his penis a long time ago," she stated as a matter of fact. Anna hung up the phone without inquiring about any more details of that incident.

Anna lay uncomfortably on the couch when her water broke. *I'm about to have my uncle's baby,* she whimpered. "Don't mess up my white couch," June demanded as she grabbed her purse and headed for the door. "You not gonna go with me?" Anna whined while holding her stomach. Mrs. Calloway ranted about Anna being a slut. The slamming door felt like a gunshot through Anna's heart. Anna wobbled to the phone and called for a cab. She grabbed her overnight bag and the fifty-dollar bill hidden in her pillowcase. She hobbled down the last step of the apartment building as the cab driver arrived.

The blood test proved her uncle had fathered Anna's son. His sentence was five years in jail. Her family believed the blood test was lying and someone obviously tampered with the results. Anna didn't need the blood test. She cringed seeing her uncle's face on her son's body. Anna tried to love baby Roger, but found herself torn between anger, hate, and guilt.

Anna's feelings didn't coincide with the Christian views she grew up on. She stifled her cries in her pillow most nights, afraid someone would hear her. She was a forced single mom with two small children. Her family abandoned her and accused her of leading her uncle on. Mrs. Calloway gave her a few months to find a new place to live.

Late one lonely night, her suicidal thoughts took over her rational thinking. She dug through the junk drawer in the kitchen and found an old rope left from the move. She resolved life was no longer worth living. Constant abuse and neglect dug in her like a tick. "I'm done," she mumbled.

Anna meandered through the apartment in attempts to find a good, sturdy anchor to tie the rope. She halted her decision when she peeked into her room and saw her innocent children sleeping on her bed. Natalie's thumb rested in her mouth, and her free arm was wrapped around her baby brother. "My babies." Anna wept.

As she took the back of her hand to wipe the bitter tears away, she concluded she couldn't abandon them. She dropped to her knees in the hallway and prayed to God for forgiveness. "Lord. I can't take this anymore. Please help me. I need you." Anna confessed defeat. She prayed the 23rd Psalms. She recited every Bible verse she had memorized. God prayed some sense into Anna. She tromped back to the kitchen and slid the rope back in the drawer. Anna crawled back in bed and held her children a little tighter. Anna unwillingly agreed to live the life she was given.

Uncle Chuck was diagnosed with skin cancer many years later. Anna worked at the same hospital where he received treatment. "I want my niece to be my nurse," Chuck demanded, refusing any other nurse to treat him.

"No. I am not going to do it." Anna held firm when the head nurse told her of his request. In all the years Anna has worked in the medical field, she never refused to take care of a patient until her uncle. *God, please forgive me, but I will not take care of my rapist*, she silently declared. She worried about the hospital firing her, but she didn't have the courage to say why she refused.

"It's fine. He will have to take the nurse assigned to him." The head nurse saw a visibly shaken Anna. She rubbed Anna's back. "I understand. I don't care too much for my uncle either." The head nurse sympathized and told her uncle that Anna had other patients she needed to help.

On her uncle's final days on earth, Anna eventually visited his hospital room. She stood at the door and just stared at him. Although the cancer rendered him too weak to do much of anything, it still scared her to be in the same room with him. As he sat in the cold hospital bed crying out in pain, Anna cried as well. Memories attacked her like muggers in the dark and starless night.

She knew the Christian thing to do was to forgive him, but she found it troublesome. She prayed hard for strength to do this. The Bible verse Matthew 6:14 came to her. *"I know, Lord. Forgive others and your heavenly father will forgive you."* Anna nodded and said amen.

As she tiptoed toward the bed, her eyes filled with water and her mouth filled with cotton. She wiped her tears and nervously stood out of arms reach of his bed. "Anna. I knew you would come." Chuck's words were raspy and faint. He stretched out his hand for Anna. She refused it.

"Although you raped me for years and fathered my son, I forgive you for what you did to me," she surmised. Anna stared him in the eyes. Anna did it for herself and not for him. She knew she needed to move forward with her life. As she turned to walk out of the room, her uncle whispered a weak thank you. He died before the sun came up.

The hospital was aware that Chuck was her uncle and asked her what to do with the body since no one came forth to claim it. Anna reluctantly called some of the same family members who accused her of lying about the rape. No one wanted to deal with the body or deal with her. Her uncle's daughter finally stepped up. "Just so you know. He was never no daddy to me. And for the record, I always believed you when you said he raped you. He raped me too," she blurted out. His daughter found the cheapest way to bury him. She had him cremated, with no service, and purposely left the ashes at the funeral home.

Chapter 4

Grandmas, June, and Cancer

"He felt that his whole life was some kind of dream and he sometimes wondered whose it was and whether they were enjoying it."
—Douglas Adams, *The Hitchhiker's Guide to the Galaxy*

Diagnosed with Cancer—Twenty-Five Years Old

In the fall, Anna begrudgingly moved in with Keith and his mom when Mrs. Calloway put her out. Anna spent her days off avoiding her mother-in-law by laying low in their makeshift apartment in the basement. Since they were already married, it was not a sin in Anna's eyes. The college kicked Keith out after failing to complete the academic probation requirements. Keith unloaded boxes off a delivery truck during the day and left Anna alone most nights while he worked as a bouncer and slept with numerous women he met at the club.

The police academy finally accepted his application, and he used the signing bonus to rent an apartment. He grew weary of his mom complaining because he was taking care of a child and he wasn't the father. Keith was keenly aware of how Roger came into this world, but it didn't deter him from raising him. Keith always wanted a son and loved Roger as if he were his own. After three years of marriage, Anna and Keith were able to live together as a couple, now a family. It seemed like a distracting dream.

Her CNA licenses helped her land a job working at a local hospital. Anna saved her money and bought an eight-year-old Nissan clunker. A few months of driving put Anna back in the driver's seat of her life. She pulled up at a light beside the public bus on one of her grocery-store runs. She glanced over at the bus riders, their faces complacent. She closed her eyes and thanked God she was not on the bus anymore. She didn't venture too far when she drove. Work and day care were her two main destinations. She made quick runs to the grocery store to get food for the family and pain medicine for her.

Coming back from dropping her kids off at June's day care, Anna lost control of the car and careened into the guardrail on the interstate. It was a single car accident and when the police arrive on the scene, she was convulsing. When the seizure subsided, Anna was barely alert and the police mistook her actions for a person drinking or on drugs. They gave her a citation and sent her to the hospital to run some tests since she couldn't consent to the field test.

The doctors forbade her from operating a motor vehicle because she has epileptic seizures. They changed the dosage of her seizure medicine and prescribed bed rest until her body healed from the bruises. Anna was relieved they didn't take her to the hospital where she worked. She neglected to inform her job about her medical condition, but now felt she obligated to tell them in case it happened at work. Again, her taste of freedom had spoiled. The department of motor vehicles determined her risk and revoked her licenses.

———— ∞∞∞ ————

Anna scheduled her yearly mammogram screening to coincide with her birth mom's birthday. This seemed a nonconventional way to honor someone who died from breast cancer. Her Aunt Cora informed Anna the disease is hereditary. "All your aunts have had cancer before," Aunt Cora told her when Anna a young girl. At age twenty, Anna repeatedly explained this to the doctors who were adamant about not giving her the screening because of her age. Anna experienced pain in her breasts for weeks. She described it as if someone laid her down and ran a car over her breast numerous times. Anna sat unprepared when the doctor called her in to explain the abnormal mammogram and the need to do a biopsy on her breast.

Two weeks later, Anna stumbled out of the doctor's office in a blurry haze. The receptionist guided her out of the building after Anna bumped into the carousel containing pamphlets about STDs and pregnancy. Anna's eyes were almost swollen shut by the time she made it to the bus stop. She just turned twenty-five a month earlier. "All I have been through, why would you give me breast cancer?' she demanded an answer from God. "Why couldn't you have left me some jewelry instead of a disease?" she peered up to heaven and asked her mom.

Anna stomped up the apartment steps, swinging her arms so aggressively she hit her hand on the railing, which added to her frustration. She slammed the door closed, and a painting of an empty forest with trees and birds fell off the wall, exposing a fist-shaped hole. Another one of Keith's greatest hits.

Keith's rage remained hidden behind cheap pictures on the apartment walls sporadically arranged. Keith's aggression toward Anna started in college. After his basketball games, Anna sat for hours in his dorm room, waiting for Keith. He snuck in way past his curfew, reeking of alcohol and women's perfume. If his team lost, he convinced himself and Anna that it was her fault and used her body as a punching bag. Anna's low self-esteem conjured this to be her life. Anna lacked the knowledge to rewrite her story. She wasn't strong enough to leave.

When he sobered up, he saw her bruises. "Anna, please forgive me. I'm so sorry for what I did. I love you so much." Keith begged for forgiveness, mostly out of fear she would report him to his coach. Anna desired someone to love her so desperately; she believed his pathetic apologies every time, hoping he would change. This ongoing routine lasted until her pregnancy. He stopped kicking and shoving her but continued with the verbal abuse. Once they started lived together, he brought his fists out of retirement and added body slamming to his routine.

Anna flopped down on the sofa and used the remote to flip though channels, wanting the noise from the television to drown out the voices in her head. Anna landed on a commercial for a movie she and Vickie watched a few weeks back. The main character was a woman in an abusive marriage, so she faked her own death so she never had to sleep with the enemy again. She saw a kindred spirit with the wife character, but lacked the resources to move away. Anna decided then that she would leave permanently.

She shuffled to the bathroom and grabbed the bottle of aspirin. As she looked in the mirror, she didn't recognize herself. She had become a shell of a woman. The pain of her existence became too much to bear. Anna believed no hope of reprieve existed, and this was the only way to alleviate her own suffering.

"Who needs this," she mumbled to her reflection as she swallowed a handful of aspirin. As she started to fade away, terrible thoughts raced through her mind. *What if Natalie found my dead body? Who would take care of my kids? I was nine when my mom died.* Anna blankly looked in the mirror, seeing her nine-year-old face. *That wouldn't be fair to leave them like my mom left me,* Anna remembered. *They say God never gives you any more than you can handle.* Why did I do this? Anna started toward the toilet. *Let not your heart be troubled.* She shoved her finger down her throat. *God loves me.* Anna assured herself. Anna understood the finality of her actions. She tried unsuccessfully to throw up the pills, and then she dialed 911.

As she staggered to unlock the door for the paramedics, she recited the first Bible verse she ever learned. The Lord is my shepherd. I shall not want. *Please hurry up.* He maketh me to lie down in green pastures. He leadeth me beside the still waters. *I'm sorry, Lord. Forgive me.* Anna was unfazed by the loud knock on the door.

He restoreth my soul.

"Ma'am we're here. Let us in please," the paramedics said.

He leadeth me in the path of righteousness for his name's sake. I can't die.

"Ma'am we're coming in."

Yea, though I walk through the valley of the shadow of death, I will fear no evil, for thou art—" She stopped breathing. The paramedic tried to revive her and then put her on the stretcher.

Anna's eyes squinted as she scanned the room to figure out where the beeping noise originated. The hospital machines were monitoring her blood pressure and heart rate. They were successful in pumping all the aspirin out of her system. She glanced over and read "Suicide Watch" written in tiny red letters on her chart. With a heavy sigh, she closed her eyes but couldn't get any uninterrupted rest with the nurses checking in on her every fifteen minutes. She needed to let Keith know the doctors would be keeping her overnight for observation. Shame convinced her to lie. She explained she was working a double shift at the hospital and asked if he would take care of their kids.

Her medical records revealed her recent cancer diagnosis, so her doctor ordered Anna to counseling. Anna turned her head away at the image of being in a mental institution. She didn't want counseling; she wanted an escape from the anguish and hopelessness.

—— ∞ ——

Her first chemotherapy appointment was met with despair. Her doctor informed her of the rapid spread of her cancer. They needed written consent to remove both her breasts as soon as possible.

"But I only came in for chemo." She could barely get the words out. They assured her it would be the only way to save her life. Anna's mind drifted to Natalie and she asked for a pen. "Can . . . can . . . can I call my . . . my mom?" she stammered as they were prepping her for emergency surgery.

"There's no time," the nurse told her. No one informed June of Anna's situation.

Just like the relationship with her birth mom, Anna's breasts were removed before complete understanding and with not so much as a good-bye. After her double mastectomy, she needed chemo to kill the remaining cancerous cells. Her job remained supportive of her situation, and a few coworkers came to visit while she recovered.

Anna accidentally caught a glimpse of her naked torso in the mirror after her bandages were removed. For months, she avoided mirrors at all cost, but Natalie used her bathroom and removed the towel covering up the mirror. Her breasts abandoned her just like her birth mom did. She studied her body in the mirror for the first time in years. Anna felt ashamed of her deformed figure. Her womanhood ripped from her chest and replaced with scars. Her breast once looked like two round eyeballs, now resembled two flat eyes, permanently closed and sealed tight with stitches.

―――∞∞∞―――

Keith came home one evening and informed Anna he was moving out. Once Anna lost her breasts, Keith deemed her no longer a woman. "If I want to sleep with somebody with no tiddys, I would of messed with a man," he hissed while packing away his stereo equipment.

"Who's going to help me with the kids while I do my chemo treatments?"

"I dunno. Ask your baby daddy to take care of them," he retorted, still not believing Natalie was his. Anna cried for ten minutes after the door slammed but then realized Keith would have delayed her already slow healing process with his negativity and potential physical abuse.

It was impossible for Anna to take care of her children in the way they needed her. For a week, Natalie fixed cereal for her and Roger for breakfast and lunch. Dinner consisted of peanut butter and jelly sandwiches and chips, while Anna lay on the bed after her weekly treatment. Her neighbor babysat the kids once when she went for her treatment, but let her know she could not do this all the time. Her neighbor harbored a brooding resentment toward Anna for banging around all hours of the night, not knowing Anna was the one being thrown against the wall from Keith's anger.

Desperation forced Anna to beg June to take care of Natalie and Roger. "If you weren't a slut, then you wouldn't have two baby daddies who didn't want you," June hissed. Anna was powerless and too feeble to put up a decent argument. She held the phone, hung her head like a dying flower, and wept.

"Mommy, why are you always crying? You want to hold my doll baby to make you feel better?" Mrs. Calloway heard Natalie in the background.

June agreed to take her kids. "I'm only taking care of them because I love my grandchildren. You're still a slut." June justified her decision.

June brainwashed Anna's children in one short summer. She exaggerated Anna's slutty ways and called her a whore. "Don't grow up to be fast like your so-called mother," June cautioned these two impressionable children.

When Anna's body was stronger, the kids would spend the weekends with her. Natalie and Roger ignored Anna when she asked them to do things. Anna thought she heard Roger call her the B word when she asked him to clean his room. Mrs. Calloway taught them they didn't have to listen to what she said. Natalie's hate was the worse being the oldest. Natalie talked back and rolled her eyes. June revealed to four-year-old Roger that he was a bastard because his mom couldn't keep it in her pants. "Keep what in her pants?" Roger asked, thinking she was talking about her legs.

It took years for Anna to gain respect back from her children. For months, June told them lies about Anna. Roger never learned to respect Anna and gave her hell for years. Natalie eventually changed. She remembered the years of seeing Anna crying.

"Mommy, I'm sorry I have been so mean to you," Natalie confessed as she hugged Anna one evening after dinner. "If you were a slut like Grandma said, you would have a bunch of men over here. I don't believe the things Grandma said about you. I think you're the best mom in the world and I love you."

Natalie kissed her Anna on her tear-stained cheek. "Thank you, Nat." Anna's voice quavered. All Anna ever wanted was to be a good mother and for her kids to love her. Natalie knew Anna had been sick, but still did everything she could for her and Roger. Over the years, Anna and Natalie's bond grew stronger. They considered each other sisters.

Toward the end of the year, things started looking hopeful. Anna was at the hospital working again. *Nineteen ninety four is going to be a good year*, she determined. Her health prevailed and she was getting stronger.

Granny—1994

Granny naturally held Anna's tiny hand when they rode the bus downtown. Anna rubbed her granny's hand as if she was trying to start a campfire. Anna checked to make sure she didn't rub the skin off. Her skin was as soft as summer peaches.

She stared at her granny's hand, wanting to ask on every trip how she could have raised such a horrible son but instead looked up at her granny and questioned, "How come you love me so much?"

Granny side-squeezed Anna and replied many times with "You're my precious baby and I love you." Granny held her until they stepped off the bus.

The best part of Anna's childhood summers were the annual visits to the soda fountain at Woolworth after a long day of school shopping with her granny. Anna was soon tall enough not to need Granny's help climbing onto the barstool that often spun Anna around too much. Even though her legs still swung as she sipped on her drink, she felt grown up. Granny pushed on Anna's back, forcing her chest forward. "A lady always sits up straight," she constantly reminded Anna. Anna adjusted herself, not taking her mouth off the straw filled with cherry flavored cola.

Anna begged to stay at her granny's house every weekend she could. Mrs. Calloway wanted Anna home to satisfy her husband, so she wouldn't have to. The safe house sheltered Anna. When Anna stayed over, Granny's only child was banned from the house. Anna referred to granny's spare bedroom as her sanctuary. She didn't mind sharing the room with Granny's clutter. It was heavenly. Anna stretched out on the bed, tracing each square of the homemade quilt with her index finger. Her eyes wandered around the room landing on the off-white vintage sewing machine slumped over in the corner. A pile of unsewn patterned cut material lay beside it begging for completion. Mothballs deodorized the air when she opened the closet door. Boxes on top of boxes lined the closet filled with clothing not worn for years. The lock on the bedroom door used a key Anna kept in the purple plastic purse her granny gave her one Easter.

Granny, apparently aware of her son's treatment toward Anna, sat helpless like in her own marriage. Evil coursed thought the Calloways' bloodline, staining everything it touched. A wide-eyed young Reginald witnessed his father victimize his mom, and he walked in his abusive footsteps. Reginald internalized that women needed to understand their place, and rape made them submissive and compliant. Her attempts to report the abuse only led to more maltreatment once the cops left.

Granny stayed under the radar when she reported finding her husband dead in the bathtub. The coroner ruled intoxication as the main cause of death. A knot on his head provided evidence that he somehow slipped and hit his head. He was too drunk to prevent himself from drowning. Granny mustered up a few tears at the funeral.

"I'm so sorry for your loss." Neighbors and friends assured she would make it through these tough times.

"Thank you," Granny replied, hiding her elation. Her husband's funeral march was music to her soul. She found crying easier when she saw others crying. Her tears gleamed like gold in her eyes. When finally alone, she cried real tears. For the first time in over fifteen years, she slept an entire night without being raped, beaten, or demoralized.

Granny tried desperately for years to gain respect from Reginald after her husband died. Her heart was a heavy stone, which she hated carrying around. "I can't have him growing up like his daddy," she promised herself. Granny purchased a new suit for Reginald. She sifted through her closet and found a dress with the tags still on it. "We're going to church this Sunday," she announced to Reginald.

"Why?" Reginald frowned his face up. She avoided the church since her husband's funeral. She needed the savior to save her.

Reginald participated in all the church activities and often begged to go to all the services. One Wednesday-night church service, Reginald met a young deacon. This deacon never had sanctified grace to fall from. His reputation and demeanor intrigued Reginald. The deacon's sexual appetite and narcissistic tendencies fell in line with what Reginald's father taught him. He fell under the deacon's marred wings and referred to him as his mentor.

Reginald studied the art of deception, womanizing, and mastered hypocrisy by the time he finished divinity school. Reginald cultivated his con-man skills and realized clergymen's morals never were the topic of discussion among the congregation. He wore a conceited cloak of ecclesiasticism. Reginald managed to conceal his faithlessness under his minister robe. The clerical collar, however, choked him as if it were the hands of God whenever he wore it, no matter how loose it was.

"Ma'am." The cops responded to Granny's accusations against her son. "Reverend Calloway is a pillar of society. Why would a man of God commit those heinous acts on his own daughter?" They dismissed all of her anonymous phone calls. Anna begged her granny not to file another report. The last incident ignited her daddy's tiger rage. He whooped then raped Anna while her June encouraged him and yelled "slut" and "whore."

Granny guarded Anna against her son until her health started declining. Her pneumonia lasted for months, and she refused treatment. Doctors diagnosed her with late-stage dementia after Anna begged her to see a doctor. Anna visited her granny on her off days. Even though the dementia rendered her unable to communicate, Anna read the Bible and rubbed her hand exactly like she did on the bus years ago.

———❧———

Anna arrived home from work when she received news that her granny died. She started convulsing moments after she hung up the phone. Natalie heard when Anna fell and rushed in to help her. "Mom. Are you OK?" Natalie asked, knowing not to grab a person who is having a seizure. Roger stood in the doorway and unknowingly cried. After the third seizures, Anna needed to rest. Natalie and Roger helped her in her bed. "My granny died," she revealed once they got her comfortable in her bed. She promised to talk to them when she woke up.

Anna didn't eat or sleep for days after the news. Her eyes were swollen shut, and they refused to shed another tear. Her protector abandoned her, and she lay exposed and vulnerable. *Why did you take my granny?* Anna fussed at God. *You know I needed her.*

Anna dressed in all white for her granny's funeral. Her heavenly look helped Anna feel closer to her grandma. As she stuffed her purse with tissues, she yelled for her kids to hurry up, or they would miss the bus.

She approached the church like a cat on the hunt for a bird in the yard. Her hesitancy was not lost on her kids. "Why we walking so slow?" Roger questioned.

"I'm just sad about losing my granny." Anna barely blurted the words out. Natalie grabbed her mom's hand and gave Roger the shush sign.

Reverend and the new Mrs. Calloway approached Anna before her foot hit the front step of the church. He grabbed Anna by the arm and yanked her close to him. Anna lost her breath. "You're not allowed to cry. This is no time for tears," he demanded through gritted teeth.

"You don't tell me how to mourn," Anna said as she pulled away from his grip. "Come on kids," Anna gathered her children and walked in the church refusing to sit with the Calloway family.

Anna used most of her tissues before the ceremony started. She loathed the fact Reverend Calloway performed the eulogy. His voice gave her haunted-house creeps. *How could he not take care of his mom when she was sick? He didn't even check up on her when she was on her deathbed.* She shook her head and rolled her eyes. Anna despised him and feared he would rape her again. She hated herself for not being Christian enough to forgive him. Her eyes were running faucets as the pallbearers hoisted her granny casket out of the church.

Anna didn't want to die as much as she wanted to stop living. Anna attempted suicide for a third time a week after they buried her granny. Natalie found her lying lifeless next to a bottle of aspirin. She resented that Natalie found her. Anyone else would have let her die. Natalie dialed 911 and calmly answered the operator's questions. Once the ambulance arrived, The 911 operator commended Natalie on being brave and staying calm, not knowing this first grader has dialed 911 numerous times before.

"This is your second suicide attempt that I know of." The same doctor that pumped Anna's stomach remembered her. He handed her paperwork for a mandatory five-day hold in a mental health facility. Anna called June, and she agreed to take Natalie and Roger for a few days while she recuperated. She didn't care if Natalie mentioned the aspirin she found. She needed an escape.

In each corner of the sterile white hospital van, a patient sat staring through their private tinted window. Sharing the three-row seating with one other person, Anna sat crowded with her thoughts. *I don't belong with no crazy people. I'm sad, not crazy.* Tears slid down her cheek like a nonstop train ride.

Anna stood near the front desk, second in line for admittance in the facility. *I hope they don't make me talk. What if they keep me here forever?* She shifted her weight from one foot to the other. *Why am I here? Why am I here? Nobody would miss me.* She gazed over her paperwork for a seventh time. A pig-like squeal interrupted her pity party. A patient, naked from the waist down, was being chased by two security officers. He managed to bypass the security doors and appeared in the lobby with all new patients and family members. A doctor holding a blanket tried calmly talking to the patient but remained unsuccessful. The patient refused the doctors' suggestion to calm down and screamed incomprehensible words. His dilated pupils communicated his fear and anxiety. He was subdued, draped in a blanket, and escorted out of the lobby behind a closed door.

"Anna," the receptionist called her name twice before Anna acknowledged her. She shuffled to the front desk and shoved the crumpled papers toward the intake person. Anna's eyes bore a hole in the closed door, hoping to see what happened to the patient.

"It's not always like this, don't be scared. You'll be safe," she unsuccessfully reassured Anna. Anna sighed, dropped her head, and lowered her shoulders.

Group therapy sessions enabled Anna to gaze at mirrors of her life experiences though someone else's eyes. A kindred spirit hugged the room, keeping ego and judgment at a safe distance. She wanted to talk about her traumatic childhood but lost her voice sometime at check-in. During her time to share, Anna spoke only of the loss of her granny. Anna wished for strength to pry open her box of demons, to share her story. She longed to crawl into her granny's bed and rub her hands, but that part of her life would never return.

Cancer—1999

Every year on her granny's birthday, Anna placed eleven white roses and one single red rose on her granny's grave. "The red rose means I love you and I miss you granny," she greeted the tombstone. As a child, she tagged along to visit her great-granny's grave. Her granny would place the same flower arrangement on her mother's tombstone. Anna asked her granny why white roses.

"They symbolize purity and innocence, and I know she is in heaven smiling down on us," her granny replied. Anna never met her great-granny but heard stories about her determination. Anna couldn't believe her granny left her five years ago. Time had passed unseen.

Anna was combing Natalie's hair when Anna grabbed her left breast and slumped down. It felt like a steel-toe boots mashing down on her breast. "What's wrong, Mommy?"

The familiar pain sent Anna's warning signal her cancer may be back. "I'm OK sweetie. Let's hurry up and get you ready for the play," Anna said, struggling to catch her breath. Natalie's fifth-grade class was performing a version of *Alice in Wonderland* for the end-of-the year program. Natalie played the Cheshire Cat. Threatened by no one. Anna admired her younger twin in the mirror as she finished the last braid. Anna wished Roger used his energy more productively. Anna sat in another meeting as various teachers rambled on about Roger's grades and behavior.

"He is very immature for his age, and he picks fights constantly."

"Roger is not developing as quickly as the other students."

"Roger sits in class and refuses to participate. His disruptions distract the others from learning."

"His work lacks the necessary foundation for him to proceed to the next level."

"Well." Anna stopped them. "Can somebody at least tell me something good about my son?" Anna needed reassurance. She stumbled on the question herself most days.

"Roger has perfect attendance," his second-grade teacher proclaimed as she thought about it. *The bad ones never miss school.* His teacher mentally assessed her years in education. The room giggled and the tension settled down. They collectively agreed that Roger would spend another year in second grade. He was small for his age and therefore would not stand out as much. Anna stuffed the paperwork in her purse, and as she stood up to leave, she doubled over in pain. One of the teachers caught her before she hit the chair. Warning signal number two.

"Roger, you are going to have to repeat the second grade." Anna sat her son down at the kitchen table to explain. "The teachers say you are struggling," she continued.

"What about summer school?" Roger pleaded in a whimper that made Anna cringe. He attended summer school since kindergarten, and his behavior forced the school to kick him out every summer.

"Not this time," Anna replied. She knew Roger ran the risk of teasing from his classmates for being held back, but she wanted him to receive a good education. Roger tried to argue with Anna. "No, Roger. You are going to repeat second grade," Anna repeated as she crossed her arms. Roger equated crossed arms with the letter x, and he knew she wouldn't change her mind.

"Well, can I go play?" he asked, accepting his fate. Before the word *yes* tumbled out of her mouth, Anna clutched her breasts and yelled out in pain. She dropped to the floor and wept. Natalie ran to the room and called 911. Roger went outside to play.

Anna's legs dangled off the hospital bed, unable to touch the floor. Her legs closed tight with ankles and feet entwined like a knot you had to loosen. Her arms crossed over her breasts as if she didn't want them to hear any bad news. "Twenty percent of cancer survivors have recurrences within the first three to five years after initial treatment," the doctor stated. Anna's spirit deflated like an old balloon. She believed by removing her breasts the cancer had no home.

"Microscopic cells can go rogue and lie dormant in the body, undetected for years. We do our best to remove as many cancer cells we detect," the doctor assured her. He left Anna in the room to get dressed. Anna's breasts cried out in grief. She stroked them gently, hoping it would sooth them. Anna missed her granny's mothering and nourishment. Cancer ate away at those memories.

Aunt Cora agreed to spend the summer with the kids while Anna's body underwent treatment. She didn't risk June destroying years of work getting her children to respect her. Anna's coworker Denise also helped Anna prepare for her second trip to the cancer center. Denise worked as an RN on Anna's floor. She started Anna's paperwork for her disability benefits, knowing Anna's lack of knowledge. Denise signed Anna up for a life insurance policy. Anna only pondered in the past about who would take care of her children; she forgot about them needing money if she died. Anna thanked Denise for being a friend during this time. Her own family didn't check up on her as much as Denise did.

Denise took Anna under her wing her first day at the hospital. Anna's shy demeanor reminded Denise of her oldest daughter who died in a car accident a few years back. She supported Anna by attending her granny's funeral. Her motherly compassion allowed limited access to Anna's personal life. Not many people had access. Anna shared pieces of her terrible childhood with Denise who related to a few of her experiences.

She mistook Anna's sadness for loneliness and introduced Anna to Wesley, a lab tech at the hospital. She figured Anna needed some male attention to get her mind off her troubles. Wesley was smitten with Anna. Men were the last thing on Anna's mind. Wesley insisted Anna be his girlfriend, but accepted the fact she only wanted to be friends. She declined his offer to travel with her to the cancer center and take care of her.

Anna returned from the cancer center, and Aunt Cora stayed a few months while Anna regained enough strength to take care of herself. Aunt Cora taught Natalie and Roger how to wash clothes, vacuum, and fix simple meals for the family to eat. "You gonna have to help your mom around the house when she gets back 'cause she's gonna be weak," she reminded Roger when he complained about doing "women's work."

It would be three months before she could start working again. Volunteering at her kid's school provided an outlet. She went stir-crazy sitting in the house listening to Prince on the radio singing about our impending doom in a few months and how we needed to party. She participated in monthly PTA meetings along with helping out with fundraisers and field trips. Natalie enjoyed her mom's participation.

"My friends think it's so cool you can come on our field trips." Natalie was all bubbly as she and her mom sat together on the school bus. Roger was not as excited. His behavior mandated Anna be a chaperone, or Roger would not be able to attend any field trips. "This sucks," he groaned when Anna sat next to him on the school bus. *This is no picnic for me either.* Anna's thoughts stabbed her like thorns.

Grandma Hettie—2003

Anna woke up to Uncle Leo tapping her shoulder. His pajama pants were slumped around his ankles as he nudged her to suck it. Anna slept in Grandma Hettie's back bedroom the weekends she didn't escape to her granny's house.

He shoved her shoulder again. "Suck it," he demanded.

When she screamed "No!" he grabbed her seven-year-old head and forced it in her tiny mouth. The corners of her mouth cracked open, and blood cried out. She gagged and then threw up. He slapped her for throwing up on him and left the room. Anna cleaned up the mess and cried herself another sleepless night.

Hettie called her a liar when she told what happened the night before. "Show me," her grandma said. "Come here, Leo." She yelled for her son. Anna stood frozen and wide eyed when Uncle Leo pulled his pants down and sat on the kitchen chair as his mom directed him to. His erection was a flagpole. Anna started to weep. "Show me what you did." Hettie pushed Anna toward her son.

Grandma Hettie's gaze was unbreakable as Anna sucked her son's dick. She lobster-clawed Anna's jaws. "Open your mouth wider," she demanded. Her eyes never darted away from Anna's face. Her grandma started fondling herself, which excited her son.

"You like watching, Ma?" he beamed. Leo shoved it down Anna's throat. Leo grunted. Anna gagged. Hettie groaned. He pulled it out before she threw up on it again. Leo sat in the chair and finished himself off. He pulled up his pajamas pants and left. Anna slumped to the floor and continued to cry.

"You liked it." her grandma determined. "I saw it in your eyes. I knew you were fast," Hettie continued. "Hot, fast girls like you have to clean your dirty mouths. If he puts it inside of you, I'ma bleach that too."

She grabbed the bleach from the cabinet and poured some in an orange-juice glass. Anna's begging and pleading fell on unsympathetic ears. "Dirty girls have to be cleaned." Hettie sneered. She shoved the cup toward Anna's mouth, but Anna refused to open up. Hettie squeezed her cheeks and poured a couple of tablespoons of bleach in her mouth before Anna spit it out. She pushed away from her grandma and ran to the kitchen sink to rinse her mouth out. Hettie walked away with her hands between her legs.

Oral sex quickly progressed to all types of sexual deviancies with her uncle and others after the kitchen incident. Anna spent weekends in Grandma Hettie's back bedroom entertaining her male relatives and neighbors. June's kinfolk refused to acknowledge Anna as a human being, let alone her being any relation to them. "She's adopted," they justified. She was made to feel less than. Hettie was Anna's pimp. She often stood at the door and masturbated while relatives and strangers violated and defiled Anna's body. Some paid, but most didn't.

One of her attackers became too aggressive and slammed her head on the bedpost, knocking her unconscious for hours. He finished raping her and left her unresponsive body sprawled across the bed. She never went in for a checkup. Doctors later diagnosed the initial cause of her epileptic seizures was repeated head trauma.

Anna pleaded to stay in the room with June when they visited Grandma Hettie's house. "No, it's grown folks talking, you go play with your cousins." Her grandma smirked. She was pleased with the knowledge of Anna's fate.

Anna moped to the back room, unaffected by a young male cousin slumped on the edge of the bed, naked from the waist down, hesitant to lose his virginity to his cousin. "It ain't incest 'cause she ain't blood," his dad justified. Anna attempted to back out of the room, but her uncle grabbed her and body-slammed her on the bed. Anna's arms flailed wildly as she fell and managed to punch her uncle square in the jaw. He slapped Anna and threatened to kill her if she ever put her hands on him again.

Anna smelled the alcohol on his breath as he sat on her chest and began to unbuckle her belt. Anna wriggled like a snake in attempts to free herself, but it wasted her energy. Uncle Leo managed to pull Anna's pants down around her ankles. One hand forced her mouth shut, and the other grasped both her wrists together, keeping her legs free to kick aimlessly.

"You'll have to hold her legs down at first," he explained to his son. He tightened his grip on her wrists, anxiously waiting for his son to lose his manhood. By the time Anna turned thirteen, she had given most her male cousins their first sexual experience. She was a sex servant of the people who were supposed to be her family.

Anna was rushed to the hospital the second and final time her grandma forced her to drink bleach. In true pimp form, she sat with triumphant boldness and explained how her fourteen-year-old granddaughter found the bleach and drank it. She asked to doctors to look at Anna in the eyes, and they would see how slow she was. The doctor stared in disbelief, but no one alerted social services. It was a mere, but significant, effect of negligence. The bleach burned half of her left lung. Anna stills functions with half a lung.

Grandma Hettie never medically diagnosed the soft swelling bulge around her belly. She figured to just cut back on her fried foods and she would be fine. A little weight gain at her age was acceptable, she convinced herself. As the stomach pains increased, she equated them with hunger pains from all the fried food she supposedly cut out. A friend rushed her to the hospital after passing out at bingo.

The doctors diagnosed Hettie with a massive hernia. Hernias are internal strains and burdens. They manifest from ruptured relationships, never given the opportunity to heal. Hettie's mom was her pimp too. That pathology of physical pain was passed down from generation to generation. Hurt people hurt people. Anna broke the cycle, vowing never to treat Natalie the way she was treated.

The hernia Hettie nourished for years now covered all her major organs and slowly strangled her. Her case deemed inoperable because of her age. The doctors had little success making her final days bearable. Pain radiated throughout all areas of her body. Every move she made created more pain.

"Somebody please help me," Hettie feebly cried out, but no one came to help. A phone was beside her bed, but it never rang. Hettie had burned many bridges in her lifetime, and no one wanted to rebuild them. Hettie died alone in excruciating pain, crying out for help.

Hettie's neighbor finally came to check in on Hettie when guilt got the best of her. She used the key Hettie gave her years ago and found Hettie dead. Her rigor mortis arm was reaching out toward the phone. The neighbor called the police and Hettie's sons. Including family members, less than a dozen people showed up for her funeral. Anna showed no remorse when her pimp died. She refused to attend the funeral. No one liked Hettie.

The Binder—2003

Anna's job required repeated bending and lifting. Nurses constantly complained of back problems. Anna's pain radiated throughout her body, which caused her concern and wonder. The pain grew increasingly worse after years of turning patients. The doctor showed Anna on the X-ray where discs in her spine were starting to deteriorate. Discs give mobility to the spine and absorb impact. "You will be limited in your ability to move. You may even be confined to a wheelchair at a young age," the doctor explained to Anna as her body grew numb.

Psychological imprisonment paralyzes victims long after the release by their captures. The slightest misalignment of the spine causes tremendous pain. Anna's was losing her support. Her backbone support was deteriorating. Her birth mom and her granny were gone. Natalie was leaving for college in a few years. Anna felt unsupported in life, and it manifested in her body as degenerative disc disease. An adult life of chronic pain mirrored her childhood trauma.

Anna's three days of bed rest gave her an opportunity to clean up loose papers lying around the house. She was singing her favorite gospel song when she stopped mid-verse. Anna shuddered when her fingers grazed her granny's funeral program. Anna tucked her program away for safe keeping, but the tic-tac-toe marks showed signs it was Roger's program.

"Roger, come get this thing," Anna yelled as she sunk uneasy on the couch. She felt a familiar pain in her breast. By the time Roger came to the room, Anna lay slumped on the couch, crying out in pain. Rogue cancer cells will present themselves when the mind and body are at their weakest. Stumbling upon the funeral program triggered the cells to reproduce. Doctors explained she would always be susceptible to reoccurring cancer based on her family history.

Natalie and Roger held Anna and cried when she announced that her cancer returned for a third time. Anna's diagnosis came months after her Grandma Hettie died. The resentment she harbored toward Grandma Hettie manifested as cancer in Anna's breast. Grandma Hettie deprived Anna of the nourishment grandmothers were supposed to give their grandchildren.

Natalie appointed herself as Anna's power of attorney. She grew up to be an assertive teenager who knew her rights and maintained her ability to control her anger. Traits she often put to use when dealing with Anna's doctors. She vocalized her views in the hospital regarding her mom's treatments. Natalie familiarized herself with the procedures and medicine the doctors suggested.

She established a routine for the household. Natalie made certain Roger wore clean clothes and attended school every day. She spoke to Roger's teachers and explained her mom's illness. The teachers promised they would let Natalie know if his grades started slipping. Since they attended the same school, she monitored his behavior without him knowing. She checked over his homework and fixed dinner. Roger was responsible for washing dishes and dumping the trash. Natalie prepared specials meals for Anna following the doctor's instructions for cancer patients.

One evening after dinner, Anna handed Natalie a black binder. "This is for you. Take it to your room and read it please," Anna softly stated. She turned and wiped tears from her eyes. Natalie bounced up the steps, not knowing what the binder consisted of. She opened the binder and wept. The binder contained explicit details for Anna's funeral. Natalie found it extreme and a little morbid.

Anna described where Natalie could find the lily-white dress she wanted to be buried in. *The new undergarments and stockings she needed were in a bag attached to the hanger of the dress,* " the paper read.

The white dress shoes were in a box in the top of the closet. *"Look in the box,"* the note instructed. Natalie went to Anna's closet and grabbed the box. Nestled in the shoe box, wrapped in tissue paper, was a gold necklace. A golden angel with wings spread wide dangled from the necklace as Natalie inspected it. Denise bought it for Anna as protection when she left for the cancer center the second time she was diagnosed. *"Please make sure I am wearing the necklace."* The instructions written in all capital letters validated the seriousness.

Anna choreographed her funeral for years. She fantasized about her funeral. Her obituary already typed for the newspaper to print. Natalie would have to fill in the death date. *"Print on pink paper,"* stated the sticky note attached to the program. Anna spent long hours pecking on the typewriter.

Specific instruction stated Reverend Calloway be prohibited from giving her eulogy. She arranged that Rev. William Clark, the pastor at her new church, officiate the funeral. Anna put in writing for Reverend Clark to find men outside of her family members to be the pallbearers.

Anna included her three favorite hymns and picked which choir members would sing them. She wanted the choir director to sing 'Take My Hand, Precious Lord" while being carried out of the church. She circled in the brochure, which flower arrangements would be around her casket. The serenity wreath she chose had a mixture of white roses, pink carnations, and white chrysanthemums. "Mom" was written on the bow attached. She settled on an all-white casket with gold trim. Anna requested the lining of the casket be pink satin. Anna insisted that Natalie and Roger wear all white. Anna had written a romantic funeral service.

Her tombstone should read "Anna Calloway—good mother." Anna put a down payment on her burial plot too. The insurance money was to bury Anna with money left over to split equally. Anna made her children promise never to fight over money. Anna felt a little more at ease during her cancer treatments. She made sure her children only had to mourn her death.

Natalie kept the binder in her bedroom but never needed it. Anna recovered from her cancer. Four months after her last treatment, June called her.

June—2005

June suffered from a stroke and needed someone to take care of her. Anna still loved her and moved back to her childhood home. Anna still pursued the approval of June and wanted to show how much she loved her. She had an obligation of loyalty. Anna loitered in each room. The place reminded her of a haunted-house museum. Nothing moved or changed since she left all those years ago.

Reginald's second wife tolerated staying in the house until they purchased a new one. It sat in solemn emptiness for years. Feeling eerie, but yet strangely comforted, Anna slumped on the plastic covered sofa and grabbed the remote. Within a year, June's health returned. She moved out after she married her second husband. Anna was elated to have the house to raise her children. Her elation was short-lived when June suffered a heart attack less than year after she left. Her second husband swindled her out of her money and left her penniless and brokenhearted.

Mrs. Calloway snuck her things back in the house while Anna was at work. She neglected to ask Anna if moving back would be a problem. A few days after June snuck back in, Anna called Mallory and explained why it was her turn to take care of Mrs. Calloway. "She's your mom too. She did more for you than she ever did for me." Anna defended her reason not to let June stay in the house. They traded valid reasons why the other should take care of her. Mallory eventually told Anna to pack up all of her mom's stuff and set it outside. Anna watched from the upstairs window as Mallory and her boyfriend dumped June's things in the back of Mallory's car.

Anna stayed safely away for fear that Mallory would attack her again. It took Anna years to overcome her fear of the steps after

Mallory tried to "knock that stupid baby out of your stomach." Mallory pushed her down two steps in attempts to hurt an unborn Natalie. Mallory was eight the first time she beat June up. As a teenager, she beat June up again when she refused her money for the movies.

Anna's reply was deadpan when Mallory called months later and told her June had died. Her dementia progressed rapidly after her diagnosis a few months before. Mallory, well aware of June's declining memory, often neglected to feed her and deprived her of the medicine she needed. Mallory would convince June that she had already eaten, so she didn't have to feed her. She locked June in a room when she went to work. "This is so nobody can get you." Mallory put in her mom's mind that people were out to hurt her. Anna regretted not taking care of her. *She may have lived a little longer if I had just taken care of her.* Anna beat herself up for years after June's death.

A second heart attack was the official cause of death. Mrs. Calloway also suffered from mini-strokes every year for the last seven years. The strokes crippled her movement and stunted her speech. June was slow to process simple tasks and cried inappropriately several times a day. The debilitating way her body tormented and betrayed her epitomized the anguish and suffering she put Anna through all her life.

Anna's body trembled as she entered the funeral home. Death disturbed her, but Anna needed to be there. Mallory moaned and sucked her teeth as Anna sat down with the rest of the family members. The funeral director asked Anna's input on the flowers and Mallory snapped. "You ain't even supposed to be here. You ain't family. You not related to us," Mallory yelled across the table at

Anna. Anna's demeanor remained calm while the papers in her hand violently shook in fear.

She reminded Mallory she was her mom too. "Then why did you put her out?" Mallory screamed.

"I took care of her when nobody else would. I have every right to be here," Anna defended. Mallory lunged over the table at Anna, knocking her out of her seat. She managed to get her hands around Anna's throat to cut off her breathing. The funeral director and a few family members tried desperately to pull Mallory off Anna. Reverend Calloway grabbed Mallory by the waist and started to drag her out of the conference room.

"If you here when I get back, I will kill you," Mallory threatened. Anna left, since no one tried to persuade her to stay.

———— ✷ ————

Mallory remained adamant that Anna not ride in the limo the day of the funeral. "So my kids can ride in the family car, but I can't?" Anna inquired as the limo pulled up to the house.

"Yup" was Mallory's only reply. Anna decided no arguing on this day. She retreated to the house and called a female cousin who picked her up and took her to the church.

Anna meandered down the church aisle, her back in excruciating pain. As she approached June's casket, a wave of emotions nearly knocked her down. Anna stood over June. Woeful waterworks fell from her eyes. Each tear filled with unanswered questions. *Why didn't you protect me? Why didn't you love me? Why didn't you believe me? How could you let them hurt me for years? What did I do to deserve this?*

Then came the question almost as deep as the mystery of life itself. *Why did you kidnap me when you didn't even want me?* As she turned around to take her seat with the family, Mallory sternly shook her head no and pointed to the visitors' section of the church where Anna could sit, away from the family and her children.

Natalie blinked back tears as Anna walked to the back of the church, banished to the last pew. As she stood up to sit with her mom, Mallory attempted to stop her. Natalie jerked her arm away from Mallory's clutches. "My mom was there for Granny. I'm gonna be there for her," she tried to whisper, but her voice carried throughout the silent church.

Natalie hugged Anna when she sat down next to her. Anna grabbed Natalie's hand like her granny used to. Natalie instinctively proceeded to rub Anna's hand. "Are you ready for your solo?" Natalie asked as she pointed to her name in the program.

Anna's eyes opened wide. She forgot that her cousin asked her to sing at the funeral. "Ready or not, I have no choice," Anna replied. She closed her eyes and steadied her nerves.

Singing calmed her spirit. When Anna closed her eyes to sing, all fear left her body. She received a standing ovation after her first church solo at age nine. Anna rejected the accolades and positive attention she received when she sang. Being praised felt unfamiliar.

"We will now have a solo by June's daughter Anna Calloway," the emcee announced. Mallory made a puking sound and some audience members gave an uneasy chuckle. Anna made the familiar, uneasy walk to the front of the church where she grew up. The silence greeted her like a friend in a crowd of known enemies.

She grabbed the microphone and made the mistake of scanning the audience members. Sprinkled throughout the family's side of the church sat her rapists. Other family members knew for years and refused to save her. An uncle licked his lips when he made eye contact with Anna. She almost threw up. She wanted to scream in the mic to have those men arrested for raping her, but the piano started playing and brought her back. Tears escaped through sealed eyes while she sang "Take My Hand, Precious Lord take my Hand." The audience assumed that her tears were for her mom, and maybe some were. She finished her song and briskly walked back to her seat. "I always love to hear you sing, Mommy," Natalie beamed as she wrapped her arms around Anna and planted a wet kiss on her cheek.

"You don't belong here," Mallory went in on Anna no sooner than she arrived at the burial site. Everyone gathered in the cemetery, giving Mallory the audience she needed to continue her fight with Anna. The flower arrangements swayed their heads nervously. She stormed toward Anna and began to push her toward the six-foot hole. "You need to be dead like my mom."

She shoved Anna closer to the hole. Anna screamed for her to stop as onlookers gasped in disbelief. Some too shocked to help, others were afraid of Mallory. Her daddy joined in the fight and began pushing Anna as well. They yelled at Anna. "You needed to be the one who died." Anna tried desperately to keep her footing. She fell to the ground as Mallory and her daddy started pushing her again. They stepped on her dress, making it even dirtier.

"Leave my mom alone," Roger cried.

"Stop doing that to her!" Natalie yelled. They tried to help but Anna's uncles held them back.

"Stay out of this," the uncles insisted.

"You not supposed to be here. Funerals are for family only," Mallory and Rev Calloway demanded. Her feet dangled inches away from the hole when a few church members finally intervened and rescued Anna. Family members knew better than to cross Mallory. Anna left before they started the committal ceremony.

Mallory made it clear no one visited Anna's house after the funeral. Anna admired the kitchen table covered with food dishes that a few coworkers dropped off. She unrested in the same chair that Mrs. Calloway sat in when Anna told her about the first rape. Anna's children were forced to stay away as well.

She reconvened with her childhood demons and sobbed uncontrollably. Her emotions bounced from anger to sadness to regret. Even though she contributed to Anna's torture and agony, June was the only mom she knew. Anna regretted not getting the opportunity to tell June she forgave her as Jesus forgave his persecutors.

Chapter 5

Party and College

The future belongs to those who believe in the beauty of their dreams.

—Eleanor Roosevelt

Birthday Party—2008

S treamers lined the family-room walls, and multicolored balloons cluttered the floor. Some balloons were placed in a box, designated for games after they ate ice cream. A silver platter on the table held enough party chicken wings to last for days. Potato chips gingerly removed from the bag and dumped in a fancy clear bowl lined with paper towels to absorb the extra grease. The crusts trimmed delicately off the sandwiches and cut into fourths. Two dozen deviled eggs were lightly sprinkled with paprika and placed on a serving dish designed to hold each egg individually. Toothpicks stabbed each cheese cube and were stacked like a small pyramid. Other finger food filled the rest of the table.

In the center of the table rested a two-layer chocolate cake with whipped butter cream icing. The cake was decorated with purple flowers and *Happy Birthday Mallory* written on it. A card table next to the food table was loaded with gifts and presents bought by the family and Mallory's friends. On the wall behind the gifts, a banner read *Happy Birthday.* Tacked next to the banner was the donkey image they used every year to play pin the tail.

Anna stopped begging Mrs. Calloway for a birthday party when she was ten years old. "Birthday parties are for little girls and not sluts like you," she reminded Anna. Anna's birthday arrived two weeks before Mallory's, and she received no acknowledgment. Mallory's friends came over every year to play board games and to listen to music. Mallory never wanted Anna to share in her celebrations. She threatened to beat Anna up if she even listened to the music. "But I live here, and I'm your sister," Anna would try to explain. "I don't care. I hate you. You ain't my family. I wish you were dead like your real mom," Mallory replied. She wished Anna dead on a daily basis. Little did she know Anna also wished the same for herself.

Anna planned birthday parties for her children every year. She didn't want them to miss out and silently suffer like she did. The parties were not as elaborate as Mallory's, but she made sure there was cake and ice cream and she invited a few of their friends over. Natalie wanted a princess party for her tenth birthday. She asked Anna what kind of birthday parties she had when she was a little girl. Anna tearfully explained to Natalie how her mom never gave her a party. Natalie wrapped her arms around Anna's neck and kissed her. She whispered in her mommy's ear, "You deserve a million birthday parties. We can share my birthday parties from now on." Anna admired how selfless her daughter was growing up to be. She hugged Natalie even tighter.

Natalie decided Anna deserved her first birthday party when she turned forty. She reserved a party room at a local restaurant and invited Anna's best friend, Vickie, Denise from work, and a few church members. She opted not to invite any family members. Even though it was supposed to be a surprise, Anna was aware of the party. She could hardly contain her excitement. A church member picked

Anna up from her house. She came out of the house wearing her favorite light blue skirt set. She carefully tucked her camera in her purse. Anna wanted to remember this day forever.

Natalie arrived early to set up the decorations. Pink and white helium balloons attached to each chair bobbed and swayed in time with the soft jazz music playing in the background. A sign announcing "Happy Birthday Mom" dangled right behind the chair Anna sat in. Roger littered the table with happy birthday confetti; most lay in clumps because he was too lazy to spread them around. Natalie handed each guest a silver cone party hat to wear. Anna wore her hat proudly while other guests laughed and joked about wearing them. It took forty years for anyone to do something this nice for her. She wiped the tears away as she hugged her daughter tightly and told her she loved her.

Anna dined at this restaurant several times before, but the atmosphere seemed a little more energized this time around. She glanced around the table and saw people who cared about her, and the tears started up again. They all wanted to be there to celebrate a big milestone with her. Anna needed to make an announcement but waited until it was time to cut her cake.

"I'm going back to school," she announced when Natalie asked her to say a few words. Anna covered her mouth in shock when the words left her mouth. She talked over the clapping and cheering. "I don't know how much time I got left here on earth, but I know I am going to get a degree." She revealed how the Calloways called her a dummy all her life and how she would never amount to anything. She planned to finish college to better herself and to prove them wrong. She shared the deepest dreams and aspirations of her soul.

"I remember what my birth mom told me on her deathbed," she continued. "She gathered all her children around her made them promise they would graduate from high school and college." Anna remembered being only eight or nine when she saw her for the last time, but those words remained imprinted and embossed on her brain.

She finished by thanking Natalie for the party and told everyone this was her first birthday party ever. By the time she sat down the entire table was in tears. Natalie bear-hugged Anna and promised she would help her mom with her studies. Anna knew she would be the first of her siblings to graduate from college, and that was enough motivation for her.

Ms. Sandy Kay—2009

Anna enrolled in a college with an accelerated graduation program. She was on the path to graduate in two years with her associate's degree in medical billing and coding. Anna's classes were in the morning, so she had the afternoons free. Anna decided to volunteer at a local soup kitchen a few times a week. "It takes my mind off of things and I enjoy helping people," Anna told the person in charge of the volunteers at the kitchen.

"Well, as long as you have a good time, that's all we ask."

Anna set tables and washed dishes for the lunchtime crowd. She enjoyed giving back to the community, and since she was unable to work, this kept her occupied. Anna quietly walked around the dining area avoiding bringing any attention to herself.

"Anna," Sandy read her name tag. "I need for you to help me empty the dishwasher, please." Anna was a little hesitant to come over when her name was called. Sandy Kay worked as a cook and had seen Anna around the expansive building, and they became fast friends.

Sandy was an older woman who instinctively took Anna under her wing. Anna shared some stories about her life with Sandy but remained private. Anna entered her final semesters of college when her doctor diagnosed her with cancer again. "I don't know what to do, Ms. Kay," Anna respected her elders and always addressed her as Ms. Kay.

"You have to talk to your professors. They may understand."

"I did." Anna sighed. She tearfully explained her situation to Ms. Kay. "This is the fifth time the cancer has come back, and I'm tired of fighting," Anna whispered between tears. Anna didn't feel as if she had enough strength to go through treatment again.

Sandy found an empty storage closet, closed the door, and held Anna's shaking hands. In front of the bulk-sized cans of string beans, creamed corn, and ketchup, Sandy prayed for Anna. She asked God to give her the strength she needed to get through this.

"You have to have the faith the size of a mustard seed." Sandy knew Anna was familiar with that Bible teaching. After the prayer they discussed having the faith and staying positive. She gestured in the direction of the spices. Anna spotted the mustard seasoning and nodded. Anna explained to Ms. Kay that her aunt was there the last time she had cancer, and her daughter would be there this time.

"Natalie left college and moved back home to help me." The sadness in her eyes was apparent when they talked.

"It's good to have your family there. Family is everything," Sandy concluded. Anna tearfully nodded in agreement.

Anna thanked her and mentioned that some of her professors were not as understanding. One professor assured Anna her grades wouldn't be affected because of the treatment. Another stated that Anna needed to leave to finish two papers that were due before she left for the cancer center in a few days. As she left out, Ms. Kay gave Anna her phone number and insisted she call if she needed. Ms. Kay hugged Anna and prayed one last time for a swift recovery. "Well, call me if you need me," she reminded Anna again.

"OK," Anna said and slipped in with a crowd of other weekly volunteers leaving to catch the bus. Anna never called.

Two days after Sandy said good-bye to Anna at the soup kitchen, she received a phone call from the transit station. Anna suffered a seizure on the train, and Ms. Kay's number was the only one in her phone. Natalie didn't own a cell phone and was unaware of the issue. Sandy directed them to take her home where her daughter would be there to receive her. She was thankful Anna saved her number in the phone. Now she also had Anna's number just in case.

When Anna arrived home, Natalie called Ms. Kay to thank her for looking after her mom. They spoke for a while, and Ms. Kay offered her services to Natalie if she ever needed it. "It's nice that you take such an interest in my mom. Nobody has ever done that before," Natalie revealed. Sandy explained that it was nothing and that her own mom taught her to be there to help others who needed it. After they hung up, Ms. Kay called her mom to tell her she loved her. "I love you too sissy." Her mom used Sandy's childhood nickname.

Chapter 6

They All Left

I think we dream so we don't have to be apart for so long. If we're in each other's dreams, we can be together all the time.
—A. A. Milne, *Winnie-the-Pooh*

Natalie—April 2010

For years, Natalie and Anna told people they were sisters. Even though Anna endured a rough childhood, she retained a youthful appearance. They considered themselves best friends. Natalie left for college on an academic scholarship. She had a free ride to any college she wanted to attend. Natalie dropped out her senior year when Anna's cancer returned for the fifth time.

She moved back home and resumed her duties in taking care of her mom. Anna felt guilty about Natalie coming back to take care of her. "But I only get one, Mommy," Natalie expressed. "I can to go school in the area. You need me, and I am here for you." Natalie gave her mom a tight squeeze, and Anna wiped both their tears away.

On the weekends, Natalie flew to the cancer center to be by Anna's side. Natalie looked in disbelief when she saw Keith sitting in her mom's hospital room. He had managed to pile in the bed beside Anna and was holding her like a doll baby. Anna had been in the cancer center for three weeks before Keith showed up. "My head hurts," Natalie complained when she called Ms. Kay to give her the news about her dad.

Natalie didn't trust Keith. For years, she refused any communication with him. She had an inkling that his motives were not pure. Keith offered to step in and resume his role as husband when he found out Anna's health was declining. Keith was a self-proclaimed "changed man." "I'm here for you, baby." That was Keith's mantra. "Are you OK? Do you need your pillows fluffed? Are you comfortable?" Keith doted all over Anna. He sat with Anna in the hospital every day. This gave Anna hope of a rekindled lost love.

Natalie's headaches grew worse when he gave Anna a promise ring. Natalie called Ms. Kay after Anna accepted the ring. "Why does he want my mom back? She is sick." Natalie cried to Ms. Kay.

"In life people will eventually show you who they are, you just have to pay attention." Ms. Kay pointed out. She explained to Natalie that everyone deserved a second chance in life. Her words offered little comfort to Natalie.

"I'm going to lie down. I don't feel so good." Natalie hung up the phone and retreated to the guesthouse offered to cancer-patient families.

Natalie complained about headaches almost every day when she talked to Ms. Kay. Ms. Kay assumed stress was the factor because of her daddy back in the picture. When she blacked out during a visit to the cancer center, Ms. Kay begged Natalie to get a doctor to check her out.

Two days later, her results came back. "They found a mass on my brain." Natalie cried into the phone. Ms. Kay asked if Natalie was going to tell Anna. "No. I'ma wait till she gets stronger. I will take care of it once Mommy is back home." Ms. Kay disagreed with her decision but went along with it.

Two months later, Anna was home recuperating. Ms. Kay asked Natalie every day if she went to the doctor to get her treatment. "I will, Ms. Kay, but my mom needs me." Natalie defended her decision not to get treated.

"Well you are not going to be any good to her with those headaches," Ms. Kay explained. "You know when you get on a plane they said put the mask on yourself before you help others," she reminded Natalie.

"OK. Okaaay," Natalie sung. She promised Ms. Kay she would set up an appointment the next morning.

The very next morning, Natalie blacked out again while in the kitchen fixing Anna's breakfast. They rushed her to the hospital, and Anna phoned Ms. Kay once they arrived. "Natalie has fluid in her brain, and she made me promise not tell you because you were sick." Ms. Kay broke the news to Anna before the doctors did.

"Why didn't she tell me?" Anna moaned. "I could have saved her." Anna called back an hour later. "My baby only got days to live. What am I going to do, Ms. Kay? I can't live without . . ." Her voice faltered. Ms. Kay comforted her the best way she could over the phone.

Anna stayed in the hospital with Natalie for two days. The scenario reminded her of when she visited her birth mom before she died. Anna lay in the bed with Natalie and rubbed her head. Keith stayed away from the situation. He barely had the stomach to nurse Anna back to health, let alone his daughter. Anna cried and prayed, then cried and prayed some more.

Natalie's body got weaker as the hours passed. Natalie kept her eyes closed because the pain was unbearable. Natalie finally opened her eyes and peered over at her mom. "I love you." Her voice sounded faint and weak. She closed her eyes and the machine flat lined. Natalie died in Anna's arms.

Anna called Ms. Kay to tell her what happened, but it sounded like senseless gibberish. Ms. Kay asked her to text instead. Ms. Kay knew Natalie died.

"*Natalie died in my arms. What am I going to do without her? She was my everything. She was not only my daughter, but also my mother, my best friend, my motivator, my support. She was everything I wanted in a daughter. I don't think I can go on,*" Anna texted. She cried as if the entire world, and all its beauty, had decided to implode.

"I'm sorry to hear she died. Natalie was a special person and I know you are going to miss her. You are going to have to find a way to go on with life." Ms. Kay texted some Bible passages for her to read and many inspirational messages for weeks after Natalie's death. Every time Anna tried to call Ms. Kay, tears strangled her words. "Just text me, Anna." Ms. Kay empathized with her.

Aunt Cora flew in to be with Anna and to help with the funeral arrangements. Cora stayed in constant contact with Sandy. Cora shared with Sandy a lot about Anna's childhood. She filled in the blanks of what Anna didn't remember or chose not to share.

"I knew Anna was adopted by the Calloways, and her birth mother died of cancer," Sandy said. Cora revealed in various phone conversations Anna's entire life story.

"Wow!" Sandy muttered during her phone calls with Cora.

The day of Natalie's funeral, Anna's drugs had her so sedated that she needed to be carried everywhere like a rag doll. Anna told Ms. Kay later that she didn't remember the funeral at all. *They told me I sang, but I don't remember singing. I wish I could remember, but I can't,"* she texted.

"Someone recorded the funeral, but I don't think it's a good idea for Anna to view it," Cora determined. "She sung "In His Arms," one of Natalie's favorite songs. Cora informed Sandy. Her voice was soft and soothing, like a tune that everyone knows. "She sang her heart out," Cora said.

The white casket with pink trim matched Natalie's pink and white polka-dotted dress. Her hair was down by her shoulders with a pink bow over her right ear. The white lace gloves she wore held her Bible and a white rose close to her abdomen. Tons of her high school friends attended the funeral. They stood in solidarity for Natalie. One of the students had shirts made with "We will miss you" on the front. On the back, written in pink bubble letters, was "Natalie." As they walked up to view the body, the teenager's tears fell like a full sponge being squeezed out. Two fainted and had to be carried out of the church before the service began.

"The one who took it the hardest was Roger," Cora said. "At the burial site, they keep holding Roger back because he tried several times to jump in the grave to be with his sister." Cora grimaced.

"He flailed his arms, kicking and screaming, 'My sister! My sister!'" Cora sighed as she revisited that memory.

"What did Anna do?"

"She was so drugged up. All she managed was a sidelong glance at Roger. I don't think she really knew what was going on." Cora determined. "After a while some people forcefully removed him away from the area. Last thing I heard was an aunt admitted him to a hospital. They think he had a nervous breakdown," Cora said with a heavy heart.

Sandy waited a few minutes then asked with hesitation if Keith showed up. "No," Cora snapped. Keith became ghost ever since Aunt Cora came back in town. He knew Cora was aware of how he treated Anna in the past. "For his safety, it is best he stayed away from me and my niece." Cora loathed Keith and didn't hide her displeasure and disapproval of him.

———— ⚬∞⚬ ————

"I'm going to take Anna back to live with me," Cora announced four weeks after Natalie's funeral. Cora and Sandy mulled the idea around a few days after the funeral, but it never came up again. Ms. Kay agreed it would be beneficial for Anna to be around family. "She can get a fresh start on life."

"It will be good for you and I will be fine," Ms. Kay assured Anna. Anna was hesitant because she didn't want to leave Ms. Kay. Two months later, Anna packed her belongings and moved to Kentucky with her Aunt Cora and Uncle Felix.

———— ⚬∞⚬ ————

Aunt Cora—June 2010

Shortly after June died, Anna enrolled in classes to become a pharmacy technician. She enjoyed working in the medical field but needed a change. A short time after graduating, she was diagnosed with cancer again. The last three times, Anna went to the cancer centers alone. Natalie was in college, but Anna didn't tell her about the cancer. She didn't want Natalie to worry. Anna and Wesley casually dated, but she wasn't comfortable having him go with her this time. She called Aunt Cora.

"It's back," Anna blabbered into the phone.

"Which cancer center are you going to?" Aunt Cora asked as she whispered to her husband that she was going to take care of Anna. Cora stepped in as Anna's surrogate mother. She had no children of her own although she and her husband tried for years. Her doctor explained infertility and the small percent of women it affects. Cora saw it as a sign from God and stopped trying after she turned thirty.

Cora stood at the door of Anna's hospital room. She appeared like sweet thoughts in a dream. Cora recognized Anna right away even though it had been years since she saw Anna. Cora always thought of Anna as her own daughter. She rushed to her side and held her so tightly, Anna gasped. Anna didn't mind as she went limp in her aunt's arms. They held each other and cried for what seemed like forever.

A wave of peace engulfed Anna. Aunt Cora made sure Anna didn't feel alone. She sat with Anna every day during her treatments. Love was Anna's cure. A real mother figure. Someone who genuinely loved and cared about her. Anna's stay at the hospital was shortened this time, and Aunt's Cora's presence contributed.

———✜———

"So how's Kentucky?" Ms. Kay asked Anna. She figured Anna should be acclimated after being there for about a month.

"It's different," Anna tried to explain. She had her own room at the end of hall away from her Aunt Cora and Uncle Felix. "It's really quiet here," she continued. "I'm used to the city life. There is hardly any traffic and most mornings I hear birds chirping." Anna smiled when she thought about the peacefulness.

Every morning, Anna and Aunt Cora walked the perimeter of her five-acre lot twice. Aunt Cora tried several attempts to get Anna to open up on the walks. Anna dawdled a few steps behind Aunt Cora, wanting not to talk. Patient Aunt Cora understood Anna needed more time. Anna was clueless as to where to begin explaining the abuse the Calloways dealt her.

Most of the walks, Aunt Cora chatted away about her garden and her desire to win biggest pumpkin at the county fair this year. Anna smiled politely and cried silent tears. One morning during their walk, Anna glanced over at her Aunt Cora. "I miss my Natalie. I still can't believe she's gone," Anna said with tears in her eyes. Her legs gave way like a wounded horse as she fell to the ground and sobbed. Aunt Cora cautiously made her way to the ground and held Anna.

Together on the cool morning grass, they shared pleasant memories of Natalie. Cora shared stories of her sister, Anna's mom. Anna soaked in all the stories. "You know Natalie and Audrey are smiling down at you right now." Aunt Cora rubbed Anna's back. Cora stretched her legs to avoid them going numb. "They are proud of all you have been through and how you still managed to survive," she continued.

"Well, I miss them, Auntie. Why did they have to go?" Anna questioned.

"Only God knows the answer to that, sweetie," Aunt Cora replied. "Now let's get up and get some breakfast your Uncle Felix cooked. I need to move before my butt goes numb too." Anna and Aunt Cora giggled as they stood up and headed back to the house.

Cora and Felix met in the grocery store where Cora worked as a part-time cashier. She started working at the store when she was a senior in high school and stayed for a year, so she could save up enough money to pay for college. Felix came in the store almost every day and always went through her line to check out. Sometimes her line would be long, and another cashier would motion for him to check out in another line. Felix would pretend he forgot something and headed back to the aisles until Cora's line died down. He was terrible at small talk, but Cora was more outgoing.

"Why not come to the grocery store once a week and not every two days?" she said with a knowing smile. She flirted with Felix for weeks and questioned his purchases.

"How else can I see you?" he replied sheepishly.

"Call me. I get off at six." Cora wrote her number down on his receipt. They dated for two years before they married. Cora attended the local university to stay closer to Felix who already enrolled in college with hopes of becoming a journalist after he received is associate degree.

Anna started enjoying her daily walks with Aunt Cora. The fresh air gave her a renewed spirit. She opened up more and felt more at peace. Uncle Felix was not an early riser like his wife but always had breakfast cooked when she came back from her walks. For fifty years, Felix fixed Cora breakfast. They sat together at the table and discussed life. Anna and Cora came in from their Saturday walk to find breakfast absent from the table. "Felix, you starting to getting lazy on me," Cora joked as she went to find Felix.

Anna nearly fell out of the kitchen chair when she heard Aunt Cora scream. She ran to their bedroom and fixated on Aunt Cora violently shaking Uncle Felix in a failed attempt to wake him. The coroner explained to Cora that Felix suffered a massive stroke and died sometime in the early morning. Anna called 911 and sat in the kitchen waiting.

Aunt Cora came out of the room shortly after and asked Anna if she wanted cereal. "Are you OK, auntie?" Anna asked, staring at her aunt who pretended everything was normal.

"Yeah, sweetie. I sat in the room and prayed with Felix. It was his time to go," she said in a voice so nonchalant Anna did a double take. As Anna ate her cereal, she listened to her aunt call friends and family to tell them the news. Anna admired how strong and put together her aunt appeared to be. She wanted her strength.

The house busted at the seams, full of well-wishers all afternoon and evening. Anna went to bed early and noted not seeing her aunt cry once. Others cried, even Anna cried, but Aunt Cora shed no tears. Anna lay in her bed and played back the story of a mother explaining to her child different reactions during adversity.

The mother put a carrot, an egg, and coffee beans in three different pots of boiling water. The carrot started strong, but it softened and became weak in the boiling water. When the child peeled the egg, the once fragile inside was now hardened. The coffee beans were different. When in the boiling water it released fragrance and flavor. The coffee beans didn't allow their circumstances to change their outcome. The beans adjusted. Anna determined Aunt Cora was coffee beans and she was the carrot.

Sunday morning they dressed for church like any other Sunday, except that Anna rode in the front seat. The view was different in the front. She held her aunt's hand as she drove to the church. When Cora parked the car, church members greeted her with hugs and offered their condolences. She assured them not to worry as she made her way into the church and took her seat on the same pew her and Felix she sat on for over fifty years. Cora and Felix were married in this church.

Church service was underway when Anna noticed her Aunt Cora twitching in her seat. "Are you OK?" Anna leaned over and whispered in her ear. Cora shook her head no. Aunt Cora clutched her heart. The pew became a sliding board as Cora glided to the floor. Her skirt was up over her thighs, and her head used the pew cushion as a pillow. She stopped breathing.

"Help me." Anna managed to get the words out before she slumped in the pew, seizing uncontrollably. Church members rushed to Cora's side, but it was too late. Cora's broken heart attacked her body, and she died instantly right next to Anna. Anna's mind changed once she recovered from her seizure. She realized her Aunt Cora was in fact the carrot, wilted and without strength to carry on.

"My Aunt Cora and Uncle Felix died," Anna told Ms. Kay through text.

"Wow."

"I'm staying at a church member's house until the funeral. It's going to be a double funeral since they died so close together."

Anna stated church members were arraigning the funeral proceeding, and she would be moving back home right after the funeral. The will mentioned that the proceeds from the house be donated to charity. Ms. Kay asked if Anna was OK even though she knew the answer. Anna never replied. Anna sorrowfully remained in a place where the only people she knew that loved her had died. She was lost in a sea of nameless faces. Anna felt more alone than ever before.

Two days after the funeral, Anna packed her belongings and caught the bus back home. Wesley met her at the bus station and drove her to his house. He knew the danger of her being alone.

Anna sat in Wesley's bed, unemotional for days. "I fixed breakfast," he announced every morning before he headed off to work. Anna thanked him and remained in a daze. Wesley returned home to find Anna in the exact same position when he left. After a week, Wesley offered his home to Anna. "You should live here until you get yourself together. Take as much time as you need," Wesley whispered in Anna's ear as he hugged her.

"You have someone who is going to take care of you, why not," Ms. Kay replied when Anna texted her Wesley's offer. *"Do you trust him?"*

"Yes I do. He is not like any other guy I ever met. He loves me for me." Anna allowed herself a delicate little smile at that thought.

"Well that is what you need right now," Ms. Kay declared. After a week, Anna moved her few belongings into Wesley's house. His answer to Anna's problem was like a bandage; it covered the cut but didn't stop the bleeding. Anna's healing would take years.

Roger—September 2010

At two years old, the doctors diagnosed Roger with cardiomyopathy, a weakening of the heart muscles. He received a heart transplant at age sixteen hoping to prolong his life, much to Anna's chagrin. "His heart appears normal but doesn't work well," the doctors explained. Anna could relate. Her own heart beat like a broken drum. Roger gave Anna heart problems on a regular basis. Roger's terror at home spilled out into the school. At least twice a week, Roger cussed out a student or was involved in a fight because he was angry. *He got his raging temper from his daddy*, Anna reminded herself when they all but accused her of being a bad mother.

Maybe I am a bad parent. This thought tossed around in her mind like a tennis ball. She raised Natalie and she turned out fine. What happened with Roger was all her fault. She didn't show up for him. Anna's obligated motherly duties were present, but she neglected to care about him. She saw her uncle when she looked in his eyes, so she avoided eye contact. Roger never understood Anna's detachment and acted out to get attention from her. An all too familiar scenario when sons are mini-twins of their no-good fathers.

Roger's heart was bad, but his mind was excellent. He was an expert at fixing things. Anna's toaster stopped working once. When she came home from work, Roger had taken the toaster apart and managed to repair it. He did this with other objects in the house as well. His services we often requested at church member's homes. The pocket change he received as a handyman, he used to buy candy, video games, and sneakers.

Anna was indifferent when she heard the news that Roger died from a heart attack. Roger suffered a mental breakdown when Natalie died and he never fully recovered. He died in the mental institution that housed him shortly after Natalie's funeral. Natalie and Roger were the best of friends. When Roger would get out of line, Natalie scolded him like a mother. Natalie became the mother figure he was missing. Roger enrolled in college with the encouragement of Natalie. He was on academic probation when he died.

The aunt who planned the funeral picked out a black suit with a yellow shirt for him to wear. A family member found a gold-plated watch his dad used to wear and put it on Roger's wrist. The casket was black with gold trim. He looked perfectly innocent lying in the casket. Anna walked to the front of the church to look at Roger one last time. Anna's mind raced as she closed her eyes and prayed. *God forgive me for not loving him. I know parents aren't supposed to hate their children. I didn't hate him, well, not really. He was a child of God so I had to love him. Lord, why did you make him look just like my rapist?* Anna's heart swelled with tears as she took her seat.

Anna doesn't remember the funeral. She sat unemotional during the service, which others erroneously assumed was a grief-stricken mother who lost two children so close together. Once the funeral was over, Anna returned to Wesley's house. A dagger of relief and guilt penetrated her swollen heart and released the sea of tears. She collapsed on the sofa and began to cry real tears. Anna was unsure how she felt about Roger being gone. She would miss him but had a hard time convincing herself.

Husband—October 2011

Anna caught Wesley numerous times staring at her at work. She would turn her head and walk in the other direction if she saw him in the hallway. "I just want to get to know you better, as friends." Wesley cornered her in the medical supply room one afternoon. Wesley's sugar spun-words didn't appeal to Anna's taste.

"I don't know you like that," Anna replied, trying to get away from him.

"That's the whole reason for us to go out. We can have lunch during the daytime. We'll be out in public."

After months of persistence, he finally wore her down. "OK. I will go out on one date with you," Anna decided. "No funny business either," Anna added.

"I will be a perfect gentleman." Wesley assured her.

On their next day off, Anna met Wesley at a restaurant. He made reservations and arrived early to calm his nerves. Wesley talked about work and some of the crazy patients he encountered. Anna shared stories of patients' family members and their insane requests. The conversation flowed without awkwardness. Anna smiled at one of Wesley's stories. She had not smiled in years. "You have dimples," Wesley commented. "How cute." Anna hadn't remembered her dimples. She still avoided mirrors.

They met for lunch twice a week, and Anna opened up to Wesley as if she knew him for years. Wesley spoke about his dreams. They bonded over failed marriages and teenage daughters. The friendship between them cultivated among the debris of past calamities and sorrows. Anna appreciated the nonsexual attention Wesley showed her.

Within five months, Anna found herself sitting at Wesley's kitchen table. He asked Anna over to show off his cooking skills. After dinner, the conversation continued on the sofa. Wesley put his arm around Anna and went in for the kiss. She pushed him away and jumped up off the sofa. "No. That is never going to happen," Anna said with force. "Take me home now," Anna demanded.

"What's wrong? Why are you shaking?" Wesley attempted to calm her down. Anna jerked away and slumped in the chair next to the sofa.

With her head in her hands, she tearfully confessed how her daddy and uncles raped her as a child. Wesley's anger came out as tears. He kneeled in front of Anna's chair and rubbed her shoulders. He questioned God how anyone could do that to another human being. Wesley held Anna and they cried together. Wesley eventually regained his composure and drove Anna home. "I'm sorry for what they did to you," Wesley said as Anna got out of the car. "If you want to talk, I'm here." Anna thanked him as she closed his car door. The weight of her secret magically lifted off her shoulders as she shuffled to her house.

Anna slept in bed with Wesley after Aunt Cora died. The times before she would spend the night, Anna slept in the guest bedroom. Wesley made one more attempt to have sex with Anna. Anna wanted to give Wesley what he wanted. She wanted to return the favor, but cringed at the act of having sex. She lay motionless while Wesley lay on top of her. She refused to remove her shirt. Anna didn't want him to see her deformed breasts. When Wesley finished, she turned away from him and cried while in the fetal position. "I won't ask you to do it again." he held her and rocked her to sleep. Wesley and Anna never had sex again.

A month after she buried Roger, Anna was diagnosed with cancer again. Anna was back in the cancer center, this time with Wesley by her side. Wesley stepped up and took over where Natalie had left off. He stayed in contact with Ms. Kay, giving her Anna's health updates. "I like him," Ms. Kay eventually revealed to Anna. "Where did he come from?" she questioned. Anna explained to Ms.

Kay how she met Wesley. Anna went on to say she felt safe being with him. She enjoyed his company and Wesley did as well.

"I'm going to ask her to marry me," Wesley mentioned to Ms. Kay when the doctors revealed Anna's treatments were not working. "They gave her a few weeks. I want to make this time with her as special as I can."

"Go for it." Ms. Kay was shocked at Wesley's confession but encouraged him.

Two days later, Anna returned from her morning treatment. The nurse wheeled Anna into the room. There were balloons dangling from the ceiling and a stuffed animal on the bed. "What's going on? It's not my birthday," Anna questioned. Wesley helped the nurse get Anna back in her hospital bed and waited for until her feeding and oxygen tubes were back in. He sat next to her on the bed like he always did. He grabbed her hand and Anna sat speechless.

Wesley rubbed Anna's hand and started talking. "I never wanted you for your money or for sex. Those things are not important to me," Wesley said. He told Anna he noticed the way she carried herself around the hospital all those years ago and he liked what he saw. "When you finally decided to go out on a date with me, you were ladylike, and that impressed me." Wesley paused. He coughed to get the words that were stuck in his throat. "You're not at all like other women I have dated in the past. I fell in love with you because even though you were sick, you pushed past the pain and it made you a stronger woman." Wesley used the back of his hand to wipe his tears away. Tears glistened in the corner of Anna's eyes.

"You are the prettiest women I have ever met, inside and out, and I would be the luckiest man on earth if you said yes." Wesley hopped of the bed and kneeled down on one knee. He pulled a ring out of his pocket. "Anna, will you marry me."

"Of course I will marry you. I look a hot mess." Anna tried to finger-comb through the remaining hair she had left after chemo.

"You are beautiful." Wesley grabbed her hand to stop her. They both cried.

Three days later, the hospital's chaplain performed the wedding ceremony in Anna's room. Anna's health improved exponentially after she got married. Their relationship was a fantastic fairy tale. Anna spent two more months at the hospital getting treatment, and soon her cancer was in remission. They spent New Year's Eve in church.

Anna moved the rest of her belongings into Wesley's house. She left her hell house and never looked back. While Anna recuperated, she stayed home and cooked for Wesley. Their evening chats focused on his day and her health. When she was strong enough, they took mini-vacations together and spent evenings playing board games with his daughter who also lived there. Nine months after her last cancer battle, Anna was ready to go back to work.

The hospital she worked at with Wesley deemed her a liability. "They won't let me work there," she explained to Wesley when he asked about returning to her old job. "But I do have an interview Wednesday at a pharmacy," she announced as a consolation. Wesley offered to drive her. "No, I have to get used to riding the bus again," she said as she kissed him on his cheek and left. Wesley had already taken the day off, so he was going to spend it cleaning up the house.

Anna's interview landed her a part-time job working as a pharmacy technician. She knew working full time would drain her energy. She called Wesley after the interview to tell him the good news, but he didn't answer the phone. *He must be really cleaning,* she thought as she hopped on the bus and headed to his place.

As the bus turned the corner, she noticed the ambulance in front of Wesley's house. Anna started shaking. She hopped off the bus and walked as fast as she could to the front door. "What's going on? I'm Wesley's wife," she demanded to know. One of the paramedics pulled her to the side. "Well, ma'am, your husband had a heart attack and he didn't make it."

By this time, Wesley's daughter ran out of the house toward Anna. "He's gone, Anna. He's gone," she screamed.

"What happened?"

Wesley's daughter, Megan, explained she was home and she heard what sounded like a crash coming from the kitchen. She ran in to find her daddy clutching his chest, barely breathing. She called 911 and curled up beside him holding his hand until he took his last breath. "Tell Anna I love her" were his last words Megan relayed to Anna. He closed his eyes and died.

Megan caught Anna before she dropped to the ground. The paramedics and Megan stood motionless as Anna had a seizure in the front yard. Wesley was only forty-four years old with no apparent signs of heart disease. Once Anna came to, she cried out, "Why does God keep taking away all the people I love? First my granny. Then Natalie. My Aunt Cora and now my husband. What did I do to deserve this?" Anna wallowed on the ground in misery. She started seizing again.

Megan found it impossible to care for Anna as well as mourn the loss of her daddy. She started hyperventilating. The paramedics rushed Anna and Megan to the hospital for observation. Wesley's body traveled to the coroner to reveal the official cause of death. Two weeks later, Anna moved back to her house. Loneliness consumed her.

Christmas—2011

Anna continued to work at the pharmacy part-time. Her hope was a fragile seed. It haunted her like the memory of some former happiness. Anna went to church and prayed for God to forgive her for questioning his choices.

The Christmas program at her church was in two weeks. She joined shortly after her last trip to the cancer center. Anna and Wesley used to attend together; now she took the bus to get there. Anna accepted the role as the lead singer for most of the Christmas carols. She sung a solo almost every Sunday, and the church looked forward to her performance for the program.

Ms. Kay suggested that Anna take a trip for a few days after the program. "Get a bus ticket, and go out of town for a few days. You need a vacation." Anna was all set to purchase the ticket when she received the news her cancer had come back. Again. Stage four.

"I can't fight anymore Ms. Kay"

Ms. Kay felt the pain in her text.

"My body is so weak," Anna announced, ready for Ms. Kay to tell her to fight.

She wanted Anna to fight but was looking through a blurred mirror of her own opinions. Ms. Kay would never understand the pain Anna endured.

"I don't want you to suffer anymore. Can you call a hospice center?" Ms. Kay encouraged Anna.

Ruby was the hospice nurse assigned to Anna. When Anna opened the door, Ruby gave Anna a big hug and a glittering, infectious smile. "I will take good care of you," Ruby promised Anna. There was an instant connection. Most hospice nurses check on their patients once a day, Ruby stopped by twice a day. "It's no problem, Ms. Sandy," Ruby explained on one of her visits. "Anna have such a lovely spirit, I don't mind at all." Her African accent was heavy, so at times she had to repeat her words. However, through the accent, Ms. Kay felt how much Ruby cared for Anna.

Ruby asked if Anna arranged for her death. "Yeah, I have a binder." Anna sheepishly admitted. Ruby leafed through the binder and was impressed with all the details Anna had provided. She called the funeral home Anna picked out to make arrangements. Ruby explained that Anna had weeks to live and needed to get everything ready. Ruby was unaware that the funeral-home director was friends with Reverend Calloway.

"She doesn't have any funeral preparations here," he said as he thumbed through her paperwork. "Someone cashed it out years ago," he reported to her. After the phone call, the funeral director informed Reverend Calloway of Anna's medical condition. A distraught Ruby informed Sandy what she found out.

"OK. I will figure out something," Ms. Kay replied. "Don't tell Anna what the funeral director said." Sandy felt like she was rowing upstream against a strong downward current.

Ms. Kay texted Anna, *"Can I be your power of attorney."*

"Sure," Anna replied. *"I don't have anyone else."*

A day later, Ms. Kay stopped by Anna's to get the papers signed. Ms. Kay explained to Anna she was not in it for the money. "What money?" Anna inquired. They both laughed. Ms. Kay helped Anna in the car. They drove to a nearby funeral home and had the power of attorney papers notarized.

Ms. Kay dropped Anna back at her house. Before Anna got out of the car, Ms. Kay handed her a pillow-sized stuffed lamb she had picked up from the store. "Whenever you get scared or nervous, hold onto the lamb," Ms. Kay instructed her. "This is the lamb of God, just like we are all lambs of God. This lamb will protect you. Hold it close. Think of me when you hold it."

Anna took the lamb from Ms. Kay and gave it a little squeeze. "It's soft," Anna remarked as she rubbed it against her face. She gave Ms. Kay a hug and thanked her for being there.

"No problem," Ms. Kay said before she drove off.

Four days after the paperwork was signed, Anna texted Ms. Kay. *"He's at my door."*

"Who?" Ms. Kay asked.

"My daddy." Ms. Kay attempted to calm Anna down and told her to call 911. Ms. Kay called Ruby and asked if she could get to Anna.

"I right up de street. I be dere in five minutes Ms. Sandy," Ruby said. Reverend Calloway beat and banged on the door using his cane. He yelled for Anna to open the door. He went around the house, checking for open windows.

Years ago, Anna installed burglar bars on her windows so she was safe. Ms. Kay called Anna and tried to calm her down. "He figured out a way in the last time," Anna revealed.

"What do you mean?"

Anna confessed what happened a few months prior. "He had an old key and used it to get in." Anna snuck out through a back door and hid in the shed out back.

"Why didn't you call me?"

"I forgot my phone in the house. I waited until I heard his car pull off and then I went back in the house."

Afterward Anna walked around the house to make sure all the burglar bars' locks were secure. She also had her door locks changed.

"The police are here and so is Ruby," Anna said with anxiousness.

"I pulling up to de house now." Ruby called Ms. Kay once she arrived at Anna's house. "He look crazy," Ruby said as she approached the front door. "Get away from de door," Ruby instructed Reverend Calloway.

"Don't tell me what to do. That's my daughter," Reverend Calloway started to get indignant.

"Anna, it's Ruby. Let me in," Ruby said as she knocked on her door. Anna didn't want to open the door, but Ruby assured her that a police officer was beside her. When Anna opened the door, Ruby blocked Reverend Calloway from gaining entrance. Ms. Kay asked Ruby to hand the police officer the phone.

"Hello." Sandy tried to calm her anxious voice. "The man at the house is her daddy who has raped her several times as a child. She is dying of cancer. She doesn't need him over there. He is harassing her. Look at how she is shaking." Ms. Kay knew Anna's mental state.

"Well, maybe he came to see about his daughter." the male police officer suggested.

"No," Ms. Kay was direct. "He probably came over to rape her one more time before she died." Ms. Kay said with crisp dialogue. Ms. Kay offered some more details about the dynamics between Anna and her daddy.

"She needs to get over being raped, that happened in the past." The police office offered no sympathy. All he offered was critical judgment.

"Hand the lady the phone." Ms. Kay snorted. She could not constrain her politeness anymore.

"Ruby. Please get Anna to the hospital before she has a seizure."

"OK, Ms. Sandy. She is shaking like a leaf," Ruby said as she called 911. Anna was in the midst of a panic attack. The ambulance rushed Anna to the hospital.

At the hospital, Anna made the decision that she wanted to go to the cancer center for treatment. "I need to get away from my family," Anna decided. "They just cause me grief."

Ms. Kay informed the nurse of Anna's condition. "Yes, we can get her to a cancer center for treatment. We have dealt with Anna before." Ms. Kay asked Ruby to go to Anna's house to retrieve the binder along with the lamb. Ruby made it back minutes before the helipad transported her halfway across the country.

Anna breathed profound relief once in the air. As the helicopter hit some turbulence, Anna squeezed her lamb and thanked God to be away from the mayhem. Her terrible past was far away, like a bad dream left behind in the night. She closed her eyes somehow knowing her sense of peace would not last long. Unfortunately, she was right.

PART 2

❦

The Nightmares

"Those heart-hammering nightmares that start to lose coherence even as you're waking up from them, but that still manage to leave their moldering fingerprints all across your day."
— Mike Carey, *The Naming of the Beasts*

Chapter 7

Family Visit

Family at the Cancer Center—February 2012

Anna's anxiousness consumed her. The helicopter seemed to crawl in the sky. She received treatment from this cancer center in the past but never by herself. The center assigned Nurse Helen as Anna's night nurse the first day of intake. Nurse Helen took an immediate liking to Anna. Ms. Kay had lengthy conversations with Nurse Helen. She provided vague details what hell Anna endured as a child, so Nurse Helen comprehended the seriousness of Anna's condition. "I understand completely," Nurse Helen said. She assured her Anna would be safe while she was taking care of her.

A month into her cancer treatments, Nurse Helen phoned Ms. Kay. "Her family is here to see her," she said in a concerned tone.

"No!" Ms. Kay practically screamed in the phone. She reiterated the urgency of Anna not having contact with her family. Mallory, her daddy, and the stepmother were persistent in wanting to see Anna.

"I told the hospital staff your request. They didn't seem to care." Nurse Helen's voice saddened with despair.

"She is my sister. I can see her if I want to," Mallory demanded to the person working the front desk. "We came halfway across the country to see her, and we ain't leaving till we do," her daddy stated. They raised such a big fuss at hospital; the head nurse came up with a way to satisfy this irate family.

Unbeknown to Ms. Kay, the head nurse heavily sedated Anna with medicine strong enough to take her out if they overdosed her. She placed a thin sheet over Anna's face and covered her entire body with blankets. She allowed Anna's family to visit with supervision. "Keep the visit short because of her condition." The head nurse relayed to the family.

"Oh. OK," Mallory agreed. Nurse Helen stayed in the room to protect Anna. The family doted on Anna, telling her how much they loved and missed her. They informed her lifeless body they couldn't wait until they were back together as a family. "I love you, sister," Mallory cooed as the family walked out of the room. Nurse Helen sat in the corner shaking her head with cautious skepticism.

"All lies." Ms. Kay pointed out to Nurse Helen later in the evening after the family left. Nurse Helen revealed to Ms. Kay what they did, and Ms. Kay went off.

"I warned them it may not be a good idea and when you found out you would be pissed." Nurse Helen worked the evening shift but stayed at work when the family showed up. "They announced they would be back in a few weeks," Nurse Helen relayed.

Ms. Kay needed to act fast. The Calloways could only pretend to be caring for so long. Ms. Kay was furious they allowed her family to have such close proximity to Anna, even after she pleaded with the hospital staff not to. She devised a scheme, but needed someone on the hospital staff who could help pull it off.

"Who has the balls to stand up to these people?"

"The social worker Mrs. Davis may be able to help you." Nurse Helen would have her call Ms. Kay in the morning.

Ms. Kay briefed Mrs. Davis on Anna's despicable family along with the pain and torture they have caused her. "They sedated her and let the family see her, even after you told them not to?" Mrs. Davis's blood started to boil. "I'm all about advocating for the patients." Mrs. Davis and Ms. Kay formed a defensive alliance. Ms. Davis willingly agreed to help Ms. Kay after hearing how terrible her family was.

"Anna needs to write a letter stating she wanted no dealing with her family," Ms. Kay instructed. She spelled out her plot to Mrs. Davis. "I also need to prohibit Anna from having any visitors while she is there," Ms. Kay added.

Mrs. Davis allowed Anna access to her laptop, and she composed a crude letter with a few sentences. It roughly described how she wanted nothing to do with her family and for them to not bother or visit her. She ended the letter with how much they scare her and that she knew they are up to no good.

"Are they coming to visit me?" Ms. Kay heard Anna's body shaking as she asked the question.

"I am working on preventing them from having access to you," Ms. Kay assured her. Anna closed her eyes and turned her head away from the phone. *They just won't stop. They are like the energizer bunny,* Ms. Kay concluded as she sighed and hung up the phone.

Mrs. Davis notarized the letter. She submitted paperwork for an emergency protective order, which provided immediate protection for Anna. She filed a restraining order on the three family members as well. Mrs. Davis certified delivery of the restraining order by having law enforcement hand deliver the paperwork to the family. Mrs. Davis proceeded with caution, taking no chances, knowing the severity of the situation.

"It's all taken care of."

"Thank you so much." Ms. Kay's smile was linked with a sigh of relief.

"It's no problem. We have to deal with aggressive family members all the time. I'm glad you told me before it got too out of hand," Mrs. Davis commented before she hung up.

Two weeks later the family came back the Thursday before President's Day weekend. "According to her file, Anna has requested no visitors." The front desk receptionist informed them.

Mallory became belligerent. "I demand you let me see my sister." Mallory's tone was hostile. "How dare someone not allow me access to my sister!" Mallory's boisterous voice scared the receptionist, so she buzzed for Mrs. Davis. "We ain't leaving till I see my sister," Mallory demanded, staring down the security officers as they approached. They continued to fuss like children who didn't get their way.

Ms. Davis approached the front desk. "What seems to be the problem?" she asked in a sly voice, knowing exactly why they were upset.

"The problem is nobody is letting me see my sister," Mallory challenged Ms. Davis. Her daddy and stepmother attempted to explain how they drove a long way to spend time with their daughter. They held papers for Anna to sign.

"I'll take the papers, but Anna requested no visitors at this time." Mrs. Davis explained as she took the manila envelope containing nicely folded, official-looking papers.

"Y'all gonna to let me see my sister."

"Look, woman. Just let us see her," her daddy started chiming in. He asked where the real doctors were who could help him. "I'm tired of talking to these so-called women," he said as he rolled his eyes. Mrs. Davis chuckled at the rising fit of rage.

"There is nothing funny here," Mallory said.

They family fussed and carried on without any sign of letting up. They were as welcomed as a fart in an elevator. The security guards approached the trio and attempted to escort them off the property. "You can't make me leave." Mallory shook the security guard's hand off her shoulder.

"Yes I can," the security guard replied as he placed his hand on his handcuffs.

"OK. OK. We're leaving," the stepmother said. "Come on." She directed the other two to follow her out of the hospital lobby. Mrs. Davis watched them leave. She eyed them with a frosty calm.

"They'll probably come back. They hate being told no," Ms. Kay said when Mrs. Davis told what happened. Do you have the letter she wrote along with the restraining orders?" Ms. Kay inquired.

"Yup. I even have the signatures stating they received the restraining orders." Mrs. Davis stomped both her feet and put her hands in a boxer's stance. "I got my dukes up. I'm ready when they come back." They both laughed.

An hour later, the Calloways were back with a local police officer in tow. "Why is the hospital refusing this family's visitation rights?" the officer questioned the receptionist. The receptionist turned the computer around a showed him Anna's request.

"Get that other lady out here. That tall one with the long, dark hair," Mallory commanded. "She seems to think she knows everything about what my sister wants."

Mrs. Davis sashayed to the front desk with papers in hand. She suppressed every sign of surprise. Mrs. Davis stood locked and loaded. She explained to the police officer the same thing she explained to the Calloways. "I have a letter Anna wrote saying for them to keep away." Mrs. Davis handed the letter to the officer.

"The letter states she don't want no dealings with y'all. It says to leave her alone," he advised the family. He attempted to hand the letter to Mallory.

"She didn't write that," Mallory screamed. "My sister ain't smart. She's a dummy." All three of them became indignant, yelling, and overtalking each other. The police officer again explained that the notarized letter was binding.

"Y'all need to evacuate the premises now," the officer explained.

"We also have a restraining order against them for harassment. They drove across country to bother her." Mrs. Kay presented the officer the paperwork along with the signed documents stating they received it. The officer used his walkie-talkie to request backup. He was all too familiar with violators of restraining orders, especially when it involved family members.

Mallory heard his request and lost it. She started screaming at the top of her lungs. "Ain't nobody harassing that stupid girl." She went on about how dumb Anna was and she never was smart enough to get a restraining order. Reverend Calloway also expressed his dissatisfaction with not being able to see his daughter. He also started getting belligerent. The stepmother was unsuccessful in her attempt to calm them down. Ms. Davis compared it to a circus.

The same police officer they brought to the hospital to help them get access their sister was the same one who helped arrest them. He hauled the guilty and baffled antagonists off to jail. They didn't get to see the judge for a week because it was a three-day-holiday weekend. The Calloways were locked up in a different state, which meant limited access to anyone who could provide bail money for three people. They missed their flight, and the hotel deemed their luggage abandoned and the items quickly donated to a homeless shelter. Mrs. Davis had the rental car towed off the hospital premises, so they had to pay towing and storage fees along with the car-rental overage charges.

"You should have seen their faces. Priceless." Ms. Davis laughed when she retold the story to Ms. Kay. "Also, I filed a report on the head nurse. She was fired for allowing her family to see Anna without your permission," Mrs. Davis revealed.

"So you're the one who has the balls?"

"I sure do." Mrs. Davis replied with a chuckle before hanging up the phone.

The amount of good in one warm hearted person is enough to over go all the cold hearted people in the world.

—Dellah Campbell

Chapter 8

The Nurses

Nurse Madison—March 2012

"Anna's sleeping," Nurse Madison replied whenever Ms. Kay called or texted to check on her. Ms. Kay never dealt with a cancer patient and was unaware of the healing process. Nurse Madison answered phone calls and texts with perfect manners that Ms. Kay didn't suspect anything. It was always "yes, ma'am" and "no, ma'am" from Nurse Madison. Ms. Kay asked about Anna's health. "She's fine," Nurse Madison would say in a singsongy voice. She assumed Anna was in good hands. If anything was wrong, Anna never mentioned it to Ms. Kay.

After two months of Anna sleeping only during the day, Ms. Kay asked Nurse Helen why cancer patients slept so much. The question caught Nurse Helen off guard. Ms. Kay explained every time she texted to check on Anna's condition, Nurse Madison responded by saying she was sleeping.

"Let me look at her chart," Nurse Helen asked if she was aware that Anna received morphine during the day. Of course Ms. Kay didn't. How would she know? She proceeded to explain what morphine did to the body.

"Anna's body never stood a chance to get stronger being on morphine during the day. In fact, too much morphine, and she would have slipped away. Usually family members ask for the

117

morphine when the patient is in severe pain," Nurse Helen revealed. Ms. Kay informed Nurse Helen that she didn't authorize morphine and demanded something be done about the situation immediately. "Sure thing," Nurse Helen promised.

While Anna lay in this coma state, her body was not getting physical therapy, which enabled her to get stronger. "You know we have social events at the hospital every day," Nurse Helen mentioned. "Nurse Madison informed us you didn't want Anna to participate."

"I never said that. I didn't even know about the events." Ms. Kay let out an audible sigh.

"They have pet day on Fridays. Every afternoon the patients gathered in the commons area for game time and Thursday was music day," Nurse Helen elaborated on the events.

"Can Anna start participating?"

"Not a problem."

She started Anna on physical therapy as well. Ms. Kay wanted Anna to get used to being around people. She needed the interactions.

Ms. Kay questioned Anna about getting the drip.

"Yeah. I knew," Anna sheepishly replied.

"Why didn't you tell me? You know what morphine does to the body?" Ms. Kay started getting angry.

"I thought I would get in trouble if I told." Anna began to cry.

Ms. Kay looked at the phone. For the life her, Ms. Kay never understood why Anna assumed she would get in trouble for being given a drug that kills people.

"How else can I fix it if you don't tell me?" Ms. Kay said. She reminded Anna she was her power of attorney and she would make sure no harm comes to her. "If something does happen, I will make sure it doesn't happen again," Ms. Kay assured her.

"Do you know what karma is?"

"No."

"Well karma is like the old saying, what goes around, comes around," Ms. Kay illustrated. "The nurse who did this to you will get hers in the end. Karma has no expiration date." Ms. Kay said it like it was no secret.

"OK." Anna secretly wondered why her family hadn't gotten their karma.

Nurse Madison's boss questioned why she gave Anna the morphine. "Cause I didn't want to do no work," she stated very casually. The new head nurse spelled out the dangers of giving morphine to a patient, but Nurse Madison had not a care in the world. She showed an icy indifference. The next day the hospital fired Nurse Madison. Nurse Helen informed Ms. Kay about her flippant attitude as the security officer escorted Nurse Madison off the property. "Geez," Ms. Kay said.

Two weeks later, Nurse Helen reported that Nurse Madison got a job at another hospital. "Those poor patients." Ms. Kay shook her head. At the time, Ms. Kay was clueless to the protocol of nurses and unaware of the Board of Registered Nurses or the Nurse Aide Registry. If a nurse is unsafe, incompetent, and unethical, on drugs, or violates nurses laws, a family member or patient can report them. They ultimately lose their nurses licenses after so many complaints (see appendix). Ms. Kay was not sure if the hospital filed a complaint against Nurse Madison.

Months later when Ms. Kay found out about the registry, no one at the hospital would provide Nurse Madison's last name. The higher-ups instructed Nurse Helen to keep silent. What bothered Ms. Kay the most was Nurse Madison's demeanor on the phone. It was a sweet severity. She pretended everything was sunshine and rainbows, hiding her laziness behind carefully chosen words and possibly threats to the patients if they complained. Nurse Madison fooled Ms. Kay and probably a number of other family members for who knows how long.

A wolf in sheep's clothing, is still a wolf

—Unknown

Nurse Penny—March 2012

Anna texted Ms. Kay that she wanted her lamb. Ms. Kay asked where the lamb was. Anna explained the nurse said she could not have the lamb.

"Page the nurse so I can talk to her," Ms. Kay told Anna. Anna tried to tell Ms. Kay never mind, but Ms. Kay didn't listen.

"What do you want?" Nurse Penny rudely asked.

Ms. Kay assessed the situation. She wanted to go off on the nurse but knew that would only make matters worse. Exercising restraint was going to be excruciating, but she needed Nurse Penny to be nice to Anna. Ms. Kay took a deep breath before she spoke in her friendliest voice.

"Please give Anna back the lamb. She doesn't have anyone there to visit her. It gives her comfort," Ms. Kay politely explained.

"Anna is a grown woman. She don't need no stuffed animals." She argued how her own kids don't have stuffed animals. Mockery crept into Nurse Penny's tone.

"I know if your kids were sick and wanted something, you would want them to have it, right?" Ms. Kay restated the lamb gives her comfort.

Ms. Kay's words must have struck a soft spot because Penny mumbled, "OK. Whatever." Ms. Kay expressed how much she appreciated Nurse Penny before she hung the phone up.

"Did you get lamb?"

"Yes."

Ms. Kay pressured Anna to talk about this Nurse Penny.

"Nurse Penny has always been mean to me." Ms. Kay asked why she never let her know. There was a long pause before she texted. Anna revealed the numerous times she had a tube down her throat for breathing issues.

"Nurse Penny pushes the tube down my throat the wrong way and then snatches it out hard," Anna reported. *"My throat is always sore and she won't give me anything to soothe it. She told me to quit being a baby*

and if I let men put stuff down my throat I wouldn't need the lamb." Ms. Kay was shocked.

"I heard Nurse Penny and another nurse in the hallway talking about me. They think I don't hear them but I do." Ms. Kay asked Anna what they said. She didn't want to say at first. Anna knew how mean Nurse Penny treated anyone who tattled on her.

"How can I fix it if you won't tell me?"

"They called me fat and ugly. They said I was too old to have no damn stuffed animal and all I needed was some dick. They made fun of the way I talk and said I stink." Ms. Kay could feel the sadness in her text.

"How did that make you feel?" Ms. Kay's anger emerged as if they said it to her.

"Sad and hurt"

"Well hurt people hurt people. You are probably was not the only patient they are mean to. I promise I will get her and she will not mess with you again," Ms. Kay assured Anna.

"Nurse Penny also takes a long time to come to the room when Anna buzzes. She said it takes almost an hour for her to get her medicine," Ms. Kay explained to Mrs. Davis along with everything else Anna mentioned the night before. "There have been several nights when Anna called me in tears saying she has been buzzing for the nurse for over an hour because she hadn't gotten her medicine and laid in intense pain." Mrs. Davis's heart sank hearing Ms. Kay's words. "You know she needs her seizure medicine on time 'cause she will die," Ms. Kay continued.

Mrs. Davis devised a scheme to catch Nurse Penny. She hid in Anna's bathroom and asked Anna to hit the call button. She timed how long it took Nurse Penny to respond.

"What do you want?" Nurse Penny buzzed into the room twenty minutes after the call.

"I need help. I messed myself."

"Well, you gonna have to sit in your mess until I get there. Didn't nobody tell you to mess yourself. You a baby." Penny laughed before she hung up. Mrs. Davis heard it all.

Mrs. Davis waited in the bathroom for over thirty minutes before Nurse Penny eventually came to the room. Mrs. Davis came out to address Penny.

"I changed her already. Why did it take you almost an hour to get here?" Mrs. Davis's unsettling question, rested in the air.

"You should have said you got somebody to change you," Penny quipped with straight attitude ignoring Mrs. Davis' question. "Made me come to your stupid room for nothing." Nurse Penny gave Anna a mean and debasing glare.

"I am going to report this to your boss," Mrs. Davis warned her. Nurse Penny shrugged her shoulders as she left out of the room.

"Stop shaking, Anna." Mrs. Davis tried to calm Anna down.

"She is going to be mean to me again. I may not get my medicine tonight if she's working." Anna expressed her fear, dread, and apprehension.

"I will make sure you get taken care of," Mrs. Davis comforted her. Mrs. Davis stayed at work overnight to make sure Anna got her medicine on time. Nurse Penny was scheduled off for the next three days.

Two evenings later, Anna coded. Nurse Helen called Ms. Kay and was frantic. "The doctors have been trying to revive her for twenty minutes. They want to call time of death. When did you change your mind about her being a DNR?" Nurse Helen sounded concerned.

"I didn't change my mind. Why would I change her to a do not resuscitate?" Ms. Kay expressed. Nurse Helen said her chart stated DNR as requested by POA (power of attorney).

"Put the phone up to Anna's ear." Ms. Kay requested.

"OK." Nurse Helen sounded perplexed.

"Anna, it's Ms. Kay. Come back. It's not time for you to go yet. Come on back to us, Anna. I know you hear me." Ms. Kay attempted to coax Anna back from her coded state. In minutes, Anna began to cough, and Nurse Helen returned to the phone.

"What did you do? The doctors are in shock." Nurse Helen was as well.

"I don't know. I just talked to her. I read the hearing is the last to go when someone dies, so I asked her to come back and she did." Ms. Kay was as surprised as everyone else it worked.

She hung up the phone, knowing Anna was breathing on her own again. Ms. Kay exhaled a silent and calm authority as she collapsed in a chair. "Thank you." Ms. Kay looked toward the heavens. Then she remembered the verse, "Oh ye of little faith." In the past, Ms. Kay's faith was tested and she didn't believe. Her faith was now in the renewing phase, and she doubted very little after that day.

Anna was still resting when Ms. Kay phoned a few hours later. Ms. Kay asked Nurse Helen to check the date and the signature on her medical chart. Sure enough, Nurse Penny wanted to snatch Anna's life away. She altered her chart on the same day Mrs. Davis spoke to about tending to the patients in a timely fashion.

"You may want to check other patient's charts to see if Penny changed anything on theirs as well," Ms. Kay mentioned to Nurse Helen. "Also, investigate the time the other patients received their medicine. Nurse Penny shows the signs of an equal-opportunity offender." Ms. Kay was sure Anna was not the only one she mistreated.

"That's a good idea," Nurse Helen agreed.

Charts from other patients revealed Nurse Penny denied them medicine and attention. These patients lay helpless on their backs for hours. She swore an oath to protect patients, and she broke it. The head nurse called Penny into work on her last day off.

"What! You're firing me?" Her face collapsed like a pricked balloon. Nurse Penny thought it was an unjust firing until they showed her the charts.

"OK. I'm out." Nurse Penny turned to leave the head nurse's office and was greeted by two security guards. "Get your hands off me," Penny said as one of the officers attempted to guide her toward the front door.

Two nurses out of the way in a matter of weeks. Now Sandy needed a strategy to deal with Anna's family members permanently.

What is done in the dark will eventually come to the light.
—**Luke 8:17 (paraphrased)**

Chapter 9 ————————

Help Is On the Way

Homeless—April 2012

In a desperate defiance, Anna's family returned to the hospital two more times with intentions to get Anna to sign some insurance policies. Mrs. Davis shredded the first set of papers they handed her in February. Being arrested didn't deter them from trying to see Anna. The front desk reminded them Anna requested no visitors. Mallory started to make a great big noisy fuss, but her daddy tapped her and pointed to the security guards who were ready to arrest anyone who caused trouble. The obnoxious gang asked if they could leave some paperwork for Anna to sign. They offered a weak "thank you" and left without incident.

Anna was aware when they were coming to visit. They called at least thirty times a day. Nurse Helen eventually turned Anna's phone off because it rang nonstop. Her family went as a far as writing a letter tell Anna how much they missed her and couldn't wait until she came back home. "You will like what we did to the place. It's all set up for you," the letter stated. Anna questioned who wrote it for them. She knew the letters were devoid of merit. Her family nursed a grudge toward Anna since childhood.

Anna lived in a constant panic fear. "She stares at the door all day," Nurse Helen reported to Ms. Kay. "Every time someone comes to the door, she jumps. She has not rested well in weeks." Nurse

Helen revealed that Anna questioned every pill or IV administered to her. "If a pill was unfamiliar to her, she would question the medicine and sometimes refuse it."

"I could hear them talking over me, Ms. Kay, but I could not respond or scream. I know they gave me something." Anna admitted she knew the hospital drugged her up, so her family could visit. Anna's presumptions were justified. She worried the nurses would sedate again. She knew it would make her too weak to fight them off if left in the room alone with them. Night terrors soaked her sheets with sweat. Anna's fear of her family outweighed her fear of cancer. Ms. Kay assured her that measures were in place to prevent them from coming to her room, but Anna's mind disregarded facts. Her woeful weariness took a toll on her health and recovery.

Ms. Kay couldn't understand the family's cynical disregard to stay away from Anna. She deduced that they needed Anna to sign insurance papers. *They want to kill Anna and collect money from her death. That's why they keep calling and visiting. They know her body can't take the stress.* Ms. Kay calculated. From Ms. Kay's point of view, these were profitable travel adventures for the Calloways. Why else would a family take off work to drive hundreds of miles to see about someone they obviously hated? Ms. Kay made sure Anna never signed any papers.

Toward the end of April, Ms. Kay received a phone call from Ruby, the hospice nurse. "When did Anna come home?" Ruby had a hesitation in her voice.

"She's still in the cancer center. What's going on?"

Ruby informed her that someone was occupying Anna's house. Ruby rode past the house occasionally to check on it since Anna was out of town.

"Two days ago, I saw some people outside de house in de front yard. I asked dem about de former resident," Ruby reported. The people explained to her they moved in about two months ago and were unaware of any former resident.

"Was dere anything in de house wen you moved in?"

"Nope. It was empty," they reported. They told Ruby they send a check for the rent to a PO box every month.

"I have to tell Anna." Ms. Kay's brain was in a daze. "I don't know how to tell you this," Ms. Kay called Anna.

"What now, Ms. Kay?" Anna said flatly, used to disappointment.

Ms. Kay hated to tell her. She closed her eyes before she spoke. "Your family took all your stuff out of your house and has rented the house to some people." Ms. Kay held her breath.

"My children's things!" Anna wailed.

"I know. I know." Ms. Kay offered little comfort to Anna. Anna never touched Natalie's room since the funeral. An unintentional memorial created by Anna's delusion that Natalie would return. Her spirits sank like a stone.

Everything else in the house belonged to June. The plastic-covered sofa. The dingy drapes. The Jesus pictures on the walls. The Bibles scattered all over the house. Anna still slept in the childhood bed her daddy raped her in. A museum filled with the horrors of her childhood. After Anna calmed down, she explained to Ms. Kay how the family always wanted the house.

"They hated the fact June let me stay there after she died."

"What about the deed?"

"It's in my parents' name."

That's why it was so easy to remove the stuff. What else are they capable of? Anger brooded all over Ms. Kay.

Her family figured getting rid of her things was the best way to get Anna back for denying them access to her. Spite allowed them to rent out the only place she had to live. Anna lay in the hospital bed devastated, knowing everything she owned was gone. The house housed bad memories, but it was her only place to live. Ms. Kay was secretly pleased with what happened. "You get to have a fresh start." Ms. Kay attempted to comfort an inconsolable Anna.

"But where am I going to live?" Anna mumbled. "I don't have any money, and they are releasing me from the cancer center in three weeks." Anna began to cry.

"Don't cry, Anna. I will figure something out," Ms. Kay assured her, but needed assurance herself.

Ms. Kay needed to find a place for Anna to live. Nurse Helen said she had family in the area who owned apartments if they needed a place to live. Ms. Kay thanked Nurse Helen but reminded her she needed money to rent a place. Sandy's power-of-attorney duties kicked into high gear. She was clueless on what to do or even where to start. Sandy was the blind leader of the blind. She prayed. *Send someone to help me. Please, Lord.*

Prayer is not asking. It is a longing of the soul. It is daily admission of one's weakness. It is better in prayer to have a heart without words than words without a heart.
—Mahatma Gandhi

The Logans to the Rescue—May 2012

Anna was days away from being discharged, and Ms. Kay had not acquired a place for her to go. Mrs. Davis attempted to set up a few nursing-home places for Anna to live. "No one wants to take her because of her age. We can try a hospice center," Mrs. Davis suggested.

"Isn't that where people go to die?" Ms. Kay questioned. Her own grandmother was placed in a hospice center and died within weeks. Anna was not sick; she just has no place to live. Ms. Kay was at a loss.

Anna's graduation day loomed a week away. Mother's Day fell on the same weekend. Sandy never had the responsibility of caring of someone. At age twenty-five, Sandy's doctor said her body stopped releasing eggs, which rendered her infertile. Sandy never felt parental, so the news bore no negative bearings on her life. It did put a strain on any man she dated who eventually wanted children. She was unaware of the responsibility and resources it took to care for someone. Sandy could barely take care of herself. Nurse Helen offered some places, but with no money, all hope leaned toward a hospice center.

On Tuesday, Nurse Helen called. "Some police officer Logan called to check up on Anna." Red flags went up in Ms. Kay's mind. *A police officer?* Her first thought raced toward her family trying to get her arrested. Nurse Helen continued. "Him and his wife were worried about Anna since they hadn't seen her since the Christmas program.

Matthew explained that Anna was an active member of their Bible study group. That's when Ms. Kay remembered. *He must be from the church she attends.* "Please tell him Anna's situation. See if knows of any place she can live," Ms. Kay said to Nurse Helen, hoping her luck would improve.

A few minutes later, Nurse Helen called back, "The officer and his wife, Jean, are on their way to pick up Anna and said she could stay with them."

Ms. Kay's jaw hit the floor. Ms. Kay mouthed a silent "thank you, Jesus." Ms. Kay couldn't believe it. Ask and you shall receive took on new meaning to Ms. Kay. "Please tell them thank you, and we will talk once they got to the cancer center," Ms. Kay said.

Ms. Kay texted Anna and asked what she knew about the Logans. She assured Ms. Kay they were nice and their four children who attended the church were nice too. Ms. Kay asked how Anna felt about living with them for a little while.

"I don't have too much of a choice now do I?"

"Well I guess you don't." Ms. Kay smiled at the phone because Anna's word ringed true.

It bothered Anna to be forced to live with strangers, but they were her only option. A day later, the Logans arrived to pick up Anna. Nurse Helen was sad to see Anna go. "I'm going to miss you," Nurse Helen admitted as she packed Anna's few belongings. Nurse Helen gave an approving smile to the Logans.

"She's going to be in good hands," Nurse Helen told Ms. Kay when she called to let her know that the Logans were about to leave.

Ms. Kay briefly spoke to Jean on the phone before they were back on the road to Anna's new home. Ms. Kay kept texting Anna the entire trip. She assured Ms. Kay everything OK and they were "very nice."

The next day, Anna informed Ms. Kay that she was attending graduation. The Logans drove her to the university to pick up her cap and gown. She thanked Ms. Kay for ordering it even though she insisted several times that she didn't want to go. Ms. Kay also did the legwork required for Anna to meet the graduation requirements. Ms. Kay was convinced that once the hospital released Anna, her attitude about graduation would change.

She remembered Anna saying her birth mother's dying wish for all her children to graduate college. Anna was the first and only one who did. Even more of an accomplishment with her being diagnosed as an epileptic. No one at the college was aware of her diagnosis, so she received no special treatment or modified classes. She earned her associate's with sheer hard work and a determination to prove to the Calloways that she was no dummy.

Other obligations prevented Ms. Kay from attending graduation. Anna beamed the entire graduation ceremony. Although her body ached, her spirit soared. Anna appeared to glide across the stage to receive her degree. "I did it, Ma," she mouthed toward the heavens as she walked back to her seat. Anna sat and wiped away her tears. She wished Natalie and Aunt Cora were there.

After graduation, Jean and Sandy spoke on the phone. Ms. Kay felt more at ease of Anna's surroundings afterward. Jean was a retired pharmaceutical sales rep with three grown daughters and one son. Her husband, Matthew, worked for the County Police Department. *Wow. A cop.* Sandy's mind started racing. *I need their help to get her family members to leave Anna alone.*

Sunday was Mother's Day. A very joyous time in the Logan household. Jean called and relayed Anna's demeanor during dinner and wanted to know what was going on. Sandy hesitantly explained to Jean how Anna's mother was no longer living, and both her children died last year. She heard Jean's heart drop.

"That explains it," Jean's voice cracked. Jean assumed Anna was unappreciative.

"She probably is angry, but not because of your family." Sandy didn't want to tell her too much of Anna's business, but elaborated a little bit more on her recent past.

Sandy described how Anna's family came out to the hospital several times and harassed her. "And because she didn't want to see them, her sister Mallory took Anna's belongings and rented the house Anna lived in," Sandy explained. "So she is going through some things, and if she doesn't feel like talking, please don't take it personal," Sandy spelled out to Jean. "Anna is not much of a talker anyway. So keep the conversations light and things will be OK."

Jean said she would pray for them. Ms. Kay thanked Jean again for taking Anna in. "Not a problem, Sandy," Jean responded before she hung up.

"Happy Mother's Day, Mommy." Ms. Kay called her mom after she hung up with Jean. Sandy's mom lived six hundred miles away. This was the first time in years Sandy didn't go home to spend time with her own mom. "I understand. We have to do what we have to." Sandy's parents understood.

Hope is a waking dream.

—Aristotle

Chapter 10

Close Encounters

The Meeting—May 2012

It was an adjustment for Anna to live with another family. She missed her own home. Jean and her daughters often celebrated girl's day out. They invited Anna to her first girl's days since moving in. Anna was apprehensive about going. She slumped in the back of the car and stared out the window.

"You OK, Anna?" Jean asked, glancing in the rear view mirror.

"I'm fine," Anna replied, holding back her tears. She wanted to relay how much she missed her own daughter. Natalie was her everything. Her whole reason for living, and now she is gone.

An empty feeling crept in the pit of her stomach. The feeling when you are up high on a roller coaster, right before the big drop. Anna hated roller coasters. Sitting with Jean and her daughters made her wanna throw up. She appreciated Jean and remembered Ms. Kay insisted that she "Fake it till you feel it." Ms. Kay gave Anna a pep talk before they left.

"I know this will be difficult, but you have to make the best of every situation." Her words stayed in Anna's thoughts for the entire outing. At the restaurant, she pretended to enjoy herself. Her parents, as terrible as they were, did teach her manners. She made polite monosyllabic replies. Jean's daughters didn't notice Anna's quiet demeanor.

Ms. Kay changed Anna's cell phone number five days after Anna arrived at the Logans. It took Mallory one week to track her new phone number down. Working for the local government allowed Mallory access to people's private information. Since she knew Anna's social security number, tracking Anna was easy.

"You didn't think I was going to find you," Mallory snapped when Anna answered her phone. Mallory called the cancer center to check on Anna when she found her phone number disconnected. They informed her that some family came and took her back home. "You know I will always find you. I am going to hunt you down." Mallory sneered before Anna hung up the phone.

The harassing and threatening phone calls continued all day and evening. It got to the point where Jean recorded one of the phone calls. Matthew traced the calls and arrested Mallory for harassment. This made Mallory furious. Two day later, she called again. This time Anna answered the phone.

"What do you want, Mallory?" Anna asked.

"I want to see you face to ugly face."

"OK."

They agreed to meet in a Walmart parking lot later in the evening.

"I don't think this is a good idea," Ms. Kay declared when Anna confessed her decision to meet Mallory. "I don't think you are strong enough, honestly." Ms. Kay worried the face-to-face would turn into a knockdown, drag-out fight.

"If I don't stand up to her now, I never will be able to. Plus, Matthew will be there with his taser." Anna and Ms. Kay chuckled at the image of Mallory being tased.

"I support your decision." Ms. Kay decided this meeting would help Anna's healing process.

Anna's emotions flooded the back of the Logan's car. *I cannot believe I agreed to have a meeting with my sister. Am I crazy? Am I strong enough? Anna, you have to stand up for yourself. Ms. Kay said I was strong. I believe her. Now I need to tell that to my gut.* Suddenly a sense of peace came over Anna. She remembered that with God all things are possible. Anna prayed for strength and released it to God.

As they approached the specified location in the parking lot, Matthew and Jean asked several times if she wanted them to stand beside her. "No," Anna decided. "I need to do this alone." They parked a little ways away, but close enough if Anna needed them. Anna was silently thankful Matthew didn't drive her in his squad car, which would have been way too noticeable. Anna's hand shook so bad she needed both hands to open the door. Her body was numb as she approached Mallory.

They exchanged hellos and without missing a beat Mallory ridiculed her. "I see you still fat and ugly."

"Well, you ain't too skinny yourself."

Mallory unloaded her arsenal stock of insults. Mallory reminded Anna she was dumb.

"I graduated from college," Anna informed her.

"They must have felt sorry for you and let a dummy graduate." Mallory laughed. Her angry words were bullets to Anna, but Anna wore her bulletproof vest. Mallory's words bounced off Anna's chest. The words stung but didn't knock her down. Graduating remained the hardest thing she even accomplished. Anna worked harder than most students in her class. In the cancer center, Anna prayed daily to live long enough to graduate.

"You ain't never gonna get a man." Mallory sized Anna up.

"I don't want no man."

"The people you staying with are only being nice to you because they feel sorry for you," Mallory mocked Anna. "They giving you a false sense of power because I know how weak you really are." She continued to blame Anna for her childhood turmoil.

"You lied about what my daddy did to you and . . ." Anna perfected the art of tuning people out, especially when they were being callous towards her. Anna knew it was rude and convinced herself if she weren't a Christian, she would have slapped Mallory. Anna tuned back in when she heard Mallory mention she had something for her.

"Well, do you want it or not?" Mallory snapped her fingers in Anna's face.

"Yeah," Anna replied as she shook her head back to reality.

As Mallory tramped to the car, Anna's mind raced, and she stood with a cold gaze of curiosity. *She told me she sold all my things. What could she possibly give me? What if she gets a gun a shoots me right here? She is going to kill me. I hope Matthew is watching.* Anna grabbed her legs to prevent her from running away. She remembered that wild animals could sense fear and will attack. Anna didn't want this animal to attack her, so she straightened her body and lengthened her spine to appear taller. She put her hands in her pocket, so Mallory didn't see them shaking.

"Huh." She grunted as she shoved a picture of Anna's birth mom into her stomach. Anna grabbed the picture.

"Thank you," Anna expressed, holding back her tears. *Don't show her weakness,* Anna thought as she steadied herself. Anna's birth sister gave her the picture one Christmas. The only picture she had of her birth mom. The only physical memory her mom ever existed.

Anna stared at the picture and then looked up to read Mallory's face. *Maybe there is a heart somewhere deep, deep down in the pit of her soul. Maybe the picture was a flag of truce.*

"Hey, dummy, say something," Mallory said, snapping Anna back.

"Thanks. Is there anything else?" Anna asked with hope.

"No, ugly. I'm done. Bye." Mallory turned on her heels and stomped away. Anna turned and stumbled back to the car, never taking her eyes off the photo. She got about five steps away when she heard Mallory's car door slam and heard her car speed off.

"You OK?" the Logans questioned as she slid in the back seat of the car.

"Yeah. I'm OK." Anna cried the entire car ride back to the house. She was careful not to mess the picture up with her tears. Calmness settled on her spirit. She couldn't wait to tell Ms. Kay what happened.

> **Each of us must confront our own fears, must come face-to-face with them. How we handle our fears will determine where we go with the rest of our lives. To experience adventure or to be limited by the fear of it.**
> **—Jean Blume, *Tiger Eyes***

The Attack at Work—June 2012

Jean found a job for Anna working as a medical biller. A friend of hers owned a convalescent home. Ms. Kay was hesitant about Anna being strong enough to work, but Anna insisted she needed to make money so she can get her own place. Before she started working, the owner asked Anna a few questions. How long had she done medical billing? What school did she graduate from? What can she offer the company? The mundane questions asked at most job interviews. Anna never thought she would be working again, let alone in the field where she obtained her degree. The job was a rope ladder dropped from heaven.

The smell of old people wafted throughout the one-story convalescent home. The head nurse gave Anna a tour of the facilities. The commons area held around forty people for game night, piano playing, and mealtime. Patients had their own private rooms. It reminded Anna of her dorm floor in college, except they traded their party flyers and sorority paraphernalia for medical charts and "oxygen in use" signs. The nurse showed Anna her office. A quiet area off to the side of check-in desk. She would be able to do her paperwork with limited interruptions. Anna secretly dreamed of working with the patients.

Anna's passionate soul connections toward the sick had bloomed years ago. It rooted from her being a suffering child and an unfulfilled longing for motherly nutrients. It branched out and flourished once her birth mom died from cancer. She nourished her dream of ambition when she worked at hospitals. Anna hadn't watered this flower in a while, and now a bud started to form.

"Thanks for letting me stay here," Anna said as she handed Jean money from her first paycheck.

"We can't take this. It's no problem you staying here."

"No, I need to give you something. It's not much, but please take it," Anna insisted.

Jean accepted the money and put it away in case Anna needed it. Anna wanted the sense of responsibility again. She longed for it. Working reminded Anna of a time in her life when she was independent. She started to get back to feeling normal. Something not felt inside her for years.

Friday was a few days away. Anna was daydreaming about what she was going to do with her next paycheck, when a UPS worker walked into her office. He abruptly closed the door behind him and locked it. He descended on Anna before she had a chance to react. He placed his hand over her mouth.

"I will stab you if you scream," he threatened. Every nerve in her body stood on end. Anna attempted to fight back, but he towered over her. She panicked and started seizing. He dropped his grip on Anna, which caused her to hit her head on the table as she felt to the floor. He left.

Moments later, the front-desk secretary walked toward Anna's office. She noticed the UPS worker's haste to leave the building. Anna lay on the floor shaking violently when she arrived. She called 911, and the paramedics waited forty-five minutes until her seizure subsided before they rushed her to the hospital.

Anna woke up in a hospital room with a vague recollection of the events in her office. Jean was at her side and Matthew, in full police uniform, anxiously wanted to ask her questions.

"Can you describe the guy and what happened?" He semi-interrogated Anna.

"She just woke up, Matthew. Give her time," Jean demanded, not liking Matthew's tone.

"We need to get him, that's all. Sorry Anna." Matthew's voice calmed down.

"All I can remember is his name tag said Vince," Anna murmured before closing her eyes back.

Jean alerted Ms. Kay of the incident. "Jean, do they have security cameras in the building?" Ms. Kay questioned. Jean asked Matthew to go to the building and pull up the security feed.

Sure enough, Matthew watched as a UPS worker entered the facility, and a short time later, he walked quickly out of the building. Matthew called UPS and inquired what driver delivered a package. They informed him that there were no deliveries scheduled for that building on that particular day. "He was an impostor," Matthew relayed to Anna's boss after he hung up the phone.

The doctors cleared Anna to resume work after a few days, but Anna remained hesitant. Anxiety hung over her like a dark, dense cloud plunged in darkness. *"You can't let one crazy person prevent you from accomplishing your dream,"* Ms. Kay reminded her.

Anna rolled her eyes up at the ceiling in the room Jean provided for her. *Forget the freedom and the independence. Forget getting a place to live and buying a rabbit. I just want to stay in the bed, pull the covers over my head, and never come out again,* Anna thought.

"OK Ms. Kay." Anna hid her true feeling from Ms. Kay.

"We will find your attacker. You have to move forward in life, even if life knocks you down." She texted Anna inspirational quotes about life handing you lemons and never giving up.

"Thanks Ms. Kay for the encouraging words. I will go back to work."

Anna sat at her desk at work staring at the door; unable to perform her duties in a timely fashion. She jumped whenever someone walked past her door. The owner stopped by to check on Anna and found her on the floor having a seizure. When Jean arrived, she called Ms. Kay. "She needs to get checked out," Jean said. Ms. Kay knew her seizures were from hitting her head. Jean stated she seized almost every day since the attack.

The doctors informed Anna her cancer had returned. She was admitted to the hospital with treatments to start immediately.

"Every time I make a step forward, I get knocked back three steps." Anna cried on the phone with frustration creeping in.

"I know it seems that way, but this is a minor setback," Ms. Kay attempted to assure her. "Be thankful you hit your head," Ms. Kay said. She envisioned Anna's perplexed look. "If you hadn't, we would have never known about the cancer. By the time it would have been detected it may have been too late," Ms. Kay explained. "We have to make the best of each situation we're placed in."

Jean stayed in the hospital with Anna during the day. It calmed her fears about being attacked. Nurse Vivian was assigned to be her night nurse. On the nights Anna coded, Nurse Vivian called and Ms. Kay revived her. Ms. Kay warned Nurse Vivian of Anna's family and expounded on how vital she remained safe at all cost.

"I will make sure she stays safe, Ms. Sandy." Nurse Vivian kept Ms. Kay abreast of all situations in the hospital concerning Anna.

No person has the right to rain on your dreams.
—Martin Luther King Jr.

Chapter 11

They're Back

Nurse Penny—July 2012

Anna's treatments were working but left her weak and vulnerable. Jean spent her retired days in Anna's hospital room. Jean attempted to brighten Anna's gloomy disposition. She read Bible passages about Job. He lost his family, health, and property. Anna, like Job, began to lose her faith. Anna remained sullen even knowing Job's wealth and health were restored before his death. She wanted to believe God listened to her prayers, but doubt tortured her at times.

"Laughter is the best medicine," Jean reminded Anna after making Anna decide between three comedy movies to watch.

"I don't really like movies or TV," Anna pouted, knowing she was going to have to watch the movie anyway. She'd rather sleep. The pain confiscated her laughter.

Anna sat unfazed at the same scenes, which made Jean laugh so loud a nurse came in once to check on them. Even the lamb sat angled as if watching the movies. Anna closed her eyes for most of the movies. She pleaded for God to take the pain away.

Anna shuddered when Nurse Penny came in her room. She clutched her lamb and closed her eyes, hoping she became invisible to Nurse Penny. Jean attempted to calm Anna who started shaking uncontrollably. "I remember that lamb," Nurse Penny revealed as she rolled her eyes at the stuffed animal.

"Do you know her?" Jean questioned.

"Why you need to know all that?" Penny snapped back.

"What is your name? You seem to be making her upset."

"Penny. It's on my name tag." Penny huffed. She left the room without seeing about Anna.

"Some Nurse Penny is here. Said she know the lamb. Anna is scared," Jean texted Ms. Kay.

"Jean, do not let her near Anna." Ms. Kay demanded when she called.

"What's going on? She is shaking and refuses to open her eyes." Jean sounded worried.

"She was one of the bad nurses at the other cancer center. Page the head nurse, please. Need to talk to her." Ms. Kay was confused how Penny was able to work at the cancer center. She gave Jean a brief rundown on Nurse Penny's antics.

Within minutes, the head nurse was in Anna's room. "I'm Nurse Miriam, the head nurse." She introduced herself to Ms. Kay on the phone. "What seems to be the problem? I see Anna is shaking. It's going to be OK, Anna." Nurse Miriam attempted to calm Anna down as well.

"She has tried to kill her. She altered her medical chart to make her a DNR. I thought she was fired and never allowed to work at a hospital," Ms. Kay exclaimed as she explained Anna's encounters with Penny.

"I need to get her file from the cancer center and I will call you back. Until then I will send another nurse to her room." Nurse Miriam handed the phone to Jean.

"Let me talk to Anna."

"You are safe, Anna. Penny will not be able to get to you," Ms. Kay said assuredly.

"OK," her words quavered out, unconvinced of her safety.

An hour later, Nurse Miriam called Ms. Kay and asked for her side of the events at the other hospital. "OK, your story lines up with what is on file," Nurse Miriam concurred. "Penny will be fired, and

I will personally escort her out of the building." Ms. Kay let out a sigh of relief.

"Also, I will be taking over as Anna's day nurse from now on." Nurse Miriam informed Ms. Kay.

Good people do not need laws to tell them to act responsibly, while bad people will find a way around the laws.

—Plato

The Family Returns—July 2012

Matthew conducted an investigation into Ms. Kay's claims of Anna's childhood rape. He collected her childhood medical records, which provided enough evidence to proceed with a criminal investigation. The district attorney took over the case and filed a formal complaint against Reverend Calloway. They served Reginald with court papers.

"Please get a copy of her credit report," she asked Jean. Ms. Kay stayed unconvinced her family had the finances to get across the country several times. Jean discovered that Mallory stole Anna's identity. She opened several credit cards in Anna's name and maxed all them out. "That's how they financed their trips to harass Anna," Jean declared as she informed Sandy of her findings.

"Damn," Sandy replied. Then her mind started racing. "Get a copy of her credit card statements. Scan those transactions and see if they got insurance policies in her name as well," Sandy requested.

An hour later, Jean called Sandy. "There are several monthly transactions paying for life insurance premiums as well as one credit card used to pay for a life insurance policy for the entire year," Jean told Sandy as she leafed through the print out copies of all the credit cards statements.

One of Jean's friends worked as an insurance specialist. Jean gave her Anna's social security number, and within hours, the insurance specialist found over fifteen policies with Anna's name on them. She faxed over the policies to compare signatures. "They equal up to over a million dollars," Jean stuttered.

"Wow," Ms. Kay replied. They already hated Anna and wanted her dead, and now they have a million reasons to kill her.

"The social worker from the cancer center said they left paperwork for Anna to sign. When she refused to sign it, they probably forged her name," Ms. Kay deduced. Ms. Kay figured it only a matter of time before they found Anna at the hospital, since they had her social security number.

Jean did more digging into the credit card transactions. She found payments for a cable bill as well as an electric bill. Jean called the companies who stated the cable bill belonged to Mallory. Reginald's address was on the electricity bill. She got a copy of the transactions. More proof her family obtained the credit cards illegally. She gave the information to Matthew to add Mallory's name to the criminal investigation.

The family went into a blind rage after they received the court papers. The family convinced themselves that if Anna died then she would not be able to testify, so they set out to find and kill Anna. Her family failed to realize the prosecutor would represent Anna, so she didn't have to go to court to testify against them.

The next day, Jean called Sandy, saying her family was leering at her from the hallway. They stood near her hospital door, masterminding their attack. "She is shaking uncontrollably," Jean informed Ms. Kay. A sudden sense of fear ran through Anna's body like the chill of an arctic blast. Fear consumed Anna at the sight of her family. She remembered the torment and abuse she suffered at their hands for years. Anna knew they were capable of severe abuse and inflictions.

Jean called for security then phoned Matthew. Three security guards rushed to her room and escorted them to the hospital lobby before they could descend upon Anna. Matthew previously submitted restraining orders against the entire family, so once downstairs the security guards detained them without hesitation.

As usual, Mallory started performing. "I demand to see my sister," Mallory yelled. "You have no right to arrest me." Mallory attempted to free herself from the handcuffs. She lunged at one of the security guards and spit in his direction. Mallory became so vile and violent it took two guards to cuff her to the bench in the front entrance. It was quite a spectacle for anyone who walked in. Matthew arrived with a copy of the restraining orders. The Calloways were read their rights and placed into the police cars.

Mallory returned to the hospital the next morning. This time, Nurse Miriam was prepared. She saw what happened the day before and positioned herself for battle. She saw Mallory getting off the elevator on Anna's floor. She immediately called for security. Miriam couldn't understand how they got out on bail so quickly.

"Um, excuse me. You're not supposed to be here," Miriam protested as she stopped Mallory in the hallway. She blocked Mallory from proceeding down to Anna's room.

"You can't tell me what to do," Mallory lashed back. Mallory started to go off on Nurse Miriam. She called Miriam all kinds of names and demanded to see her sister. Nurse Miriam stood with her arms crossed, trying desperately to maintain her professionalism.

"You're bothering Anna as well as the other patients. You need to leave now."

"Bitch. Don't tell me what to do." Mallory stepped toward Miriam with the intentions of putting her hands in Miriam's face. Miriam unfolded her arms. A hostile skirmish was about to ensure. Miriam began to ball her up her fist at her side. Then Miriam stepped back and chuckled.

"Ain't nothing funny," Mallory growled. Mallory's back was to the elevator when security grabbed her by the shoulder.

"What the—" Mallory yelped. Miriam saw them coming and never let on. Security escorted her off the floor and downstairs where she was arrested again.

"You should have seen her jump when the security guard grabbed her. She didn't know he was behind her. Mallory's eyes got so big." Nurse Miriam laughed when she told Ms. Kay the story of what happened. Ms. Kay thanked her for keeping Mallory away from Anna. Anna lay in the bed unaware of Mallory's returned.

"Now we need to find out why she's able to get out of jail so fast." Ms. Kay mentioned the incident to Jean so she could tell Matthew.

The next afternoon, Reverend Calloway came back to the hospital. Nurse Miriam was working a later shift, so a different nurse was tending to Anna.

"You promised Ms. Kay. You promised they would leave me alone." Anna shook, terrified as she texted Ms. Kay that her dad was at her hospital door.

"I can't help what crazy does," Ms. Kay tried to assure her. Ms. Kay explained she was doing the best she could.

"That crazy dad of hers is up at the hospital again," Ms. Kay texted Jean. Matthew called security and decided to come up to the hospital himself.

Ms. Kay called and asked Anna to hand the phone to the nurse. Her mean disposition was apparent when she spoke. Ms. Kay explained to her the man at the door is only there to cause Anna harm. "Well, he keeps saying he is her father," the nurse said with an attitude.

Ms. Kay asked the nurse if Anna was shaking and crying. "Yeah she is. So?" the nurse argued back, showing a clear lack of sympathy.

"When you get a visit from your dad do you shake like that and cry?" Ms. Kay asked her.

"I guess not," she replied sarcastically.

"Then don't let him in her room. It's in her chart."

"Well, I have to get the chart and see."

"Don't leave her there by herself," Ms. Kay pleaded.

"Well, how can I get the chart then?" she said in a tone that made Ms. Kay twitch. Ms. Kay asked the nurse several times to stay with Anna until security got there.

"Whatever." She snorted and handed Anna back the phone. Ms. Kay attempted to comfort Anna until security arrived a few minutes later. By then Matthew and Jean were at the door.

Jean sat next to Anna to comfort her while Matthew handcuffed Reverend Calloway. The nurse started giving Matthew lip.

"Why you need to arrest this man when he says he is her father?" she questioned Matthew.

"This matter doesn't concern you."

"Yes, it is my concern," the nurse announced as she put her hands in Matthew's face. Matthew, donned in full police gear, grabbed her hands and put her in handcuffs before she even knew what happened. She continued flipping off at the mouth as the security guard escorted her to the police car. It seemed like the nurse took sides with the Calloways without even knowing the story.

Ms. Kay stayed on the phone with Jean during Matthew's altercation. "Matthew needs to check Reginald to see if he has anything on him. He keeps coming back to the hospital." Ms. Kay was sure something was going on. *There had to be a reason,* Ms. Kay thought. When Matthew patted him down, he found a syringe. The lab at the hospital ran a test on the contents.

"Bleach, rat poison, and a plethora of cleaning products were in that syringe," Matthew informed Ms. Kay less than thirty minutes later. "He will be staying in jail until his trial," Matthew assured her.

"Good."

They finally found enough evidence to hold him permanently. His trial was a few weeks away, which gave Anna a few weeks of peace. That evening, Nurse Vivian gave Anna a sedative to calm her down.

"Mallory will probably be up there tomorrow when she find out about her dad's arrest, Miriam. So be ready." She informed Miriam of all the action she missed.

"I got this." Miriam chuckled, remembering her last encounter with Mallory.

Mallory arrived at the hospital early that next morning. Nurse Miriam greeted her at Anna's door. Mallory screamed at Anna from the door.

"You had my dad arrested, Anna, I'm going to kill you," Mallory said with a taunting accusation. Anna turned her head away from the door.

"Shut up. He got his own self arrested," Miriam retorted, placing her hand on the doorframe, not allowing her access to the room. Miriam and Mallory argued back and forth. Security came within minutes. They handcuffed and escorted Mallory downstairs again.

"Please have Matthew find out why this family keeps getting out of jail so quickly." Ms. Kay called Jean once she found out Mallory came back. Ms. Kay was extremely perplexed.

Later on that same evening, Mallory returned to the hospital. She didn't make it past the front desk. They recognized Mallory and security detain her until the police arrived. Matthew realized that the counties were not synchronized. The county police that arrested Mallory didn't have the restraining order paperwork because it was filed in a different county. Matthew refiled the restraining orders with all adjacent counties. Mallory's arrest took this time because they had the paperwork, and she too remained in jail until her court date.

Collect calls from jail started coming to Anna's phone. Mallory started harassing Anna from behind bars. Miriam called her cell phone provider and blocked collect calls. Mrs. Calloway started calling from a blocked number.

"We gonna get you, Anna. You too weak to live," Janice threatened Anna. Miriam blocked calls as well. Matthew insisted to keep her phone number the same so their calls are evidence for stalking and harassment.

Two days later, Mrs. Calloway came to the hospital. Janice hoped coming at night would throw the nurses off. Her husband

and stepdaughter were in jail, and she sought malice and revenge on Anna. She had a stubborn disregard that Anna was the victim.

When Anna opened her eyes, Janice was standing over her with a cold glare. Anna stared back in helpless bewilderment. Anna buzzed the nurse and her scream pierced the silence. Nurse Vivian appeared in the room quickly. Janice's paralyzing self-doubt didn't allow her to harm Anna. Maybe in her heart she knew it wrong which caused her to hesitate. She was arrested as well.

They searched Janice and found a syringe with the same concoction her husband had. They also confiscated a pocketknife from her purse. She tried to explain she worked nights and needed the knife for protection. Further investigation found she retired three years ago. Escorted away in handcuffs, Janice never returned to the hospital.

Matthew decided to post a security guard at Anna's door. There needed to be a full time nurse in her room at all times at Ms. Kay's request. Anna never took her eyes off the door. They positioned her bed so she could see whoever entered her room. Anna wasn't taking any more chances of being snuck up on by anyone.

Days after all the madness, Anna suffered a grand mal seizure and suffered temporary memory loss. The doctors said her memory would return. It was just a matter of when.

Dreams so often become nightmares. Family can so easily become foes. And people are always more stupid than you give them credit for.
—Mike A. Lancaster, 1.4

Chapter 12

The Other Sister and Cancer

Alisha—August 2012

Eight years into their marriage, Reverend Calloway cheated on June and produced Alisha. As a child, Anna admired Alisha. Growing up, Alisha lived a few states away and visited her dad during the summertime.

"Alisha took me to the hospital when my dad raped me," Anna confided to Ms. Kay when she first talked her about the rapes.

"Whatever happened to her?" Ms. Kay questioned.

"I don't know. She just left and never came back for me." Anna recalled with a flat tone. Ms. Kay assumed the family found out that Alisha helped Anna so they kept her away.

Alisha and her military husband lived in Germany for the past ten years. They were on leave visiting family members when she found out her daddy faced a slew of other charges as well as raping Anna. She attended his last days of court and found out Anna's whereabouts. She needed to see Anna. The penetrating cries of a young Anna begging to go back with her assailed her memories as something unforgettable. Alisha's guilt returned as well.

"Who is this at the door?" Nurse Miriam asked Anna when a small but round woman stood at her hospital door, hesitant to come in.

"Hey, Anna!" Alisha stood at the entrance to her room. Alisha wore a big smile on her face.

"Sisssteeer." Anna's eyes lit up. She was unable to remember Alisha's name but knew who she was. Anna's words were slow and deliberate. Her memory came back in certain areas, but after weeks, it still was not 100 percent. She glided past the security guard and attempted to embrace Anna.

"Who are you?" Nurse Miriam snapped as she blocked Alisha from getting too close to Anna.

"I'm her sister. I haven't seen her in years. I needed to stop by."

"Well, you have to speak to her power of attorney." Vivian called Ms. Kay. "Some lady is here saying she Anna's sister," Miriam cautioned. She never took her eyes off Alisha.

"Yeah. Jean explained to me that she saw her in court. Let me speak to her." Ms. Kay assured Miriam.

Ms. Kay spoke to Alisha and explained she was Anna's POA and was taking care of Anna for a while. Ms. Kay was aware Alisha bled Calloway blood, so she chose her words carefully.

"She has cancer and she's getting treatments," Ms. Kay stated.

"You can look at her and see she is not strong," Alisha commented. She expressed her gratitude toward Ms. Kay for stepping up and taking care of Anna. "I just wanted to spend a few days with her before we go back to Germany."

"That's fine as long as you don't stay long. She needs her rest," Ms. Kay insisted.

"OK. Thanks again for taking care of her," Alisha praised Ms. Kay before she handed the phone back to Miriam.

"Watch her," Ms. Kay told Miriam.

"Like a hawk," Nurse Miriam replied, giving Alisha a sideways glance then rolling her eyes.

"Are you OK? How have you been? Do you need anything?" Alisha's questions bombarded Anna.

"I . . . OK . . ." Anna stammered.

Alisha accepted her response and continued doing most of the talking. She caught Anna up with what has been going in her life. Anna politely listened. Alisha neglected to ask Anna anything about her life.

Before she left Anna's room, Alisha called Ms. Kay to ask if they needed anything. "No, we're OK. She needs her rest. Her memory is fading in and out," Ms. Kay assured her.

"OK." Alisha mentioned she noticed that during her visit.

"So where have you been?" Ms. Kay demanded to know.

"Well . . ." Alisha paused before she answered. Guilt tried to rationalize her answer. "I didn't live close to them growing up. My mom messed around with my dad while he was married to Mrs. Calloway. After I was born, my mom moved us out of the state and away from him," Alisha recollected. "I tried to help Anna when I could, but I had my own life to live as well. I visited during the summer and helped her. I told her what she needed to do, but she never did it. "Alisha found herself defending her absence and pulling the victim card.

"For the record, he was no daddy to me either. His absence stood out when I needed him. That's why I had issues with men in the past." Alisha's sobbing sounded like a beached whale. Her guilt manifested as tears. Ms. Kay rolled her eyes at each sniffle Alisha produced. Alisha was unaware Ms. Kay knew the whole story. Alisha needed a few minutes to regain her composure.

"When do you go back to Germany?" Ms. Kay switched subjects. She needed all Calloways out of Anna's life.

"In two days. Thanks again for taking care of her," Alisha expressed several more times. She handed Nurse Vivian the phone and left.

"We gotta watch her," Miriam stated as she stood at Anna's door making sure Alisha got on the elevator. Ms. Kay was well aware.

Alisha returned the next day, and Anna smiled when she stood by her bed.

"So are you hungry?" Alisha inquired.

"Anna doesn't have too much of an appetite because of her cancer treatments. She is getting her nutrients through a feeding tube. It's also difficult for her to swallow," Nurse Miriam answered for Anna.

"Oh," Alisha replied, "Can she have a smoothie? They are easy to digest." Before Miriam could reply, Alisha turned toward Anna. "Sister, would you like a smoothie?"

Anna murmured a vague agreement. Anna didn't have the heart to tell her sister no. She hated when people were mad at her.

An hour later, Alisha returned carrying a super extra-large smoothie. Anna politely took a few sips and stated she didn't want anymore. She placed the cup on her table.

"Throat . . . hurts . . . can't . . . drink . . . no . . . more . . ." Anna's speech was still delayed from the amnesia.

"I went and spent my money on this smoothie and you don't want to drink it." Alisha fussed at Anna. She grabbed the smoothie and pushed it in Anna' face. "You gonna drink it," Alisha demanded. Anna's body was too frail for Alisha's moods. Nurse Miriam was in the bathroom when she heard Anna crying.

"What are you doing to her?" Miriam raced across the room to protect Anna. The security guard peered into the room, waiting to take Alisha away.

"She won't drink this smoothie I spent money on." Alisha tried to force-feed Anna. Anna turned her head away and closed her eyes. Nurse Miriam demanded that Alisha calm down and she didn't need to yell at Anna. "Well, she is my sister and I have to right to say what I want to her," Alisha snapped.

"Not in this hospital you don't." Miriam stood her ground.

"It don't matter 'cause Anna will be moving back to Germany with me and my husband, so I will be taking care of her," Alisha announced. Anna turned toward Alisha with disbelief in her eyes.

"She is not even strong enough to stand on her own, let alone move out of the country. Plus she has cancer." Miriam's words fell on deaf ears.

"She is my sister and you all are not taking good care of her." Alisha spelled out her ploy to get custody of Anna and take her back to Germany in a few days.

Alisha asked Anna if she wanted to move with her. "I'm . . . happy . . . here," Anna proclaimed. The thought of moving away gave Anna a stronger voice. "I love . . . you," she paused, "but I don't . . . want to move away to . . . someplace . . . I . . . don't know." Tears filled Anna's eyes.

"Well, you don't have a choice." Alisha replied. Anna turned her head away from Alisha again. "How dare you turn your head away from me?" Alisha was belligerent. She towered over her bed and reached around Miriam in an attempt to grab Anna's face toward her.

Miriam used her body to push Alisha back away from Anna. "You got some nerve." Before Alisha could finish going off on Anna and Miriam, the security guard grabbed her under her arm and escorted Alisha out of the room to the parking lot.

Miriam called Ms. Kay with the details of what transpired. Ms. Kay could not contain her laughter. "First, Anna doesn't have a passport to leave the country. Second, you cannot get custody of a grown woman. Third, she is crazy." Ms. Kay laughed even harder.

"You should have seen her, Kay." Nurse Miriam described Alisha as a short portly woman with glasses too big for her face and lenses too thick for the frames.

"Something evil flows in the Calloway blood, which makes 'em crazy," Ms. Kay commented.

"You ain't lying about that," Nurse Miriam concurred.

Ms. Kay assured Anna that there was no way she was going to live with Alisha. "You . . . promise . . . Ms. Kay?" Anna questioned.

"Yeah. Don't worry. I'll take care of everything. Try to rest," she reassured Anna.

Alisha and her husband, Nick, returned to the hospital the next evening. Nurse Miriam and Nurse Vivian were both on duty. She flashed the plane ticket with Anna's name on it. "That must have cost a couple of thousand dollars," Miriam whispered to Vivian.

Alisha announced she was leaving for Germany and they were taking Anna with them. "I don't think it's a good idea," Nick piped in. "Let's wait till she is strong enough. I told you when we got the ticket that this was not a good idea." He observed Anna's body language. Anna's body tensed up as she gripped the lamb for dear life. "She needs to stay here," Nick stated loudly so the nurses knew he was on the side of common sense.

"She is not leaving this hospital," Nurse Miriam protested.

"Yes she is," Alisha challenged Miriam's authority. She glared at her husband, threatening him to stay quiet.

"You don't even have a passport for her," Nurse Vivian reminded her.

"Yes I do." Alisha reached in her bag and shoved the accordion folded card stock toward Vivian. The dingy, yellow faded document indeed had the word "Passport" printed on the front, but was Anna's immunization shots from childhood. The last entry was stamped 1977.

"This isn't a passport. It's her shots from a long time ago. You can't get on a plane with this. It don't even have her picture on here." Vivian smirked as she gave it back to Alisha, who snatched it from her hand.

"I don't need that. I have connections." Alisha snorted.

Vivian thought, *So do we.* She paged Matthew.

"No doctor is going to release her from the hospital with stage 1 brain cancer." Nurse Miriam tried again to reason with Alisha.

"European doctors are the best in the world at curing cancer. They will also help with her seizures." Alisha huffed.

"You are not her power of attorney, so you have no rights to take her anywhere." Nurse Vivian interrupted Alisha's rant about how terrible they have treated her sister.

"Sister, don't you wanna go with me?" Alisha glowered over at a terrified Anna.

"No . . . you . . . mean." Anna stared Alisha in the eyes before she turned her head away from her again.

"Anna will die before the plane lands," Vivian divulged, well aware Alisha had no clue about Anna's health.

"What do you mean die before the plane lands?" Nick's words were thick with apprehension and curiosity.

"Well, sir," Vivian began, "it's a ten-hour plane ride with someone who is epileptic. The change in cabin pressure may cause her to have seizures, and with no nurse to help out she could have a terrible seizure and die midflight." Vivian paused and Miriam continued.

"She is also getting treatment for cancer. Her pain meds only last a certain amount of hours before she starts screaming out in pain." His eyes got bigger as Vivian spoke again.

"She also has to get dialysis three times a week, and she may be confined to a wheelchair for the rest of her life because of a nerve disease, which leaves her writhing in pain some days." Vivian and Miriam scanned Alisha's face for any sign of acknowledgement of the severity of taking her. There was none.

Then Vivian turned to Alisha. "What about insurance? Anna would not get your military insurance because she is not your child?" Vivian questioned.

"I'll pay out of pocket for everything." Alisha snorted.

"Oh no we won't," Nick chimed in. "She needs to stay here and get well." He turned toward Anna. "I am sorry about all of this." He sighed, gesturing in Alisha's direction. "I hope you get better," he sympathized as he squeezed Anna's hand and attempted to get Alisha to leave. "We gonna miss our flight. Let's go," he demanded.

"Not without my sister!" Alisha yelled, showing her true Calloway side.

"She don't want to go with you," the words pushed passed Vivian's gritted teeth.

"I have every right to my sister, and I am not leaving the United States without her," Alisha announced.

"Oh yes the hell you are," Miriam threatened as the police officers came in the room.

155

"This woman is attempting to remove this patient from the hospital illegally," Miriam explained to the officers. The officers eyed Anna who was weeping and rocking back and forth.

"Do you want to go with this lady, ma'am?"

"No!" Anna screamed. "Tell . . . her . . . leave . . . me . . . alone." Anna closed her eyes and turned her head away.

"She has no paperwork or legal rights to the patient, and she needs to be removed from the property." Miriam looked around for Nick, but he had made it to the elevator. They escorted Alisha and her husband to their car. Matthew asked the officers to give them a police escort to the airport so they won't miss their flight.

> **He who establishes his argument by noise and command, shows that his reason is weak.**
> **—Michel de Montaigne**

The Cancer Spread—September 2012

A week after all the commotion with Alisha died down, things were almost back to normal. Anna continued to stare at her hospital door for any more family members who wanted stop by to kill or kidnap her. The doctors checked Anna's vitals and determined she was healthy enough for surgery. Her medical team decided to operate on her brain to remove the cancer.

No one explained to Ms. Kay the risks involved in removing cancer from a cancer patient. When cancer is exposed to air, it spreads rapidly and that's what happened with Anna. She went from stage 1 to stage 4, which has a less than 10 percent survival rate. The doctors informed Ms. Kay there was nothing more they could do but to make her comfortable.

The doctors wanted Nurse Miriam to ask for consent to start the morphine drip. "No," Ms. Kay snapped. "I'm not giving up on Anna," Ms. Kay quipped.

"I know you mad, Kay." Miriam heard the frustration in her voice.

"I cannot believe they didn't tell me the risks." Ms. Kay was irate.

"Yeah, Kay. They could have given her chemo instead," Miriam pointed out, sounding helpless about the situation. Anna writhed in excruciating pain. The meds they were giving her were not strong enough. Ms. Kay determined that the stress from her family and the brain cancer combined caused her to have more seizures.

Ms. Kay explained the cancer spread.

"*I just want to give up Ms. Kay,*" Anna texted. "*The pain is too much.*"

"*I know. I know, but you're a fighter. You have come too far to give up now.*"

"*But it hurts so bad. My body hurts all over,*" Anna replied in a dreary depression. She held the phone and cried. "*I don't have any family. The family I do have is trying to kill me. My kids have died. So has my husband. I have nothing to live for.*" Anna's text was riddled with despair.

"*I know Anna, but God has you here for a reason. You have to believe and the faith of a mustard seed. Fight one more time.*" Ms. Kay's words gave Anna little comfort and security. Ms. Kay sent positive messages and inspirational quotes to Anna's phone. Nurse Vivian reported Anna cried all night long as she squeezed her lamb for dear life.

"You know they opened a cancer center in our area. Maybe they can help Anna," Nurse Miriam mentioned the next day. Miriam already applied for a nursing position at the center and was only a matter of days before she would be on their staff. Miriam made some calls, and later that afternoon, an ambulance transferred Anna to the cancer center. Nurse Miriam vested in Anna health and made sure she remained Anna's day nurse at the cancer center. Ms. Kay called the agency and requested Nurse Vivian as her full-time evening nurse. Anna would be their only patient. Ms. Kay knew these two would fight for Anna.

That evening, Ms. Kay received a call from Dr. Caley Calabretta, the head doctor over Anna's teams of doctors. "Call me Dr. C," she requested. Dr. C was the first doctor who called to discuss Anna's health and was willing to listen. "We gave Anna some heavy-duty pain medicine. This should help," Dr. C assured Ms. Kay. "When people are in as much pain as Anna, they don't want to fight anymore," Dr. C explained.

"OK. She didn't want to live," Ms. Kay said with hesitation.

"That's the pain talking. Let's give her few days for it to get into her system and then try to talk to her," Dr. C aptly suggested.

A breathless eagerness came over Ms. Kay. She prayed this would work.

Ms. Kay forewarned Dr. C about Anna's crazy family. "She transferred to you all a few days after her sister came to the hospital and tried to take her out of the country." Ms. Kay needed Dr. C to understand the severity of keeping her family members away.

"Aren't you her family?" Dr. C said with a qualm of apprehension.

Ms. Kay explained she was Anna's power of attorney. "It's less drama and questions if everyone believes that we're sisters. I am very protective of Anna," Ms. Kay cautioned. She explained to Dr. C what transpired the last few months with her family's failed homicide attempts on Anna. "They are absurdly dangerous," Ms. Kay explained.

"Wow" was all Dr. C could muster up. "So that's why she has two full-time nurses." It started making sense to Dr. C.

"I call them her bodyguards." Ms. Kay laughed.

Dr. C assured that Anna would be safe while at the cancer center. She decided to remove Anna's name from her room door. "We also took her name out of the computer system. We don't want to take any chances if the family is a crazy as you say they are," Dr. C told Ms. Kay.

"Does she have a husband or any children?" Dr. C asked. Her heart sank after learning both of Anna's children died as well as her husband. "OK, well, no wonder she doesn't have any fight in her." Dr. C held back her tears as she thought about her two youngest children who came to visit last weekend. "No mother should bury her child let alone two children," Dr. C mumbled to herself.

"She is to never be left alone with any male staff members," Ms. Kay stipulated. Ms. Kay revealed to Dr. C about several incidents where male nurses have molested and raped Anna.

"My word. She has really lived a life," Dr. C lamented.

"You have no idea." Ms. Kay sighed. "We will . . . wait. I will personally make sure your sister is taken care of. Her story has touched me." Dr. C quickly hung the phone up so Ms. Kay would not hear her openly weeping.

Once Anna's pain was under control, she announced her readiness to fight one more time. "I'm so proud of you, Anna. You can do it," Ms. Kay reminded Anna of her strength and that she could accomplish anything if she put her mind to it.

Ms. Kay ended the conversation by singing the chorus to the song "Survivor." "I'm a survivor. I'm not gonna give up. I'm a survivor. I'm gonna work harder . . ." Ms. Kay always sang off-key and out of tune. She knew it would make Anna smile. "How did I sound?" Ms. Kay asked, smiling.

Anna hesitated. "My grandma said if you don't have anything nice to say about someone, then don't say it." Anna and Ms. Kay both laughed.

"I love you, girl."

"I love you too, Ms. Kay," Anna replied.

Dr. C explained a new procedure they were using on cancer patients. "It's a type of radiation therapy in which lasers slice away the cancer and dissolves it. The machine uses 3-D imaging so they can focus on the cancer cells and not destroy other parts of the body." Anna's body sighed in relief.

"No more chemotherapy?"

"Nope. This will be less severe and painful on your body Anna."

Anna started her twelve weeks of TomoTherapy, and it removed most of the cancer and purged her soul of her family's nonsense.

Anna's health and spirit improved. Anna's hope outweighed years of sorrow and grief.

> **You may tire of reality but you never tire of dreams.**
> —**L. M. Montgomery,** *The Road to Yesterday*

Alisha Is Back—October 2012

A month into Anna's treatment, Nurse Miriam observed an older woman roaming the hospital floors with a photograph of Anna. The photo captured Anna as a teenager. Nurse Miriam recognized Anna in the picture right away. After she passed Anna's room for the fourth time, Miriam approached the woman.

"You seem lost, can I help you?" Nurse Miriam noticed that the woman donned an outdated nurse's uniform and had no work badge.

"I'm looking for Anna Calloway. I am her nurse for the day," the woman stated with a matter-of-fact tone.

"What agency sent you? Where is your identification? You're not wearing any badge," Miriam grilled the woman, waiting for her to lie. The woman shifted her weight from one leg to another. Miriam thought that the woman was going to run.

"I don't have any identification," the woman finally admitted.

"Well, you have to leave. We don't have a patient by the name of Anna Calloway." Nurse Miriam guided the confused-looking woman toward the elevator.

As they proceeded off the elevator, Nurse Miriam caught a glimpse of Alisha out of the corner of her eye. Miriam doubled back onto the elevator but held the door open button. She watched at the woman walked toward Alisha and sat down to talk.

"That crazy sister of hers sent some woman up here to find Anna." Miriam was pissed as she relayed the story to Ms. Kay. "Why won't these people leave her alone?" Miriam sighed. The phone was silent.

"Why you quiet?" Miriam asked.

"I'm thinking." Ms. Kay's mind raced. As they sat on the phone in silence, the intercom buzzed. "Nurse Miriam, you are needed in the lobby, you have a visitor."

Miriam started going off. "Why is this woman calling for me? They keep coming up here bothering Anna. All is she wants to do is get better and they just won't—"

"Tell her Anna's dead." Ms. Kay said solemnly, interrupting Miriam's rant.

"What? Are you crazy?"

"No. We have to get her sister to leave Anna alone. I don't know what else to do." Ms. Kay was fresh out of ideas. Matthew filed a restraining order against Alisha, but like a true Calloway, she ignored it.

"Miriam, I need for you to go downstairs and convince her Anna is dead." Ms. Kay knew Miriam needed to sell it in order for it to work. By this time, Dr. C stopped by to check on Anna and to find out who was in the lobby for Miriam. Ms. Kay let Dr. C know her plan.

"If that's what you feel you need to do. Go for it." Dr. C knew the stress her family caused Anna. "Our first priority is to care for the patients' health and well-being," Dr. C pointed out.

Together Dr. C and Ms. Kay coaxed and prepped Nurse Miriam on what to say. "Nurse Miriam, you have a visitor," the loudspeaker announced again.

"Will she give me a minute? Damn." Nurse Miriam didn't want to talk to Alisha. "If she says anything out the way to me, I will punch her," Miriam informed them as she left to go deal with Alisha.

"Keep your hands in your pocket, Miriam." Ms. Kay reminded her.

Miriam drew an indignant breath before she stepped off the elevator. As she made her way toward Anna's sister, anger consumed her. She shoved her hands in her pockets and pinched her thigh to calm down.

I have to protect Anna, she reminded herself. Alisha scurried over in the direction of Miriam. *Stay calm, Miriam. You can do this.* Miriam rolled her eyes, but Alisha was too far away to notice.

"Where is my sister?" Alisha demanded to know.

"What are you talking about?" Nurse Miriam played dumb. Alisha admitted she went back to the other hospital and they informed her she no longer was a patient.

"They said they couldn't tell me anything because discharged patients don't give forwarding information." Alisha sounded frustrated. "They couldn't tell me if Anna was admitted at another hospital or anything." Alisha continued to tell Miriam about her quest to find her sister. She combed the city searching for Anna. Alisha called every hospital within a hundred-mile radius. "Then someone told me about this new cancer center, so this is the last place I looked," Alisha explained.

"Why are you not in Germany?" Nurse Miriam switched subjects. Alisha said she informed her husband of her intentions to come back to the states to take care of her sister.

"What did he say? He didn't seem too happy before." Miriam was being messy.

"He argued and I should wait till she got better. He concluded she was not strong enough to travel," Alisha responded. "So I decided to stay here in the states to take care of her until her health improved, but now I can't find her. It's been almost a month," Alisha said, hoping Miriam would show compassion. "Do you know where my sister is?" Alisha's sad eyes stared directly at Miriam.

Miriam bit the inside of her bottom lip before she spoke. She hoped the pain would help her shed some tears. Nurse Miriam's expression was deadpan when she announced Anna's passing and she sympathized for her loss.

"She died!" Alisha screamed. "Why didn't anyone tell me? She is my sister. Where is she? Where is my sister?" Alisha began to pace back and forth in the lobby in disbelief. "This can't be. I saw her a month ago." Alisha rambled on, giving no attention to her surroundings.

Other families in the lobby glanced in their direction and whispered to each other. One approached the front desk to ask the status of their family member. If Alisha paid any attention to Nurse Miriam, she would have seen the smirk on Miriam's face. Miriam pinched her leg to keep from laughing at Alisha's antics.

"Well, where is she? What happened to her? Where is her body?" Alisha interrogated Miriam.

"I don't know where the body is," Nurse Miriam stated as she poked her leg again.

"What do you mean you don't know where the body is?" Alisha snapped. Nurse Miriam explained when a person dies and there are no family members, the city takes the body.

"So no one claimed the body. Where's the body then?" Alisha sounded confused. Nurse Miriam almost giggled. "I have to find my sister's body. She's cold," Alisha expressed concerned.

Of course. Dead people are supposed to be cold, duh, Miriam thought.

Nurse Miriam claimed she understood why Alisha was upset because she searched for the body as well. "I was taking care of her and Anna died on my day off. I can't find the body either." Miriam offered an excuse. Alisha calmed down a little knowing someone else was searching for her sister too.

"So they didn't tell you either?" Alisha asked.

"No. I'm not family. I put in a request to be notified when her body turns up." Nurse Miriam didn't know where that lie came from.

Alisha made Nurse Miriam promise if she found the body she would let her know. "Oh of course I will." Nurse Miriam gave Alisha a false assuredness. She thanked Nurse Miriam and gave her a bear hug for being there for her sister. Alisha broke down. She babbled on about how she wished she had been a better sister to Anna and how she wanted to thank Nurse Miriam for being there. Alisha heard about Nurse Miriam through the other family members.

"They were wrong about you. You're not a bad person," Alisha said as Nurse Miriam rolled her eyes. Alisha hugged Nurse Miriam too tight for her liking and left the hospital. The woman roaming the halls caught up to Alisha and linked arms as they walked toward the parking lot. Nurse Miriam giggled to herself as she got on the elevator.

She can't find the body. Ms. Kay is going to love this, she thought as she proceeded to Anna's room to retell what happened.

Days later Dr. C received a phone call from the medical examiner. He was inquiring about an Anna Calloway. Alisha stopped by his office, desperate to claim her sister's body so she could bury her properly. Alisha revealed she called all over the city seeking Anna's body.

"She called morgues and funeral homes," the ME stated. "She even called the city to find where unclaimed bodies were and they sent her to me." Dr. C heard his frustration. "She is a persistent little thing," he mentioned.

He noticed Alisha appeared a little disheveled and her request was stranger than most he had encountered. "I explained to her we did have a few bodies matching Anna's description, but she had no idea when Anna died," the ME said.

All the unidentified female bodies the medical examiner received were badly decomposed and had been there for months and not weeks. "She picked one and claimed that was her sister." He paused. What is so funny?" He could hear Dr. C snickering on the other line.

Dr. C took a deep breath before briefly explaining to the medical examiner the events of what they did. He chuckled and said he would inform Alisha her sister's body was not there.

"We don't want this lady burying somebody else's daughter," he said before he hung up. Dr. C could hardly tell the story to Ms. Kay without giggling.

"Guess she's still looking for the body." Dr. C and Ms. Kay both fell out laughing.

Alisha sent flowers to the hospital about two weeks later. "Kay. You know her sister sent some funeral flowers to the hospital for us." Dr. C scoffed when she called Ms. Kay. The all-white wreath flower arrangement was mounted on a tripod stand.

"Why would she send a funeral arrangement to the hospital?"

"No flowers are even allowed at the cancer center." Dr. C shook her head. "Let me read you the note." Dr. C insisted. In the note, she thanked the hospital for taking care of her sister, and she was headed back to Germany to be with her husband.

Good riddance. Ms. Kay exhaled.

Strange, I thought, how you can be living your dreams and your nightmares at the very same time.

— Ransom Riggs, *Hollow City*

Chapter 13

Happy New Year

Happy New Year—December 2012

Things quieted down after all Anna's family members were out of the picture. Ms. Kay revealed to Anna how they faked her death. She didn't find it amusing. "I did what I needed to do to get Alisha away from you." Ms. Kay justified her decision. She couldn't fathom why Anna would be upset.

"I know you did Ms. Kay. It's just strange to hear that I died. That's all," Anna said. Anna dreamed for years about dying, but hearing someone else say it sounded strange.

"I'm trying to get her home before Christmas," Dr. C declared to Ms. Kay.

"How are the treatments going?"

"A lot better now." Dr. C noticed that Anna's health improved greatly once her family stopped harassing her. Anna's blood pressure returned to normal, and her seizures subsided. Her memory came back although spotty at times; Anna's recovery was making a remarkable step forward.

"Anna, as long as you continue to stay positive and work hard on healing your body, Dr. C believes you can be home by Christmas," Ms. Kay explained to Anna, hoping it would motivate her.

"OK" was all Anna could muster up.

Knowing Christmas lurked around the corner saddened Anna. Memories of the holidays with her children raced through her mind. She closed her eyes and flashed back to Natalie's first Christmas. Anna spent two paychecks buying Natalie gifts. "You will always get Christmas gifts," she whispered to Natalie as she squeezed and held her young daughter.

She wiped away tears remembering all the years the Calloways denied her Christmas presents. "Whores don't get gifts," they taunted when they handed Mallory gift after gift. Mallory gloated and stuck her tongue out at Anna with each gift she opened. Anna shut her eyes and struggled to get those images out of head.

Anna's cancer was in remission, and she moved back into the Logans' house a few days before Christmas. The Logans decorated the outside of the house with Christmas lights, and an eight-foot Christmas tree stood erect in the family room. Anna smiled when she saw the tree.

"How beautiful," Anna marveled at the various angel ornaments on the tree.

"I've been collecting angels for years," Jean told Anna when saw her admiring the tree. "I know it's difficult during the holidays." Jean thought about the first Christmas without her parents. "But what helps me cope is thinking now I have two angels in heaven watching over me." Jean grabbed Anna's hand and placed a small box in her palm.

In the box lay a silver guardian angel pin with clear crystal stones. "When you wear this," Jean said as she pinned the angel on Anna's shirt, "focus on the happy times with your children, Aunt Cora, and your granny. They're now your angels in heaven watching over you." Jean offered Anna some hope. Anna hugged Jean, and the two women cried in each other arms, silently consoling each other for the loss of their loved ones.

Nurse Vivian insisted Anna attend watch night service at church on New Year's Eve. Ms. Kay started to object, but reconsidered. "Bringing in the New Year in church will set the tone for Anna's new beginning," Ms. Kay said.

"Plus she has been talking about how much she misses church." Vivian remembered Anna's talks in the hospital. Ms. Kay sent church service videos to her phone, but there was nothing like sitting in a real church, Anna had confessed once.

Nurse Vivian dressed Anna in all white from head to toe. Anna pinned her angel on her blouse and caressed it whenever she started feeling down. During the program, a warm sensation touched her soul. It felt like someone wrapped their arms around her and refused to let go. Anna knew for sure her children and Aunt Cora's spirit embraced her. Telling her they loved her. Telling her, they were proud of all she accomplished.

"*Church was good,*" Anna texted Ms. Kay when she arrived back home. "*Loud, but good.*" Anna had a resilient spirit. She left church with a new sense of direction and happiness. Ready to face the New Year with optimism.

As the crazy year was about to end, Ms. Kay reflected on all the people who had a positive impact on Anna. *Anna had a strange adventurous year, mostly while sitting in a hospital bed,* Ms. Kay thought while still wrapping her mind around the events of the past year.

She reached out to everyone who was a considerable help through this journey. She thanked them for their invaluable kindness and unhesitating faith. Sandy reminded them that karma is real. She stated how they will be blessed for everything they did for her and Anna. Most replied how blessed they already were. They seemed more than happy to oblige. When you treat people with a genuine respect, most of the time they will do anything they can to help. Sandy's parents taught her that lesson as a small child. Her parents were often the recipients of good karma.

Karma: every act done, no matter how insignificant, will eventually return to the doer with equal impact. Good will be returned with good; evil with evil.

—Nishan Panwar

PART 3

———— ⚜ ————

The Awakening

Don't waste your time on revenge. Those who hurt you will eventually face their own karma and if you are lucky, the Universe will let you watch.

—Unknown

Chapter 14

The Attackers

First Husband—Keith 2010

Anna and Keith stayed legally married for years after they separated. Neither one wanted to pay for the divorce. After five years apart, Keith wanted to remarry, so they split the cost of the divorce in half. Keith already paid child support for Natalie and had weekend visitations. Even though Roger was not his son, Keith gave Anna an extra two hundred dollars a month for him and took Roger along with Natalie on the weekends.

Anna met Keith's second wife during a weekend visit. Anna came to pick up her children and found Joyce outside playing with all the children. His second wife had two children from a previous relationship and was pregnant again. As a police officer, Keith spent a lot of time away from the house policing and doing side jobs. Anna was relieved to know his second wife treated Anna's kids with the same love she gave her own children.

She smiled lovingly at Joyce as she scooted her kids in the cab. Joyce came to the cab and gave Anna a hug. "I really love Keith and I love your children too. If you ever need anything, please let us know," Joyce insisted as she let go of an embrace lasting too long for Anna's liking.

"Thank you and good luck with him," Anna warned her as she closed the cab door.

Keith flew to be by Anna's side when he found out her cancer returned. Anna wanted to give Keith another chance. She has recently buried Natalie and vulnerability replaced common sense. She desired something familiar in her life. Aunt Cora had returned home to attend the funeral of her husband's mother. Anna moving with Aunt Cora was still up in the air.

"Keith wants to move in."

"Just give it time." Ms. Kay heard a hesitation in her voice "People can only pretend to be someone else for a while, but eventually the real person comes out."

The cancer treatments left Anna in pain and often unable to complete simple tasks. A way too familiar feeling for Anna. At the cancer center, Keith promised a recommitment to her with a ring. As he put the ring on her finger, he promised he would be there for her and help around the house. He tried to convince her he changed. Anna was unsure whether he changed, but it comforted her to have someone there.

Keith showed up weeks after Anna buried Natalie, making sure he stayed away from Aunt Cora. He claimed that work prevented him from attending the funeral. Anna needed help and excused his weak absence from his own daughter's funeral. When he first moved in with Anna, Keith kept up his side of the bargain. He worked a lot but cooked meals for the week and set out her medicine. He often canceled side jobs in order to carry Anna to her doctor appointments. The honeymoon lasted less than three weeks. His outpouring of tenderness was reawakened with remorse and disdain.

Anna first noticed the bubbles forming in the pot when she heard Keith grumble, "I always have to bring everything in from the car. And I have to get you out of the car too."

"I'm sorry," Anna replied, trying not to agitate the already warm water.

"You too heavy for me to pick up. Maybe you should lose some weight." Keith's attitude simmered as he complained about how fat she had gotten.

The water started to sway in the pot. Anna felt steam from his body as he grunted and groaned helping her up the stairs to bed every evening. The boiling point happened after a visit to the doctor's office. It took five hours out of Keith's life, and he reminded Anna the entire car ride home. When they reached the house, Keith's harsh words spilled over onto Anna, burning her feelings. They both agreed it was time for him to move out.

Two weeks after Keith moved out, Anna received a phone call from an insurance agency. The agent inquired about a life insurance policy Anna signed up for with her husband. The agent mentioned Keith called about two months ago to update the policy. She reminded Anna she needed to comply in thirty days and make a payment.

"Your husband gave a two-thousand-dollar down payment and has only made one payment since." The agent told Anna. Anna informed the agent she was divorced from Keith for over ten years now. "Well, that changes everything." Anna heard the agent typing on her computer. "I see." The agent logged into a system that showed her the divorce decree. "Thank you, ma'am. I will take care of this," the agent said as she hung up the phone.

"That no-good, dirty dog. I can't believe this Ms. Kay." Anna came to the ugly revelation. "He only wanted to marry me for a million-dollar life insurance policy," Anna said with a disgusted tone.

"So what happened?" Ms. Kay knew Keith's motives were not pure.

"The agent gonna send me the refund check since he lied and forged my name is on the original form." When she said the words out loud, Anna's heart dropped to her stomach.

"They not gonna to file charges against him because they neglected to investigate the validity of the marriage," Anna said.

The company believed giving Anna money would prevent her from suing them.

Keith received a letter stating the company cancelled his policy. When he called, an agent informed Keith he was not entitled to the refund check because he lied and forged documents. An outraged Keith drove straight to Anna's house. He banged and kicked on the door to gain entry and to get his money.

"I know you in there, Anna!" Keith yelled. "Lemme in! You stole my money." Anna lay on the sofa, frozen. Fear and pain rendered her unable to move. Her phone was on the other side of the room, charging. The door eventually gave in at the hinges, and he descended on her. He repeatedly kicked and punched her. She crumbled to the floor too weak to defend herself. He screamed, "Give me my money, bitch. I will kill you." He pinned her down under his knees and repeatedly bashed her head on the floor. Anna started seizing. He fled the scene before she came to.

A neighbor heard the commotion and saw Anna's front door open with Anna sprawled out on the floor bleeding and seizing. She called 911. The neighbor grabbed Anna's phone. She scrolled through the phone and found the only name in the phone was Ms. Kay. The neighbor notified her of Anna's situation.

"I saw a tall thin gentleman fleeing her house as I walked over." She handed the phone and Anna's purse to the EMT. The ambulance rushed Anna to the hospital. The neighbor closed the door the best she could. She called a handyman to fix the door frame and paid the bill.

Anna came to from her seizure and texted Ms. Kay. "*Keith beat me up. He wanted the money.*" Ms. Kay was furious. While Anna recovered at the hospital, a nurse called Ms. Kay.

"Who's the nice-looking man at the hospital asking for Anna?"

Ms. Kay instructed her to call the police because he was her ex-husband, the one who beat her up. "Don't let him near her," Ms. Kay pleaded. "Look at what he did to her."

Keith's voice was so boisterous, Ms. Kay heard him through the phone. Everyone in earshot heard him. The nurse buzzed for security.

"You need to call the police. I need to press charges on him," Ms. Kay directed the nurse.

Keith was a bellowing bull, exclaiming how he needed to see his wife. He needed to talk to Anna. Anna heard him in the hallway and had another seizure. One of the police officers who arrived to assess the commotion informed the nurses that Keith was a fellow police officer.

They walked into Anna's room and asked if Keith had assaulted her. With tears in her eyes, Anna nodded and mouthed "Yes." She turned her head away.

"That bitch is lying!" Keith screamed. "I ain't even touch her." I will get you, Anna!" They escorted him out of the hospital in handcuffs.

<hr />

Anna wanted to stay in bed, mourn the loss of Natalie, and not leave her house to go to court. She cried for weeks. Aunt Cora returned to collect Anna but was surprised to learn that Anna needed to stay to testify against Keith.

"I knew that man was up to no good." Aunt Cora sighed as she hugged her still visibly bruised niece. The emotional bruises lay undetected by her aunt. Keith attacked Anna in the past and only received a petty punishment. Anna remained adamant that the court would downgrade his charges to a mere misdemeanor. Anna changed her tune when she heard he had more charges besides the assault.

The police arrested Keith at the hospital and ran a routine background check. They discovered long-standing arrest warrants in another county. His second ex-wife filed charges against him for molesting her daughter years ago.

<hr />

Anna testified against Keith but refused to make eye contact with him, even when the lawyer asked her to point to her assailant. If Anna had looked in Keith's direction, she would have seen him mouth the word "bitch." He was an unrepentant criminal.

His second ex-wife took the witness stand and testified to Keith's lewd behavior toward her. She cried on the stand as she recounted when her daughter, Amy, said Keith raped her. The prosecutor called Amy to the witness stand. Her words regurgitated in gory details what Keith did to her. He molested and raped her for years, she described.

"Why didn't you tell your mother when it first happened?" the defense interrogated Amy. Anna's heart went out to Amy. She knew far too well the sexual abuse from a father and the judgment received from it.

"Cause he threatened to kill my mommy if I told." Amy dropped her head like a broken branch.

"I'm sorry it took me so long to tell you," Amy's tear-filled eyes looked over toward her mom.

"You eventually told me, baby, that is all that matters," Joyce said, wanting to run to the stand and embrace her daughter.

"He raped his other daughter Natalie too," Amy revealed, feeling like she betrayed Natalie's trust. Anna's gasp was audible throughout the courtroom. Aunt Cora held Anna close.

Anna openly wept in the courtroom. "I didn't know," Anna whispered. Anna's powerless stare looked to Aunt Cora for help. The prosecutor turned to Anna to ask where Natalie was so she could testify.

"Heee hiiide," Anna babbled. Aunt Cora decoded Anna's words.

"My great niece was buried about two months ago, your honor." Aunt Cora refused to hide her tears. She gave Keith a glare of scrutiny. He held his head in shame.

Keith received twenty years in prison for the assault charge and the rape and molestation of minors. Time was also added for the insurance fraud.

After court, Anna thanked Joyce for including Natalie in the charges. "I'm sorry to hear about Natalie," Joyce said. She wrapped her arms around Anna and held her as they cried together. Anna always wondered why Natalie was adamant about not wanting to visit her dad after he and Joyce separated. Joyce protected Natalie during her visits. It hurt Anna's soul knowing her daughter's pathology mirrored her own. Anna had been unable to stop it. Now it was too late to console her because Natalie was dead.

> **The power of the harasser, the abuser, and the rapist depends above all on the silence of women.**
>
> **—Ursula K. Le Guin**

Vince UPS Worker—June 2012

Matthew used an unmarked police car to sit in the parking lot of Anna's job, waiting for Vince to return. Matthew was all certain Vince would likely return because Anna's seizure prevented him from finishing the job. Matthew dealt with a few hit men in his twenty-eight years on the police force. The attack seemed too specific not to be a contract hit.

Vince pulled into the parking lot in the same borrowed UPS truck an hour after Matthew arrived. He parked in a spot closest to the exit and pulled to the front of the parallel spot for a quick getaway. Vince sat in the truck, talking on the phone for fifteen minutes. He seemed locked in a heated discussion with the person on the other end. He banged his fist several times on the steering wheel and threw the phone in the seat when the phone call ended. He sat for a few minutes with his eyes closed to gather his nerves.

He adjusted his UPS hat as he checked himself out in the mirror. Vince popped open the antacid bottle and chewed on two tablets. His girlfriend suggested he had a stomach ulcer. He slammed the door to the truck and proceeded to walk to the building. Vince strode several car lengths away when he remembered he needed a package to gain entry to the building. As he walked back to the truck, Matthew jumped out of his car and headed toward Vince. Matthew feared he changed his mind and was getting ready to flee. He paged for backup before he approached.

Matthew quickly started a conversation. "Hey. I know you. Ain't you Vince?" Matthew inquired while scratching the back of his head as if trying to remember him.

Vince made no eye contact as he assured Matthew he had the wrong guy. "Your name tag says Vince," Matthew pointed out. Vince ignored Matthew and focused on getting the package and getting to Anna.

"We went to middle school together," Matthew continued. Vince stopped and cocked his head to the side, giving Matthew the once-over.

Matthew's boyish face and lack of facial hair made him appear younger than his actual age. The baseball cap, printed T-shirt, and designer jeans aided in Vince thinking them going to school together could be plausible. Matthew shook his hand and mentioned how they grew up in the same neighborhood.

"I'm Matt. Marcus's younger brother." Matthew tried to sell it. Vince rubbed his chin several times in an attempt to place Matthew. Vince was still not remembering Matthew from any of the places Matthew suggested.

Vince looked at his watch as he started getting agitated. He convinced himself he didn't need the package, turned on his heels, and started heading to the building while Matthew yammered on. Matthew heard the dispatcher on his earpiece saying backup was five minutes away. Matthew changed the subject and started walking with Vince toward the building.

"What are you doing up here? I see you parked in the parking lot. You must not be working or you on your lunch break," Matthew asked.

"I'm visiting a friend," Vince replied, rather bothered with Matthew's questions.

"Who is it? I know lots of those pretty nurses in the building. I need to make sure you ain't trying to see my girl."

"Anna," Vince mumbled her name so it sounded like "and."

"OK. What? Y'all going to lunch or something?" Matthew stepped in front of Vince to slow his pace.

"You don't need to know all that." Vince sneered as he sidestepped Matthew.

"Oh an old flame you sneaking around with?" Matthew questioned jokingly, trying to keep Vince outside of the building.

Vince stopped in his tracks and turned to Matthew. "Look, man," Vince started.

"It's Matt," Matthew reminded him.

"Look, Matt. You asking a lot of questions, and I don't even know you for real," he snarled as his bird chest started puffing up. Matthew saw beads of sweat starting to form on Vince's forehead. Vince wanted to be done with Matthew and finish his mission. Before Vince had a chance to turn around, three police officers surrounded him.

"Sir, place your hands behind your back," one office commanded.

"What I do? I ain't even do nothing. This guy is the one harassing me." Vince tried to explain. The officers patted Vince down and found a knife and a gun. They handcuffed him and took him down the station.

Once at the station they placed Vince in a secluded room and left him there. He noticed the dried blood on the table in front of him. He pushed himself away from the table. Vince rocked back and forth in the wooden chair like it had rockers. He shook his head and sniffled to prevent himself from crying. He was aware the cops watched him through the double-sided mirror. Secrets and guilt manifest themselves as ulcers in the body. He couldn't stomach what he was going to do to Anna, and it ate away at him. He screamed out as he pushed his handcuffed hands into his midsection in an attempt to lessen the pain. After about ten minutes, the police officers heard Vince yelling he was ready to talk.

He confessed to beating up Anna earlier in the week. "I had to come back and finish it, or she would kill me." Vince broke down. He disclosed he once dated Mallory. He confessed Mallory gave him two thousand dollars to "beat up and take care of my sister."

"Those were her exact words," he recalled. He pleaded with Mallory several times how he was no killer. "That's when she threatened to kill me." Vince's right leg started shaking, and he bowed his head in shame as he continued to talk.

"Mallory told me how she used Anna's social security number to track her down and she would find me if I didn't do what she wanted." Mallory worked with a government agency and had access to millions of people's personal information.

"She described where to find Anna and gave a description of what she looked like," Vince explained. She recommended that Vince wear his old UPS uniform, and she would provide him with a truck to use. Mallory expressed to Vince he needed to act soon, or she would find someone to shoot him dead. Vince admitted he was scared of Mallory. "She was borderline psychotic when we dated. Mallory beat up two of my girlfriends after we broke up. She fought a dude at a club once." He stated he felt he had no other choice.

"You could have contacted us," a police officer reminded him.

"I already got a record," Vince admitted. After his confession, he slumped back in the wooden chair with an unrestricted relief. His stomach pain eased up a little. Vince faced charges of conspiracy, gun possession, carrying a weapon with unlawful intent, and assault and battery. He was sentenced to serve eleven years in prison. His testimony against Mallory lessened his sentence.

Killing is not so easy as the innocent believe.
—J. K. Rowling, *Harry Potter*
and the Half-Blood Prince

Chapter 15

The Nurses

Nurse Penny—July 2012

Nurse Miriam and two security officers escorted Nurse Penny out to the employee parking lot at the hospital. "Don't try to come back her, or we will arrest you for trespassing," Miriam informed Penny. Nurse Miriam stood a few feet away as Penny opened her car door. Penny attempted to reach for something in the side pocket of the car door. The security officers advised her to get in the car and go home. As the officer spoke to her, Penny saw his fingers on the gun's trigger. She flipped Miriam the bird as she slammed her car door and sped off.

Later on in the evening, Nurse Vivian phoned Ms. Kay. Her voice was frantic. She explained when she left for her dinner break that Anna's vitals were normal and now her body was lifeless.

"Anna's barely breathing and her blood pressure is deathly low," Vivian lamented. Vivian mentioned that Anna's lamb disappeared from the room.

"I don't think it got up and walked away." Ms. Kay chuckled, trying to calm Vivian down. Ms. Kay was confident this was Nurse Penny's doings. Somehow, she managed to finagle her way back into the hospital undetected.

"Nurse Penny had to have given Anna something in her IV," Ms. Kay deduced. She asked Vivian to have Anna's blood drawn to see what coursed through her system. Anna's blood work came back a few minutes later with high levels of morphine and hydromorphone.

"What's hydromorphone?"

"Both drugs mess with the nervous system. The hydromorphone is now experimental for lethal injections," Nurse Vivian informed Ms. Kay. "The amount she had in her system would have killed her in a few hours," Nurse Vivian said with an eternity of silence afterward.

The only way to remove the drugs was to start detoxing Anna. This four-hour process removes all medicine from her body. Anna underwent hours of painful agony, and the convulsions from the multiple seizures almost killed her. Nurse Penny assumed that the toxins would kill Anna instantly; it only prolonged her intense suffering.

Ms. Kay needed to prove Penny had committed this passive-aggressive act. She had Vivian page Nurse Miriam.

"Are there cameras in the hospital?" Ms. Kay asked. Nurse Miriam explained there were no cameras in the room for patient privacy, but each floor has a camera monitoring the hallways.

"I'll let you know what I find," she said as she left to get the footage.

The camera feed showed a clear view of Nurse Penny entering Anna's room shortly after Nurse Vivian left for dinner. Penny was stealthily walking the hallway, darting her head from side to side, checking her surroundings. She was a prowling animal. She made it to Anna's room completely unnoticed. She did one final check of the hallway and proceeded to enter her room. The time stamp on the video revealed she stayed in the room for three minutes. She haphazardly grabbed the lamb before she left. The video shows the lamb appearing to be choking under her armpit as she walked down the hallway as quiet as she entered. Security guards found the lamb in a trash can next to an exit door by the stairwell.

Three police officers appeared at Penny's apartment like thieves in the night. They knocked several times before her oldest daughter answered the door. The ten-year-old yelled for her mommy. "Come to the door, Ma, the policemen are here." Penny shuffled from her bedroom, her pajama bottoms lazily dragged on the floor as she walked. The officers asked Penny to identify herself.

"Its three thirty in the morning, why are you here?" Penny wiped her eyes and yawned, demanding answers to why they disturbed her sleep. She shot a look at her ten-year-old as if to say, "Why did you open the door?" The ten-year-old sat on the sofa and cried.

The officers explained she was under arrest for the attempted murder of Anna Calloway. Two officers moved toward Penny to place her under arrest, but Penny flailed her arms away from the cuffs and screamed, "You arresting the wrong person!" She tried in desperation to convince them she didn't do anything wrong. Her screams woke up her two younger children.

The ten-year-old wanted to make things right so she called her grandmother. "Gramma. Ummm. The police are locking my mom up." A few more details were exchanged before the daughter hung up. "Gramma on her way," the words stammered out of her tiny mouth.

Penny continued to struggle with the officers, so they tased her. The projectiles from the taser gun subdued Penny's combativeness. The electric charge dumped more confusing information in her nervous system than when her nerves decided that ending Anna's life was a good idea. Now the taser got on her nerves. It locked up every muscle in her body, rendering her too weak to move. She resembled Anna, lying on the ground, writhing in pain.

The handcuffs rested right below the cluster of stars she had tattooed on each wrist. "Soon you will be wearing stripes to match those stars." One police officer chuckled as he lifted her still-twitching body and guided her outside. Her mom arrived as they were placing Penny in the back of the police car. She pleaded for her daughter's release.

"There's nothing you can do for her, ma'am," one of the officers interrupted Penny's mother. "You have to pick her up at the station." They drove off, and Penny's mom embraced the two-year-old as she wailed and sobbed for her mommy. The other two children sat on the sidewalk and bawled.

Matthew escorted Jean down to the police station later that morning to identify Penny. She happened to be the last person to see her in the hospital room with Anna. The police needed a non-cancer center worker to identify her since the cancer center was pressing the charges. Jean pointed her out in the lineup right away. Penny, dressed in cotton Tweety Bird pajamas, was barefoot. Her hair was strewn about her head and her eyes were bloodshot red. "She looked a mess. Like they forced out of bed and body-slammed on the ground." Jean laughed as she retold the incident to Ms. Kay.

They initially charged Penny with falsifying documents and two counts of attempted murder. More charges were eventually added. Matthew persuaded the courts to prosecute her right away. He volunteered to be the bailiff when she went to trial. In court, the judge reminded Penny that nurses were to uphold a level of professionalism.

"You knew what putting those meds in her IV would do to her," the judge scolded her as he read the hospital reports. "Why did you do it?" he questioned Penny.

"Because she got me fired," Penny quipped with a huff.

"This woman is in the hospital with cancer. Her body is weak. She is getting painful treatment to help fight off this disease, which eats away at her body," the judge noted. "She's in constant pain and needs twenty-four hour care. She has already been dealt a bad hand in life, and you're trying to get her back for getting you fired. Do you hear how crazy that sounds?" The judge offered no sympathy toward Penny. Penny dropped her head in shame.

"So how did she get you fired? She is sitting in the hospital bed," the judge questioned, still in disbelief. Penny remained silent.

The prosecution asked the judge to look through Penny's file. She would see Penny's name as Anna's nurse at the other cancer hospital. The documents also showed where Penny forged Ms. Kay's name on Anna's medical charts. The judge asked if there were stalking charges because this was not the first incident she encountered with this woman. Penny mustered out a quiet "No."

Penny proved herself an equal-opportunity offender as well. Three more patients who filed complaints about her were in court as well. Matthew called the other cancer center and retrieved their information. He flew them in for court. The judge read out loud the horrible things Penny did to those patients. The list included denying patients their pain medicine, letting them sit for hours in their own urine and feces, leaving vomit on their clothing, taking away their blankets and pillows, pushing her fingers inside their bed sores until they bled, and smacking them to wake them up. The judge stopped reading when she noticed Penny's former patients sobbing in the back of the courtroom. "You're a bully. Plain and simple."

Penny remained dead silent with no explanation when she had her turn to address the judge. She darted her eyes from the judge to the floor as her sentence was being read.

"You should have walked away from the Anna situation and found another job. You have tried to kill her twice," the judge scolded her. "People like you need to be taken out of the medical profession. You lack compassion. These people depend on you and this is how you treat them. You need help. You are a sick person."

Penny was sentenced to fifteen years in prison. Her mom went limp like a wet noodle then fainted in the courtroom.

A few weeks later, Penny returned to the hospital. She traded in her nurse's scrubs for a faded orange prison jumpsuit. The letters DOC (department of corrections) replaced the cute teddy bears and other designs on her scrubs. Her plastic name badge was now Inmate #45657 as printed on her jumpsuit. Her feet once donned sensible white walking shoes. Now she shuffled around in black slip-on shoes with a white rubber sole. Handcuffed to the bed, a police officer stood outside her room guarding the door. The hospital where she used to work happened to be the closet hospital from the jail. Penny's face was almost unrecognizable.

Both eyes were swollen shut, and gashes covered her face and arms. She had patches of hair missing all over her head, and her busted lip bled profusely. Her jaw was broken in three different places and needed to be wired shut to set correctly. She was also getting medical treatment for the rest of her injuries. Penny mouthed off to the wrong prisoner, and they shut her mouth for her.

The nurses whispered throughout the hospital. Some even went past her room to get a peek at her. Penny caused trouble as a young girl. She was kicked out of a few elementary schools and high schools for fighting. She eventually graduated from an alternative school. Penny always was the big bully fish in a little pond who never met her match until she went to jail. The bullies in jail were more aggressive and had nothing to lose. Most were lifers.

Penny's mother walked around the hospital for days, wanting to get to the bottom of what happened. She stopped every nurse she could and bombarded them with questions. "Why are people lying on my daughter? Who would set my daughter up like that? My daughter isn't capable of doing what they accused her of doing. They have the wrong person." She convinced herself the more she spoke. She talked to anyone who would listen to her ramble. "My Penny is a good girl. She made a mistake. Everyone deserves a second chance," she pleaded.

Penny's mother approached Nurse Miriam asking for a meeting with Anna. She wanted to see who wrongly accused her daughter.

"That is never going to happen," Miriam snapped.

"Well, can you call the judge and tell him you want Penny to be freed. Then she can work for the hospital again," she begged.

"No." Nurse Miriam not-so-nicely protested. She threatened Penny's mom that if she didn't leave the hospital she would call the police and file a harassment charge. As her mom turned to leave, the security guards were there to help escort her off the property.

Remember the unkindness, dishonesty, and deception you display toward others . . . don't be shocked when it comes back to bite you.

—**Sarah Moores**

Nurse Madison—July 2012

Four months ago, Nurse Madison married the father of her four children and anxiously wanted to start a new life in a different part of the country. Her work ethic in her current city preceded her.

"Madison. I didn't want to believe your former boss when she warned me about you. You're apathetic and callous toward your patients. Your services are no longer needed here," her boss stated when she handed Madison her pink slip.

"That's fine," Madison replied as she shrugged her shoulders. Her attitude remained indifferent. *Someone will hire me,* she thought. These words were not new to Madison. She was hard of listening.

Nurse Madison applied for a job across the country at a cancer center, which recently opened. This opportunity would provide her a fresh start and a chance to make a better name for herself. She convinced herself of this as she omitted certain jobs on her résumé. *"They don't need to know I worked all those places."* She assured herself everything would be OK.

The cancer center hired her, paid for her move, and provided a signing bonus. She spent two weeks looking for the perfect home in an area with the best school system for her young children. Madison spent her bonus check on big-screen televisions, a stereo system, and other lavish items for her new home. She needed to start working because her money quickly depleted, and her husband had not yet found employment.

New nurses spent the first week at the cancer center shadowing a doctor to get the feel of the new hospital. Patients at a cancer center required more attention than at a regular hospital. The nurses were to care for and educate the patients who have cancer. They were responsible for assessing any side effects the patient may have based on the various cancer treatments they were given. These nurses need to always be on high alert and stay observant.

Human Resources paired Nurse Madison with Dr. C. They made their rounds to various rooms to be acquainted with whom she would be working with. Dr. C attempted to explain the lay of the hospital, but Nurse Madison constantly interrupted. "Oh. I know how to do this," Nurse Madison would chime in. When Dr. C gave instructions on various procedures, Nurse Madison often finished her sentences.

"Have you ever worked at a cancer center before? Because you seem very familiar with the policies and procedures."

"No," Madison abruptly lied.

Dr. C and Nurse Madison stopped in Anna's room. Madison walked in seconds after Dr. C. She spotted the lamb right away. The lamb's position on the bed was that of protector. Madison swore the stuffed animal growled at her. The lamb stared at her with dark, judgmental eyes. Madison shuddered. She hated that lamb, convinced it was peering into her soul. Anna smiled when she saw Dr. C, but the smile left her face when she saw Nurse Madison. She remembered her from the other cancer center. She turned her head away and squeezed her eyes shut so tight, her premature crow's feet radiated outward from the corner of her eyes.

"What's wrong, Anna?" Dr. C questioned her.

"My head hurts," Anna replied, refusing to open her eyes.

"You shouldn't have a headache. You got your pain medicine a few hours ago," Jean reminded her. Jean had been sitting by Anna's bed all morning and noticed Anna's body starting to shake. Her attempts to console her were futile.

"We'll be back," Dr. C addressed Anna by touching her arm. She shook her head as she left Anna's room. Something was not right with Anna, but Dr. C hadn't put her finger on it.

"I remember that stupid lamb from the other hospital," Nurse Madison blurted out as they left her room to see about another patient.

"What else do you remember about this patient?" Dr. C's interest was piqued. Her radar sent off warning bells.

Madison described how Anna would hold on to the lamb for dear life. She didn't understand why a grown woman needed a stuffed animal. "What she needs is some . . ." Madison giggled.

"Some what?" Dr. C asked.

Madison made a fist with her right hand and placed her left pointer finger inside. She proceeded to move the finger back and forth to simulate her fingers having sex. Dr. C curled her lip up and shook her head in disbelief. *This girl is dense to the point of stupidity,* Dr. C thought.

Nurse Madison went on to mention Anna's power of attorney. "She was a bitch. I never met her, but she was so demanding. Ugh." The words flew out of Madison's mouth like a trapped animal that finally had a chance to escape. "She always wanted us to do stuff for Anna. Why should she get special treatment?" Nurse Madison scoffed.

"So what did you do when her power of attorney wanted things?" Dr. C set the bait.

"Her power of attorney was dumb. Whenever she called, I informed her that Anna was sleeping." Madison grinned, confiding in Dr. C. Madison, and was quite pleased with herself as she confessed to drugging Anna at the other cancer center so she would sleep all day.

"Really?" Dr. C said in shock. She looked at her watch. It happened to be close to lunchtime. "You can take your lunch break now." Dr. C allowed Nurse Madison an extended lunch break so she could contact Ms. Kay.

Ms. Kay confirmed Nurse Madison's confessions. "She said I was dumb?" Ms. Kay chuckled. "What dummy tells her boss she drugged her patient? My parents always told me, Sandy, give people enough rope and they will eventually hang themselves." Nurse

Madison placed her own noose around her neck and began to tighten it herself.

Dr. C investigated and found that Nurse Madison had been fired from the cancer center and another hospital shortly after that. Madison neglected to put all her past employment on her résumé, which is illegal. This is especially important to know in the nursing field. Getting caught was the furthest thing from Madison's mind. Ms. Kay advised Dr. C to dig deeper. Nurses like Madison were equal-opportunity offenders. She remained convinced Anna was not the only one who suffered. Dr. Calabretta pulled twenty-five records of Nurse Madison's former patients. Nurse Madison held patients' pain meds for more than twelve hours. She also violated patients' rights, and thee patients died under her care because of neglect.

Madison returned from her extended lunch and met Dr. C at her office. Outside of her office, two security guards stood.

"Come in. Leave the door open." Dr. Calabretta motioned for Madison to come in. Dr. C explained to Madison what she discovered in her file after further investigation.

"You seemed to know a lot of information about working at a cancer facility. Then when you admitted to seeing that lamb before, it made me do some research on your past." Dr. C grabbed a piece of paper off her desk and walked toward the door. She handed her the termination papers.

"You firing me?" she demanded to know. Her lackadaisical attitude vanished like a dream.

She stood square to Dr. C, with her hand on her hips. "That's some bull." Madison tried to jump at Dr. C, but one security guard grabbed her and escorted off the property. Dr. C handed the other security guards her photo and informed them she was banned from the hospital.

"If she comes on the property, have her arrested immediately," she directed them. She remembered Ms. Kay's warning about the Calloways and didn't want a repeat at her hospital.

Madison was required to pay back the relocation bonus check they gave her. She was sued for medical malpractice and falsifying documents. Dr. C also reported her to the nursing registry, so any other agency who wants to hire her will have the report. Dr. C contacted the other cancer center and demanded to know why they didn't report her earlier. Nurses have their licenses suspended and ultimately revoked after a certain number of complaints. Months later, the police arrested Madison on nonrelated hospital charges, and she received five years in jail. Her husband and her kids moved back home.

You can't get away from yourself by moving from one place to another.

—Ernest Hemingway

Chapter 16 ───────────

The Family

Reverend Calloway—August 2012

"You are to have no contact with Anna, do you understand?" The bail bondsman handed Reginald a contract to sign.

"Yeah, yeah. Whatever." Reginald signed his name, anxious to taste the sweetness of freedom. The taste soured two days later. Reginald's bond was revoked after his last encounter with Anna in the hospital. He remained in jail until his trial.

The prosecution needed two weeks to prepare for court. Reginald spared no expense when he called one of the most expensive law firms in the country. Charged with attempted murder, rape, sodomy, aggravated stalking, forgery, and aggravated assault. He convinced his lawyer the rape and sodomy charges wouldn't stick because it would be Anna's word against his.

"They don't have no proof I did those things to her." Reginald's air of confidence left a stench in his lawyer's office several hours after he left. His lawyer gathered key witnesses to testify in Reginald's behalf. The lawyer believed his years as a minister would help build his character. "Lots of church members will vouch for me," Reginald beamed. Reginald fantasized a slap on the wrist as the worst-case scenario.

The courtroom was a beehive. It was a swarming population of religious folks. Ministers and members of his church buzzed around the benches and outside the courtroom. Rumors swarmed around looking for people to pollinate. The nectar ranged from disbelief to anger to curiosity. No one minded its own beeswax. The queen bee was now an attempted killer bee. The honey in the hive began to crystalize; it became transparent. A few honeycombs sugarcoated the rumors, while others delineated the outcome knowing he was guilty. The bailiff asked the buzzing to cease and ordered the colony to take their seats. The queen bee then entered the hive.

A gasp fell over the courtroom when they saw Reginald escorted in wearing an orange jumpsuit and shackles. He shuffled in with his head held high and a smirk on his face. He made a beeline to his seat. He blew a kiss to his wife. She smiled and gave him a wink, assured her husband was not guilty. Janice and other family members sat together and held hands. Matthew stood in the courtroom in his police uniform. Jean was there to report to Ms. Kay.

The pompous judge swaggered in the courtroom. His robe swaying as he walked. He floated to the bench on his high self-esteem. He patronized the spectators by making them stand for two minutes before he perched on the edge of his seat, looking down at the commoners.

"This is my courtroom," he stated in an attempt to establish his authority. Other judges dismissed him as a joke after a few trials he preceded over were debacles. His facial expression seemed indifferent as he read over the case. He looked up and inquired why the plaintiff chose not to show up in court. He scoffed when informed she lay in the hospital sick.

"This is a serious case. She should be here," he uttered to no one in particular.

"She is battling cancer," the prosecution lawyer defended her absence.

"She should show up in court and be woman enough to face the man she claimed did all these things to her." The judge sneered. The prosecution lawyer cleared his throat and adjusted his tie. He looked down at his paperwork, hoping the judge would not postpone trial and force Anna to show up. He knew Anna was not strong enough to testify.

The judge looked over the paperwork one more time and frowned. "OK. Let's begin," the judge said with haughtiness.

"What do you want?" he asked the bailiff as he approached the bench. The bailiff informed the judge he was need in his chambers. Court recessed for twenty minutes.

Judge Laura Walker replaced the first judge when court resumed. Her walk commanded attention. As she entered the courtroom, everyone sat up straight without even knowing why. Judge Walker's reputation preceded her. Criminals shuddered at the sound of her name.

No defense attorneys wanted to come up against her when they went to court. Some even attempted to postpone their court dates in hopes that she would retire. A no-nonsense judge who always stood on the side of right, she was fair and impartial. Her BS detector stayed on ten, ready to call anyone out who attempted to make a mockery of the courtroom. Judge Walker never was persuaded with kindness or flattery, nor did she entertain any foolishness.

"Where is the plaintiff?" Judge Walker read the documents then looked where Anna should have been seated.

"She is confined to a bed in the hospital, battling cancer again," the lawyer disclosed. Her lawyer explained to the judge Anna's medical condition. The judge asked her lawyer and Matthew to meet in her chambers. The judge was made privy to Anna's current health status. The lawyer gave a quick overview of all the charges against Reginald.

"This is her father, right?" the judge inquired with a scowl.

"Yes. Her sister Mallory is also being tried for similar charges," Matthew added.

"I'm taking that case as well," the judge asserted, disgusted with the entire family.

When court resumed, the judge inquired how Anna was going to testify if she was not present. Her lawyer waved one of the tattered and worn-out-looking composition notebooks like a black-and-white marbled victory flag.

Anna kept journals because no one ever believed her. June found some of the journals when Anna was a teenager and burned them. She determined they were full of lies and whipped Anna with an extension cord. The handwritten journals narrated the words of a little girl molested, raped, beaten up, and tortured her entire childhood.

Mallory lied when she claimed she threw away all of Anna's stuff. The search warrant Matthew filed discovered a majority of Anna's items were stored in Mallory's house. Cops confiscated over thirty childhood journals written by Anna. Mallory unknowingly helped put her own daddy in jail by holding onto all the proof needed to convict him for rape. Never was there a greater mistake and a benefit for the prosecution. Those journals would testify and take the witness stand for Anna.

A jury was picked and the trial soon underway. A sense of uneasiness came over the lawyer as he opened his case by reading aloud Anna's journals. He felt as if he were violating her privacy. He needed to convict this monster, so he closed his eyes and whispered a prayer before he began to read.

The courtroom rendered dead silent as the lawyer began reading. His voice captured Anna's helpless words and desperate cries for help. He quoted explicit details of Reginald's attacks on her. He forced a young Anna to suck his dick before she hopped on the bus for school. Reginald raped her before he preached his Sunday sermons and threatened to kill her if she mumbled a word to anyone.

June's job kept her from the house fifteen to twenty hours a day, so Anna spent ample time alone with her daddy with no one to save her. There were several entries, however, where June stood in the doorway watching, yelling "slut" and "whore." She watched her own husband rape their daughter and stifled Anna's cries for help. No one loved her but her granny, she wrote.

Reginald sat in the courtroom with head bowed, listening to the words of a child being molested by a beast. His face remained hard to read, wrinkled and scored like a dried-up apple. It showed a look of sadness and shame, but at the same time, his face concealed a hint of a smirk. He almost seemed guilty proud of what he did.

In the midst of the journal readings, two jurors requested a dismissal from the case. One expressed that her own famous pastor was in the news for been accused of having sex with minors and didn't want to go through that ordeal again. She cried for several minutes before she left the jury stand. The other juror stated she had a young daughter and couldn't listen to another reading from the journals. She expressed her desire to inflict pain on Reginald. She couldn't wrap her mind around anyone mistreating an innocent little girl. Two alternate jurors joined the jury stand.

The journal readings lasted two more days. The courtroom was flooded with tears and tissues. The final journal entry read was her vacation to Disney World. A twelve-year-old Anna, her family, and a few cousins drove to Florida. Donald Duck had always been her favorite character and was excited at the opportunity visit Disney World. Once they arrived, she was informed they didn't buy a ticket for her to go to the park. She was to be holed up in the hotel room. She was beyond heartbroken. She wrote about how her daddy would come back to the hotel before the others and rape her. Since she had no escape, he would rape her for hours then fall asleep. He would wake up and molest her again. Her cousins and Mallory came back to the hotel worn out from a day at Disney while Anna worn out from a day of forcible violations.

Anna's lawyer wiped his eyes, closed the journals, and look toward the jury. Most were dabbing their eyes with tissues. A male juror openly shed tears. The evidence stacked up against Reginald with two more days left of testimony from the prosecution. Fear replaced Reginald's smug look as he too saw the jury weeping. His lawyer also brushed a few tears away from his eyes as well as he glanced at his own thirteen-year-old daughter in the back of the courtroom.

Reginald's phone records tracked that he called Anna 107 times in a row. Keenly aware his voice alone would cause Anna to have seizures, he left abrasive messages, permanently scarring her mind. A few of the messages played on speakers in the courtroom. In one message, Reginald threatened to come over to Anna's house and rape her so hard "her stuff would fall out." He promised to kill her and determined no one would believe a minister would be capable of these things, so he would get away with it. He illustrated in specific details how he would hunt her down and rape her before he stabbed her in her private parts.

Another message expressed now that his ex-wife and mom were dead, he could do whatever he wanted to Anna. "I never loved you, but I do miss effing you. You always put up a struggle, and I liked the challenge." His sickening confession oozed out of the voice mail like a weeping lesion. Most of the messages contained the same agenda of raping and killing Anna. His daily voice mail rants lasted for weeks.

The prosecutor had a bewildering labyrinth of facts and documentation. He submitted several sets of forged documents along with other documents to seal their case with Reginald. Some were life insurance policies totaling one million dollars. Reginald and Mallory were aware that if the policies were too large, Anna would have to provide a physical for the insurance companies. The insurance policies, from six different companies, ranged between ten thousand dollars and thirty thousand dollars. Reginald visited the funeral home where Anna paid for her entire funeral services. The funeral director, a friend of the family, disclosed how much Anna paid for her funeral. Days later, Reginald handed the funeral director forged documents stating that Anna wanted a refund. The lawyers submitted to the documents along with the canceled check with the deposit made to his bank account.

Arrest records provided proof that Reginald violated the restraining order Anna filed against him. The four times the officers arrested him, they released him almost immediately without any background check. He pulled the minister card and managed to persuade the arresting officers to release him without incident.

"We need to look into the arresting officers and file charges against them," the judge ordered.

"Here is the proof that he received the restraining order." The lawyer handed the judge the receipt requested form from the Calloways' household.

Most of the arrest took place in a different county than where Matthew filed the restraining order for Anna.

"The arresting officers claimed they were *uninformed* about the restraining order against Reginald," the prosecutor air-quoted the word uninformed.

"It's protocol for adjacent counties to research other violations from the perpetrators," Judge Walker asserted as she wrote down notes to follow up on the counties' protocol on restraining orders. "We cannot let this fall through the cracks again. People's lives can be in danger." Judge Walker let out a discouraging sigh.

The last document submitted contained the contents of the syringe found at the hospital. "Rat poison, bleach, borax?" The judge cocked her head to one side and her lip turned up with distaste in her mouth. The lawyer's final submission was Reginald's last arrest at the hospital along with the contents of the body search as proof he was in possession of the syringe. Anna's lawyers rested their case.

Reginald's lawyer shook his head as he placed his hands on the desk and gradually stood up. He leaned forward over his desk. His expression was solemn as he viewed the faces of each member of the jury. His audible heave let out all the air in his lungs as he became a bit lightheaded. The relatively new lawyer had been railroaded on his second case ever. He moved from second to first chair lawyer when his first chair conveniently backed out the morning of the trial. This lawyer's only job was to find character witnesses for Reginald. He was unaware of the magnitude of the offenses until the morning of the trial. 'That was all they asked me to do," he mumbled under his breath in the courtroom.

"Speak up," Judge Walker insisted.

"Ladies and gentlemen of the . . ." he paused. He attempted a counterargument. He shook his head again and scratched the back of his head by his neck. "You heard the evidence," he concluded as he motioned his hands toward the prosecution. He then threw his hands up in the air like "I surrender." "I have nothing to say," he divulged as he slithered back down in his chair.

"Can you call my character witnesses in?" Reginald nudged his lawyer's leg. The lawyer glared at Reginald, almost unable to speak.

"They won't be able to help you," he hissed through gritted teeth. He wondered if Reginald even heard the evidence stacked up against him. The jury went to deliberation. They were back in twenty minutes.

When the jurors returned, Judge Walker commanded Reginald to stand up. She asked if he had anything to say before she read the verdict. Reginald offered a weak apology for what he did and convinced himself he didn't know it hurt Anna.

"I did the best I could trying to raise her with an absentee mother," he claimed. He pleaded that the judge to show mercy on him. "I'm an old man. I didn't know it hurt her." The crocodile tears Reginald shed were useless in persuading the judge to go lenient on him.

"Are you kidding me?" Judge Walker scoffed. The judge gave him a surprised look, like a child catching an adult in a lie.

"Guilty on all counts," the judge read. The courtroom erupted as if something had attacked the beehive. These fools and underlings were outraged. Some church members gasped. Some boohooed loudly. Some expressed they knew he would be found guilty the whole time. The judge banged her gavel.

"Order in the court!" She directed them to quiet down. The judge's mouth opened in disbelief at the church members' reaction to the verdict. She reminded them they heard all the things he did to his child, not his flesh and blood, but still a child of God.

"He is supposed to be a man of God," she continued to fuss. "People looked up to him for guidance, and all along he was doing this horrendous things to his own daughter, whether she was related by blood or not," Judge Walker affirmed. She warned them they were following the wrong thing.

"You are to have faith and show loyalty to God and not in a person." Judge Walker reminded them about worshiping idols. She showed the courtroom a grim face like a carved masked. "You all know the elementary principles of right and wrong," she continued.

"You are a pathetic old asshole who has shown no remorse for what you did." She stopped preaching to the courtroom and directly spoke to Reginald. "I cannot believe a seventy-six-year-old self-proclaimed man of God harassed this poor woman, knowing her illness. You raped and tortured her for years. God only knows what else you did to her. You will now suffer in the same hell you put her through." She rolled her eyes and audibly let out all the air in her lungs.

The verdict was a total of twenty-five years plus life in prison. His wife, Janice, fainted. His head hung so low it looked as if he lost his spine. He appeared headless as police officers escorted him out of the courtroom back to sleepless hollow.

Reginald suffered a heart attack shortly after his arrival at the prison. He agonized through six heart attacks as well as eight strokes in his lifetime. Karma punished him for all his misdoings. Prison granted Reginald the same courtesy he presented Anna. His health rapidly declined. His imprisonment was plagued with anguish and affliction. Only after serving a year and a half of his time, he died in the prison infirmary.

Karma is like a rubber band, you can only stretch it so far before it comes back and smacks you in the face.

—Unknown

Mallory—August 2012

Mallory remained adamant that she did nothing wrong. She retained a lawyer from the same law firm that couldn't save her daddy. After a few meetings, Mallory's demeanor convinced the lawyer she needed psychiatric help and was delusional. She accepted no responsibility for her role in Anna's potential demise. "She's lying. My sister is a bold-faced liar," Mallory repeated in excess.

"There's lots of evidence stacked against you," the lawyer attempted to explain. Her lawyer sat as co-counsel when Reginald went to trial.

"You're my lawyer. You're required to believe I'm innocent. You will get me out of this," she demanded from him, pointing her finger in his direction.

"I will do my best to help you with this case," he proclaimed. His body language contradicted his words. He sat back in his chair, stifled his disgust, and contained his eye rolling.

Mallory stood in her orange jumpsuit before the same judge who sent her daddy to prison for twenty-five years plus life. Scattered on the courtroom benches were faithful family members along with curious coworkers. Mallory's friends extinguished any relationship they had with her. Her caustic behavior ate away at any lasting friendships.

Her charges were forgery, conspiracy, aggravated stalking, and attempted murder. As soon as Judge Walker entered, a gasp fell over the courtroom.

"She's the same judge Reginald had." Janice turned around and whispered to anyone in earshot. "This is not good," she mumbled to herself. Janice closed her eyes and prayed for God to grant the judge some compassion for Mallory.

Judge Walker addressed Mallory straight away. "I tried another case with the same last name a few days ago. It's not a common name. What is your relationship to him?" Judge Walker played ignorant.

"My daddy. She lied on him. Anna gonna get hers." Mallory snarled at the judge.

"Something's wrong with this family," the judged determined with a sneer. She tilted her head and turned her lip up. The courtroom chuckled. The jury was chosen and the trial soon underway.

"Jury," Anna's same lawyer stood up and turned toward the jurors. His hand gestured in Mallory's direction. "Mallory was keenly aware her sister, Anna, had health issues. She battled cancer as well as other health afflictions since she was a small child. Mallory traveled halfway across the country to harass Anna. Anna sprawled out on the hospital bed, her body inflicted with pain from a chemical substance coursing through her body to kill the cancer cells. All she wanted was to make the pain go away, but the real tormentor lurked around the hospital looking to terrorize this innocent woman."

The lawyer paused and shook his head slowly and deliberately, sympathizing with Anna's suffering. His own mother died two years ago from pancreatic cancer.

"Mallory snatched Anna's life away from her," Anna's lawyer suggested.

One juror gasped.

"Her identity, I mean," the lawyer clarified with a slight smirk. "Mallory's job allowed her access to Anna's social security information. She knew Anna was in the hospital and wouldn't check her credit report," the lawyer lamented. "Mallory applied for seven credit cards and two gas cards in Anna's name." The lawyer submitted the credit card bills along with Anna's hospital records proving it impossible that Anna applied for or used the credit cards.

"Ladies and gentlemen of the jury, Anna has epileptic seizures, and her licenses were taken away over twenty years ago. One credit card charged several times to rent luxury cars." The lawyer proceeded to explain how Mallory and her father traveled to the cancer center to pursue and harass Anna using credit cards in her name. They purchases first-class plane tickets, stayed in upscale hotel rooms, and dined in expensive restaurants in the same city where Anna received treatment.

"The cost of these wild, extravagant purchases didn't matter to Mallory. Anna would ultimately be responsible for the bill," the lawyer stated, looking over at Mallory who stuck her tongue out at him.

"Mallory may have gotten away with it, but she made several mistakes," the lawyer pointed out. "I will show you facts to support this." He knew the jury was not convinced, and he needed to prove a random identity thief didn't steal her information from hospital records.

"One credit card shows payments for a cable bill and a light bill. My investigation discovered that those bills were Mallory's address." He submitted the address where the cable company had service. He had a copy of Mallory's licenses, confirming her current address.

Other charges revealed an assortment of frivolous purchases from hair appointments, new bedroom furniture, massages, car detailing, and over two thousand dollars for an entertainment system. Most of the credit cards were maxed out before the first bill came due. "Two credit cards were used to make down payments for two forged life insurance policies," Anna's lawyer revealed.

Mallory forged Anna's name on eight of the fifteen different life insurance policies. Her dad admitted to forging the other seven for a lesser charge. The insurance companies charged the credit cards for monthly payments on the policy. The lawyer submitted copies of the policies into evidence. A copy of Anna's identification card proved that her signature didn't match the one the policies.

"She said we could get those policies," Mallory proclaimed as she jumped up, almost knocking her chair over.

"Control your client," Judge Walker warned Mallory's lawyer. He pulled Mallory by the arm and yanked her back to her seat. Mallory's chest rose and fell with each huff and puff. She grumbled under her breath a few times before her lawyer motioned to her the "shush" sign with his finger.

Phone records showed Mallory called Anna's phone an average of sixty times a day for three weeks straight. Mallory, unlike her daddy, was smart enough not to leave voice mail evidence. Matthew needed proof the unknown number belonged to Mallory. He asked Anna to answer the phone a few times when Mallory called. "Don't be scared," Matthew assured her. "She can't get you. I just need to be able to get a transcript of the calls."

"No matter where you move, Anna, I will find you and make your life miserable." Her lawyer used a sinister and mockery tone as he quoted Mallory's transcribed words. In one transcript, Mallory stated her intentions to torture then kill Anna. She planned to "destroy her life for telling those lies on her daddy for all those years." The lawyer scoffed at her ignorance.

Other transcripts were along the same lines of harassment. Mallory promised to send men to Anna's house and rape her. "Let the record show the phone calls caused Anna's health to decline, and she had seizures after each incident," the lawyer reported to the jury. He submitted the dates and times of the phone calls as well as the nurses' log stating her health condition.

"I ain't hire nobody to kill that bitch." The prosecution brought up the attempted murder charge, which lit Mallory's fuse. Her explosive words shattered the courtroom walls. She leaped out of her seat in a failed attempt to bombard the prosecutor. Both her lawyers had to contain the volatile defendant.

"Calm down, Ms. Calloway," Judge Walker's gavel packed a wallop when it hit the desk.

"I ain't do those things they said I did," Mallory snapped. Her gradations of outrage bothered the judge. Judge Walker warned Mallory that if she didn't calm down the bailiff would dismiss her from the courtroom. "The proceeding will continue without you if you don't get yourself together, young lady." Judge Walker diffused another potential explosion. Mallory rolled her eyes at the judge and begrudgingly sat down. She rocked forcefully in her chair as hit man Vince's confession was read to the jury.

———⦿———

All Mallory's arrests were a result of her refusing a legal order to stay away from Anna. "The restraining order made Mallory more aggressive," Anna's lawyer concluded. "What person in their right mind would keep coming back after being arrested for the same violation?"

The lawyer submitted proof that Mallory was aware of the restraining order. "She is like a pit bull," the prosecution reasoned. Mallory growled. Her lawyer nudged her to be quiet.

"Pit bulls give no warning before attacking. When challenged or confronted by authority, they readily engage and don't normally back down. They become more aggressive and will fight to the death even when not provoked," the lawyer theorized. Mallory's barking and snarling startled a few jurors. She demonstrated a lack of restraint. Her lawyer attempted to cover her mouth, and she nipped his finger. He let out a tiny "Ouch you bit—"

"Be careful," the Judge warned them both, shaking her finger in their direction. Anna's lawyers rested their case.

The defense had nothing. Again. The fifteen minutes it took for the jury to decide the case coincided with the length of a bathroom break. The judge asked Mallory if she wanted to speak before the verdict was delivered.

"You have to believe me. All these things are lies. Anna has been lying on me for years. She is the one who has been harassing us." Mallory stood and insisted in her most loving voice how she cared about her sister and would never do anything to hurt her. She slightly smiled in the direction of the jury. Judge Walker's jaw dropped, and she tilted her head to the side. It took a few seconds before she could speak.

"You have been bothering this poor woman for years," the judge started in on Mallory. "You know this woman is sick and you kept harassing her. You even flew across country to torment her on her dime no less. You're not her family. You don't deserve to call her your sister. This Calloway clan are a bunch bullies with no remorse for all the damage they have caused her," the judge continued. "This family is like bleach. They destroy everything they touch or come in contact with."

The jury found her guilty on all counts. Mallory was sentenced to fifteen years in prison. Her stepmother fainted again. Mallory screamed and proclaimed her innocence. Her lawyer's papers flew everywhere as Mallory knocked over the table and started running toward the judge. It took two police officers to handcuff and subdue her. The officers carried Mallory out of the courtroom screaming, still trying to plead her innocence. Tears of outraged arrogance blurred her vision.

Mallory unsuccessfully tried to call Anna from prison on several occasions, but all collect calls remain blocked from her phone. Judge Laura Walker retired two months after this trial.

Some people just aren't happy unless they're making someone else's life miserable. Watch out, karma always comes back.
—Nishan Panwar

Janice—August 2012

"Janice has a weak mind and is easily persuaded," her second-grade teacher observed as she shared this with Janice's parents at a parent conference. "Proper guidance would help her tremendously, or I can see her heading down the wrong path," her teacher warned. In desperation, Janice's parents dragged her to church, hoping "the word" could educate and enlighten their impressionable daughter.

Janice sang in the church choir and attended Bible study faithfully. She recited Bible passages at a young age and was prepping to become a church leader. Church kept her focused until a twenty-three-year-old Janice fell for a much older man at a church revival. Reverend Reginald Calloway awakened a fire in her soul.

"The way he preaches just does something to me," Janice confided to a close friend after the second night of revival. By the third night, Janice couldn't contain her desire for Reverend Calloway. She approached the altar where the sinner was saving sinners and slipped the reverend her phone number. By the last night of the weeklong revival, Reverend Calloway and Janice had been intimate several times.

They secretly dated for months, with Janice believing her parents were none the wiser. Her family disowned her after learning that she was dating a married minister. They labeled her a home wrecker and refused to support her lifestyle. Janice and Reverend Calloway wed three years after meeting, and her family refused to attend their oldest child's wedding.

<hr />

Janice had a soft spot for Anna. Janice's youngest brother was riddled with health infirmities for years. He reminded her of Anna's suffering.

"Anna seems like a nice quiet girl. Why are you so mean to her?" she accidently questioned Mallory at dinner on evening. Mallory went ballistic.

"You don't know anything just because you married my dad. Anna tore our family apart and I hate her. If you want to stay in this family, you will do what I say," a teenage Mallory asserted with a tone that made Janice wince. Mallory brainwashed Janice for years into believing Anna was a horrible person. She actively participated in the callous and cruel treatment toward Anna.

After a while, Mallory's handbook of torment replaced her Bible scriptures of compassion. She prayed less as her heart hardened more.

<hr />

After her last arrest at the hospital, Janice remained silent and distanced herself from Anna, sensing it useless to harass her now. Her husband and Mallory's shenanigans sentenced them to prison, and she feared the same fate. Fate had twisted and turned her life in a thousand ways.

Janice appeared in court for aggravated stalking and forgery. She was relieved when Judge Walker didn't enter the courtroom. She faced the judge without a support system. Reginald provided no siblings as in-laws. After the second Calloway trial, friends and church members wanted no association. Some even fled the church to baptize themselves from the Calloway stink. Her family unfazed to find Janice in this predicament maintained their lack of support. Jean sat in the back of the courtroom to relay information to Ms. Kay.

Anna's lawyer failed to produce adequate paperwork showing Janice forged any of the life insurance documents. "Her signature doesn't match the forged documents," Janice's lawyer protested. Janice used a different law firm. She needed a lawyer with no bias based on her last name. The prosecution submitted Janice's phone records showing an excess of thirty-five calls a day to Anna's phone. The restraining order and multiple arrests after the restraining order were also submitted as evidence.

During proceedings, Alicia sent a text message informing Janice of Anna's death. Janice broke down in the courtroom as her lawyer relayed the news of Anna's passing to the judge. Her cries sounded like a wounded animal, and she jerked away when her lawyer attempted to console her. The remorse she felt for Anna's passing was palpable only to her. Others viewing her outburst were barely able to discern her tears for the death of Anna or the lighter sentence she was bound to receive. Her lawyer requested a ten-minute recess, so she could get some air. When she returned, the judge sentenced her to two years' probation.

Jean called Ms. Kay frantically after the verdict. She wanted to know why no one told her Anna died. Ms. Kay laughed so hard she snorted.

"It's not funny, Sandy." Jean sniffed as she wiped her nose. "I was sitting in court, and it took everything thing I had not to leave and call you," she managed to blurt out between sobs.

Ms. Kay laughed even harder.

Jean didn't find Anna's death comical until Ms. Kay described in hilarious detail how Nurse Miriam convinced Alisha that Anna died.

"How did her face look when she got the message?" Sandy inquired.

"Priceless." Jean giggled as she was now in on the joke. The nurses, Jean, and Ms. Kay still have a good laugh when one of them says, "I can't find the body."

> *People pay for what they do, and still more, for what they have allowed themselves to become. And they pay for it simply: by the lives they lead.*
> *—Edith Wharton*

Alisha—February 2013

"I got served papers to appear in court." Miriam was in tears as she dialed Ms. Kay's number.

"What is going on?" Ms. Kay attempted to get clarity. Before Miriam could respond, Ms. Kay received another call.

"Hold on, Miriam," Ms. Kay said as she clicked her call waiting.

"Girl. That stupid Alicia is taking me to court," Vivian blurted out before Ms. Kay had a chance to say hello.

"Wait." Ms. Kay cut her off. "I have Miriam on the other line. Let me call you on three way." Ms. Kay hung up with Vivian and before she could dial her back in, Dr. C called.

"Kay. What is this mess I got today about being sued by that stupid woman?"

"Wait." Ms. Kay interrupted. "Let me get all of you all on the phone." Miriam, Vivian, Dr. Calabretta, and Ms. Kay had a four-way phone conversation.

"I got served papers from Alisha," they all blurted out at once in unmixed astonishment. Alisha was suing each of them for Anna's remains since she had been unable to locate the body. She wanted reparations because she felt they should have notified her when Anna died. Alisha was also suing for defamation of character. Ms. Kay assured them she would take care of the situation.

"She still can't find that body?" Vivian chuckled as the rest joined in on the comic relief. As the laughter died down on the phone, an idea came to Ms. Kay.

"I am going to write a letter stating Anna is alive and doesn't want to be bothered by anyone in her family.

"How's that gonna work?" Miriam was skeptical.

Ms. Kay explained her idea to write the letter as if she were Anna. "Judge Walker retired, so it needs to be written where the new judge will understand her plight and have compassion for Anna," Ms. Kay noted.

"OK." Dr. C agreed.

"It's crucial the letter is read out loud in court," Ms. Kay stated. Alicia needed to hear the letter. They all agreed it was a solid ruse and eventually calmed down.

After the phone call, Ms. Kay constructed the letter and e-mailed it to Anna. "Anna, your crazy sister is trying to sue your nurses and Dr. C," Ms. Kay explained on the phone.

"I need you to read the letter I wrote in your behalf and sign it please. We need to get your family to stop bothering you." Ms. Kay hoped Anna agreed.

"I wish they would just leave me alone," Anna whined.

"I know. They will after this. She is the last one," Ms. Kay assured her. Anna read over the letter and thanked Ms. Kay. Jean's friend who was a notary stopped by the house and notarized the letter after Anna signed it. The letter was officially ready for court.

<hr />

A week before court, Dr. Calabretta was leaving work and spotted Alisha in the employee parking lot. She jumped in her car and headed toward her house, hoping Alisha didn't see her.

As she drove along the interstate, she noticed a car trailing her. She made it to her exit off the interstate. The other car followed her as if playing Simon Says. Not taking any chances, Dr. C drove into a neighboring subdivision. She pulled into the driveway of a house and parked as if she lived there. The car following her parked on the street a few houses down. Dr. C called 911 to report that someone in a red sedan followed her home and she feared for her safety.

The police arrived and approached the red car. Alisha was behind the wheel, and Janice sat in the car looking very nervous.

"I am on probation. I can't go to jail," Janice reminded Alisha.

"We gonna be OK. Just act cool," Alisha assured a doubting Janice.

Alisha gave the police office a lame excuse about being lost when the police approached the car.

"I need to see your license and registration. The woman in the car reported you followed her from the cancer hospital. You traveled through three counties. That's considered stalking," the police officer warned them.

"We're leaving," Janice stated. Janice was on probation and needed to stay out of trouble. Dr. C obtained a police report of the incident in time for court.

Dr. C retained a lawyer. Vivian and Miriam applied for council.

"She's still alive, right?" the lawyer's secretary asked.

"Yes," they confessed.

"You don't need a lawyer then," the secretary surmised. The day of court arrived. In the courtroom, the three sat together on the defendant side. They wanted a good look at Alisha once court started.

"All rise," the bailiff commanded. Judge Laura Walker entered the courtroom. Her decision to return to the bench after retiring made the news. Judge Walker had been a pillar in the judicial system and made her name for herself after forty years in the court system. Judge Walker was quoted in the newspaper as saying, "I was called back to the bench. A higher power drew me back. There was more work to be done." Miriam, Vivian, and Dr. C quietly cheered as they squeezed each other's hands. Some grunts and a few groans of aggravation were heard in the courtroom as well. Alicia was facing an impending fate.

The three looked around the courtroom to see if Alisha's face recognized the judge. Alisha was not in attendance. When the judge called their names, all three stood up.

"Where is the plaintiff?" the judge asked.

No one knew. The three shrugged their shoulders and looked around.

Judge Walker tried the other cases on the docket. Lunchtime was approaching, and Alisha was still a no-show. Judge Walker called the three into her chambers. Judge Walker looked over the paperwork and scowled.

"I remember Anna Calloway. I remember that crazy family of hers too," Judge Walker noted. "What family member is out to get her now?" she questioned.

Vivian informed the judge that her sister was suing for Anna's body.

"Did she die?" The judge held her breath. She remembered Anna being sick.

"No, she isn't dead." Vivian affirmed.

"We have a letter she wants read out loud," the three blurted out in unison.

"This must be an important letter." The judge glanced over the letter when Miriam handed it to her.

"If Anna would be willing to talk on the phone, this would go a lot faster," the judge suggested.

"We have to ask her power of attorney," Vivian interjected. Vivian called Ms. Kay and gave a quick summary of events, and asked if they could contact Anna.

"Of course."

Ms. Kay phoned Anna to let her know she would have to testify over the phone. "Don't be nervous, Anna. This is the last one we have to deal with," Ms. Kay promised her.

"OK, Ms. Kay," Anna unenthusiastically agreed.

Dr. C reported that Alisha followed her home about a week ago. "I have the police report." Dr. C presented the document to Judge Walker. "I guess maybe she figured I hid Anna's body in my basement," Dr. C joked. Everyone laughed.

Alisha and Janice arrived in court after the lunch break. Alisha attempted to explain to the judge she didn't think her case would be heard right away, so she took her time to get there. "That's not how the system works, young lady. You need to get your priorities straightened out," the judge snapped. Alisha gasped as she clutched her imaginary pearls. Courtroom proceeding began.

Alisha stood up and pointed. "Those people have my sister's body. I am the only family she has left. She was moving with me before they let her die." Alisha presented the judge with paperwork allegedly signed by Anna agreeing to move to Germany with Alisha and her husband. She submitted two thirty-thousand-dollar life insurance policies Anna supposedly signed as well. Janice whispered to Dr. C, "That's why she was so determined to find the body."

Alisha continued with her rant about "how these people tried to keep her from her sister and she needed the death certificate." The judged interrupted her lies and asked for the defense to provide something with Anna's signature on it. Alisha interrupted. "Excuse me?" Suddenly, like death, the truth appeared.

"These signatures don't match," the judged informed Alisha. Dr. C's lawyer handed the judge the letter signed by Anna. She looked over all the documents presented.

"Let's call Anna and see if she signed these," Judge Walker suggested.

"My sister is dead." Alisha was sure of it.

The judge used Vivian's phone to call Anna. She used the phone's speaker. Alisha's jaw dropped like it was off its hinges when she heard Anna's weak voice say "Hello." Everyone in court looked over at Janice, who shook her head in disbelief.

The judge asked a few questions to confirm it was Anna Calloway. After confirmation, Judge Walker questioned Anna.

"Do you want to be reunited with your sister Alisha?"

"The Calloways are not my family. I have a new family who cares for me, and they treat me nicely." Anna spoke slow and deliberate. "No. I don't want to live with Alisha," Anna said firmly.

The phone got eerily silent.

"Hello?" The judge thought the call dropped.

"I just want everybody to leave . . . me . . . alone!" Anna screamed and then broke down. Judge Walker assured Anna everything was going to be OK and her safety was the most important thing.

Judge Walker inquired if Anna signed any paperwork stating Alisha would be her caretaker. Anna insisted she never signed anything.

"Last time I saw my so-called sister, she was mean to me in the hospital. The nurses and Dr. C kept her away from me," Anna said. "The nurses made it clear to Alisha I didn't want to go to Germany with her," Anna revealed as she snorted snot back up her nose.

"Did you get my letter?" Anna inquired.

"I sure did." The judge wished Anna good health and thanked her for talking to her before she hung up the phone.

"She's not bright enough to write a letter," Alisha alleged as she jumped up and insisted there was no way Anna wrote a letter.

"Sit down," the judge stated. Alisha sat down with a look of disgust. "Why do you want to take care of Anna, then, if she's not bright? Maybe you have a hidden agenda," the judge suggested.

Alisha shrugged her shoulders then crossed her arms. Alisha sat on the edge of her chair as the judge read the letter out loud [full letter at the end of the book].

The letter went into details of Alisha's knowledge of Anna's childhood sexual abuse. Her much older sister grew up in a different state and visited during the summer. For years, Alisha neglected to get Anna help. Alisha reluctantly drove Anna to the hospital twice. Once she forced Anna to blame it on a boy at school so "daddy wouldn't get in trouble." It also explained how aggressive Alisha became after she reconnected with Anna a few months ago. Anna admitted it was wrong to pretend to be dead but felt that was her only option to stop the harassment. The letter concluded with Anna not wanting any dealings with her family. She recommended something be put in place if any family member tried to find her.

"Anna ain't write that. She ain't smart!" Alisha yelled out in the courtroom.

"Well, she was smart enough to fool you into thinking she died," the judge said with a grin. Dr. C and the nurses giggled.

The judge glared at Alisha then shook her head. "What is the deal with this Anna woman?" The judge asked. "Is she rich?"

"No," Vivian replied, shaking her head.

"Well, there's something going on with her and this family." The judge was confused. Judge Walker asked Alisha if she was a Calloway by blood.

"Yes. I am," Alisha replied, chest puffed up like a proud peacock.

"That explains everything. It must be the genes. Crazy flows through the Calloway blood like water from a faucet," the judge concluded.

Miriam covered her mouth to prevent from laughing aloud. Vivian nodded her head in agreement, and Dr. C smiled. They glanced over at Janice whose face was unreadable.

"After reading the letter, anything said about Alisha was probably true," The judge threw out the defamation of character charge. Judge

Walker also dropped the charges for reparations, but added more charges. The charges were against Alisha.

"Based on the information presented in court, I am charging you with contempt, aggravated harassment, stalking, and forgery." The judge ruled.

"I didn't do nothing wrong," Alisha insisted. "I just came here for my sister's body." Alisha words cracked.

"It must be the blood because Malory said the same mess." The judge chuckled.

Alisha didn't realize coming to court late resulted in a contempt charge. Following a doctor across three counties gave her a stalking charge. Once the judge heard about the phone calls and broken restraining order, she added harassment charges. Alisha's most sinister act was bringing forged documents to court. The judge concluded Alisha knowingly tried to profit from her sister's death. Alisha almost fainted when she heard the verdict. Janice put her head in her hands and whimpered.

Alisha was sentenced to ten years in prison. Her passport was confiscated, which prevented her from ever living in the home her husband just purchased in Germany. Alisha remained adamant she was innocent. She attempted to flee the courtroom, but two cops blocked the door.

"I need to call my husband!" she wailed. "All I wanted to do was help my sister." She begged the officers to release her from the handcuffs. The judge left the courtroom witnessing Alisha screaming, flailing her legs, and almost tripping the arresting officer. One month later, Judge Walker retired again and never returned to the bench.

A person may cause evil to others not only by his actions, but by his inaction, and in either case, he is justly accountable to them for the injury.

—John Stuart Mill

Chapter 17

The Medical Staff

Dr. Caley Calabretta

Caley competed with David ever since middle school. Their love for academia sparked a love-hate relationship. In high school, David's academics started to falter when he realized he was in love with Caley. In class, Caley concentrated on math theories and physics. David studied Caley's anatomy and the mathematical probability she would give him the time of day.

"See. I told you David I was going to be valedictorian of the class," she gloated when she got the news.

"It don't matter, 'cause I love you," David admitted. He pushed her up against the lockers and kissed her hard. Caley didn't resist. They attended prom together and were a couple before graduation.

Caley and David attended the same prestigious university. They both graduated in four years with science degrees.

"Let's go to different medical schools," David suggested. He loved Caley but knew she needed her space to grow. He also knew he would not be able to concentrate with her on campus. He struggled in undergrad.

"That's fine," Caley agreed. They were already living together and the break would do them both good.

"We can compare notes on different professors. It will be fun." David chuckled as he kissed Caley. "Plus, I want to give you this."

David got down on one knee and proposed to Caley. "You are the smartest woman I know. I love you and want to spend the rest of my life with you. Caley, will you marry me?" David held up a three-karat ring for Caley to admire.

"Yes, David. Yes." Caley beamed like the full moon.

Caley maintained her competition with David in medical school even though they attended different schools. David felt like he had already won the prize. His grade point average shot up once they went to different school. Before they started their residencies, they got married at the justice of the peace. Their parents attended the ceremony but secretly wished they had a traditional wedding. "We will once we finish medical school," they both explained to their parents.

Caley was no stranger to hard work and determination. She graduated with a 4.0 GPA, which she maintained her entire educational studies. Caley worked at a local hospital for seventeen years. In a very short time, she moved up in the ranks to obtain the status of attending physician. Caley's impressive work ethic caught the eye of the director of a cancer center in her area. The director called Caley personally and offered her the job as chief physician as well as a signing bonus to transfer to their hospital. She worked at the cancer center for seven years when they asked her to help open up a new cancer center close to where Anna lived.

Her new job title was liaison to the doctors. The move looked like the dawn of a new day, full of promises and potential. The Calabrettas were ready for a change of scenery. David was a dermatologist, and the move allowed him to open up his own private practice. Dr. Caley transferred to the cancer center two months before Anna arrived.

Dr. C remained Anna's doctor whenever she needed to return to the cancer center for treatments or any checkup necessary for cancer patients. She treated Anna like a mother treated her own child. Dr. C went the extra mile for all her patients but went two miles when it came to Anna.

"There's something about her," she would often say to Ms. Kay. "Yes. Anna is something amazing," Ms. Kay replied each time.

"She is always so polite. She's so mannerly. I know if I were in her shoes I would not be saying please or thank you," Dr. C commented.

"Me either," Ms. Kay chimed in.

Dr. C fought for Anna when other doctors wanted to give up on her. Some doctors on her team were naysayers, and their flippant attitudes didn't benefit any patient they cared for. "Some doctors only want to treat patients who are not needy. Some only offer various surgeries because they get a cut from each surgery they perform whether the patient needs it or not," Dr. C revealed to Ms. Kay after one of many intense meetings on Anna's health.

Dr. C dismissed any doctor on Anna's team she deemed not playing for "Team Anna." She researched alternative treatments to combat Anna's various health issues. Doctors with a level of compassion like hers are rare nowadays.

Dr. C receives thank-you notes and gifts from her patients on a weekly basis. She is always highly praised at the center for her dedication to her patients. After years at the cancer center, she and David decided that retirement was not too far in their future. They retired within months of each other. Caley spends most of her retirement time riding horses and playing golf. She too calls Ms. Kay to check in on Anna's progress.

> **You can easily judge the character of a man by**
> **how he treats those who can do nothing for him.**
> **—Johann Wolfgang von Goethe**

Nurse Helen

At four years old, Helen mixed her mom's medicine in applesauce and fed it to her dolls.

"Mommy, I am going to be a nurse when I grow up," Helen declared when her mommy found out and fussed at her.

"Stop wasting my medicine. It's expensive." Her mom warned Helen various times. Helen was five years old when she used all her mom's bandages to "heal" her stuffed animals. Helen only knew her mom to be sick, so she mocked what she saw the nurses do.

Helen's father died in an attempted robbery when Helen was nine. Although she was an only child, Helen never felt obligated to care for her mother. She jumped at the chance. Helen came straight home from elementary school every day and donned her makeshift nurse's uniform. She prepared her mom's meals and administered the meds she needed. Helen bathed and dressed her mom. She called in the doctors' appointments and found transportation to get her there until having a license to drive.

Helen's mom fell gravely ill a few days before Helen's prom. Helen didn't bat an eyelash when she canceled her plans and stayed at the hospital with her. Her friends knew of Helen's commitment, so they came to the hospital after prom and sat with Helen until her mom took her last breath.

After the funeral, her favorite aunt stayed in town for a few weeks to help Helen. Her aunt convinced Helen to pack up and move to California. "You can stay with me rent-free and attend college," her aunt suggested. Since Helen had no family where she lived, she sold her mom's house and moved to California after graduation.

Helen finished college in four years with a 4.0 GPA. She wanted to work at a cancer center to help cancer patients like her own mom. She applied at the local cancer center, and they hired her immediately. They paid for her schooling where she received her master's degree in nursing. Helen worked at a few cancer centers in different states until she found one that was the right fit. It was the center Anna would receive treatment from years later.

Nurse Helen saved Ms. Kay's number and called six months after Anna left her cancer center. She needed to know how things were going but hesitated, not wanting to hear Anna passed away. A smile crept on her face when she heard Anna's health had improved. She asked about the lamb and was happy to know she still had it.

"I have thought about you all a lot. I pray for the both of you on a daily basis," Nurse Helen confessed.

"Thanks. We need it," Ms. Kay replied.

"The way you cared for Anna who is not even family is beyond amazing. You will surely be blessed for this," she stated with admiration for Ms. Kay.

"I already am." Ms. Kay smiled as she thought about the angels on earth who have continuously protected Anna.

Months after the phone call, Nurse Helen transferred from the cancer center across the country to the cancer center close to Anna around the same time as Nurse Penny. On her first day, she was shocked to find Anna back in the cancer center. Shock turned to elation when she was assigned to be Anna's nurse.

"Guess what. Nurse Helen is my nurse. The one from the other cancer center."

Ms. Kay heard the happiness in the text message. Nurse Helen is still at the cancer center and loves being able to take care of Anna whenever she has an appointment.

To do what nobody else will do, a way that nobody else can do, in spite of all we go through; is to be a nurse.

—Rawsi Williams

Ruby

Ruby was born in the United States when her family came to visit. She was three when her family relocated back to Africa. She graduated from high school in Zimbabwe and desired a better life for herself. Ruby set her mind on going back to America. She applied to several state colleges that were happy to accept her.

After getting her RN degree, she worked at a few hospitals in her area. Ruby found her calling comforting the terminally ill patients. She applied at a hospice center that hired her immediately. Her sympathy and compassion left her patients longing for her daily visits. Ruby played card games and prayed with the patients if they requested. She educated the family members by creating personal-care instructions for them to follow. When one of Ruby's patients died, she attended the funeral and sometimes spoke on behalf of the center. Family members were in awe knowing Ruby went an extra mile.

—

Ruby flew across country to the cancer center to visit Anna. Anna longed for a familiar, friendly face in the midst of all the turmoil.

"Ruby!" Anna's eye lit up when Ruby walked into her hospital room.

"Hello, Anna. I missed you. I came to take care of you," Ruby said. She washed Anna's hair and tended to her the days Nurse Helen didn't work. Ruby even fussed at a few nurses. Anna loved to hear Ruby fuss. Her African accent was more prominent when she became upset.

Ruby is really mad. Ms. Kay, Anna texted one afternoon.

Why you say that?

Cause she talking that language. I don't understand what she is saying.

Somebody must be getting it. Ms. Kay giggled.

I like the way she talk when she fuss, Anna admitted.

A few moments later, Ruby called Ms. Kay to give the details about the nurses. "I sorry for talking like dat in front of her, but dees nurses make me so mad," Ruby tried to explain.

"What did Anna say?" Ms. Kay wanted to know.

"She just laugh at me. I told her it not funny. Then we both start to laugh. Anna has a pretty smile you know," Ruby informed Ms. Kay. Ms. Kay smiled at the phone. Anna hadn't smiled or laughed for months.

Ruby stayed for two weeks and Anna was elated. She cried the last day that Ruby stopped by.

"I will miss you." Anna feared her bad treatment would resume after Ruby left.

"Anna. I will be back soon. You are going to be OK," Ruby assured it.

In the spring, Ruby and her husband relocated back to Africa to be close to Ruby's family. "There is so much going on back home, Ms. Kay. Good and bad," Ruby explained. Their daughter Mia was graduating from a new all-girls school that opened up. This was the first graduating class of the school, and Ruby needed to be there. Her only daughter would soon attend college, and Ruby was not going to miss that.

Her mama's health took a turn for the worse around the same time.

"Nobody can take care of me Mama like I can. She need me," Ruby said.

"I understand that. Family should always come first," Ms. Kay added.

Ruby is currently working as a nurse in Zimbabwe, along with taking sole responsibility for the care of her mama. She is working on a project to open her own hospice center in the United States in a few years. Ruby reaches out to Ms. Kay once a month to check on Anna. "You and Anna have an open invitation anytime you want to visit me country," Ruby lets Ms. Kay know after each phone call or e-mail. Ms. Kay thanks Ruby every time she calls.

> **To make a difference in someone's life, you don't have to be brilliant, rich, beautiful, or perfect. You just have to care.**
> **—Mandy Hale**

Nurse Miriam

Miriam finished her rounds at the cancer center and was in Anna's room when her phone rang. "Paul overdosed on pills, and they are trying to revive him," the frantic voice said on the line. The doctors were pumping his stomach, and she needed to get to the hospital. Miriam reached the hospital too late.

"We tried. We could not save him." The doctor met her at the door of the ER.

"He's gone?" Miriam shrieked in disbelief. "I need to see him," Miriam demanded. The doctor escorted Miriam to the back. When she saw his lifeless body on the gurney, she collapsed.

She woke up in a hospital bed with a splitting headache. *How could he leave without even saying good-bye?* Miriam questioned herself. *Why didn't Paul talk to her if he suffered from depression?* Her head pounded with every difficult and abstruse question she asked herself.

Miriam and Paul were together for twenty years. High school sweethearts. She figured she knew everything about him. *Was it something she did? Why was Paul too scared to talk to her? Why no note or letter explaining his actions?* So many questions ran through Miriam's mind she would never know the answers to. She dreaded going home, but she didn't want to stay at the hospital. She mustered up enough energy to drive herself home.

Miriam reached out to his friends for answers, but they were just as dumbfounded. One friend finally admitted that Paul mentioned taking his life earlier in the year but assumed the alcohol was speaking for him. Miriam wanted to crawl through the phone line and choke him.

"Don't you think that's something I needed to know?" she wailed.

"I didn't know he would actually do it. I'm sorry." The friend gave a weak and uneasy apology.

Miriam hung up before he said another word. Her eyes cleaned themselves with tears in search of answers. She searched and cried every night after Paul died.

Her favorite aunt traveled with her to the funeral in the neighboring state. "She was solemn the entire trip," her aunt reported to Ms. Kay. Paul's family insisted he be buried in the family plot even though he purchased one next to Miriam shortly after their honeymoon. Although Miriam was his wife, they treated her like a part-time girlfriend of Paul's. Her input was not acknowledged during the arraigning of the funeral and was requested to not ride in the family car.

Paul's parents never cared for Miriam and provided no substantial reasons. They had hopes of him marrying his childhood neighbor, Lana. Lana and Paul dated in middle school for a month and decided they were better off as friends. Paul constantly explained to his parents his love for Miriam. "Like it or not, Miriam is my wife, and she is not going anywhere." Paul constantly defended Miriam.

On holidays, Miriam requested to work at the hospital. "I can't stand his family, and they can't stand me," she explained to her bosses. Paul spent the holidays with his family and then celebrated the holiday evenings with Miriam.

Miriam fell into a sinkhole of depression after the funeral. It was a collapse in her surface layer, a shift in her soil and her soul. It swallowed her will to live. The hole grew daily, making it almost impossible for anyone to get close enough to save her.

Miriam traded her nursing position to become a full-time drunk. She put down the blood pressure kit and picked up a bottle of booze. Her hands gripped the bottle like a knotted cord. Miriam's drinking binges were irresponsible and borderline dangerous to herself and others. "Don't tell me what to do." Miriam snarled. She cursed out at anyone who suggested she needed help getting out the sinkhole. "I'm fine," she convinced herself as she sat in the sinkhole, refusing help. Ms. Kay felt talking to Miriam was like trying to put toothpaste back in the tube. Almost impossible, but Ms. Kay refused to give up on her.

One morning right at sunrise, Ms. Kay called to check in on Miriam. Miriam informed Ms. Kay she was sitting in her car outside of Paul's job.

"Why?"

"I just miss him, Kay," Miriam lamented.

"I understand." Ms. Kay's words did little to comfort Miriam.

"No you don't!" Miriam yelled. "Don't nobody understand what I'm going through," Miriam determined.

Ms. Kay stayed on the phone while Miriam ranted for fifteen minutes. Her garbled words were barely audible.

Ms. Kay eventually talked Miriam into going home and getting something to eat. "I'll meet you at Denny's," Ms. Kay urged Miriam as she started to get dressed.

"Can't go nowhere. I'm in my pajamas," Miriam quipped.

"Well, please just go home," Ms. Kay begged. Ms. Kay stayed on the phone and silently prayed until Miriam arrived back home.

"I'm home, Kay," Miriam announced.

"All right. Try to get some sleep please," Ms. Kay said. "OK," Miriam murmured.

Several hours after Miriam arrived home, Ms. Kay called to check in on Miriam.

"I'm packing my bags." Miriam grunted.

"Where are you going?" Ms. Kay inquired.

"I'ma gon ta get Paaaul. I wantsta be wit him." Miriam slurred her words. She hadn't stopped drinking from the night before.

"Well, you can't dig him up from his grave. That's illegal." Ms. Kay tried to rationalize with her.

"I wantsta be wit him. I'ma kill myself so I can be wit him," Miriam snapped.

A frantic Ms. Kay talked fast. "You can't kill yourself over a man," Ms. Kay pleaded with her. "He is just a man. I know he was the love of your life, but if you kill yourself, you will be in hell with him," Ms. Kay theorized. Ms. Kay offered Miriam various avenues to cope with a loss. She provided Bible passages, quotes, sayings, and personal stories from her own experiences. Two hours of a heavy saturation of positive thinking, Miriam concluded a life on earth without Paul was better than an eternity in hell. Before the call ended, Miriam promised to stay at home. She unpacked her bag and slept for two days.

———— ❧ ————

A few weeks after the funeral, Miriam lay in her bed wallowing in a wave of self-pity when a faint smell of smoke wafted past her nose followed by the sounds of the fire truck's whistle. She peeked through her window and saw her neighbor Kellie pacing back and forth outside. Her oldest stood with his Tonka truck and Kellie's youngest rocked in her arms. Kellie was delusional as part of her home burned to the ground. Miriam threw on some clothes and stood outside with Kellie for support.

Miriam and Kellie were friendly neighbors for years, and without hesitation, Miriam offered her home to Kellie and her children for as long as they needed. Miriam's home needed a shift in the dynamics.

Too many things in the home reminded her of Paul. Kellie and her two children made a smooth transition in her home. Kellie's home was deemed a total loss. "Bad wiring," the report showed in a letter Kellie received alongside a check from her homeowners insurance.

Miriam's house filled with a different energy. The sadness melted like a late spring frost. Children's laughter and a kindred spirit now occupied the home. Kellie's stepdad killed himself two years earlier. The bond Miriam and Kellie formed would be forever. Their symbiotic relationship worked. Kellie cooked every night, and Miriam babysat the children when Kellie worked evenings. They found comfort in their daily talks, and it helped Miriam deal a little better with Paul's death, but the sadness remained evident.

After Paul died, Miriam complained for months about a headache she couldn't get rid of. She tried a plethora of medicines to no avail. Kellie convinced her to see a doctor and drove her to the appointment. Doctors found a tumor in her head the size of a lemon and prepped her for emergency surgery to remove it. Tumors manifest from nursing old hurts and dealing with shocking news. Remorse causes the tumors to grow. Releasing the past and focusing on a new day aids with the tumors not returning.

The surgery was a success. The doctors warned if Miriam waited any longer, that it would have been too late. Miriam recovered in the hospital, reflecting on her next path in life. Her silence seemed heavy and dark, like a passing raincloud. Unsure of what direction she wanted to travel in. She contemplated moving forward without Paul in her life. She needed guidance.

"Have you tried praying?" Ms. Kay suggested. Miriam admitted she never actually prayed before. As a child, she went to church, but she never knew the Lord. Ms. Kay gave her Bible passages to read. Miriam found her faith one quiet night in her hospital room. She left the hospital with a renewed strength and a different outlook in life.

Prayer changes things. Miriam learned having a little talk with Jesus could make things better.

Once fully recovered, Nurse Miriam applied at the same agency Nurse Vivian worked for so she could still be Anna's nurse. Anna resided with the Logan family. Miriam worked the morning shift, and Vivian continued working nights.

Six months after Paul died, Kellie believed Miriam was ready and set her up on a few blind dates. As all blind dates go, some were less horrible than others were. The last blind date was with Eric. A reluctant Miriam suggested they meet at her house for the first few dates. Kellie was the unsuspecting chaperone. One of Eric and Miriam's conversations started with growing up and led to schools they attended. Miriam was shocked to learn he attended the same elementary school as Anna. Eric remembered Anna being quiet and a little weird. "It's such a small world, Kay," Miriam disclosed to Ms. Kay that Eric knew Anna.

Eric was instantly smitten with Miriam and spent every waking moment working on his relationship with her. Miriam was hesitant to date at first, but eventually Eric softened and mended her harden and broken heart. They have agreed to marry in 2015.

> **"Incredible change happens in your life when you decide to take control of what you do have power over instead of craving control over what you don't."**
>
> —**Steve Maraboli,** *Life, the Truth, and Being Free*

Nurse Vivian

Nurse Vivian limped into work donning a black eye. The brand-new uniform she wore refused to hide the fresh bruises on her arms and legs. Her hair was a rat's nest. Vivian looked as if she had fought a wild animal and lost. Dr. Calabretta questioned her appearance. "This my Halloween costume," Vivian sheepishly tried to convince Dr. C.

Not only did she look beat down, but her mannerisms were off as well.

"She snapped at Anna," Dr. C informed Ms. Kay about Vivian's demeanor.

"OK, I will talk to her." Ms. Kay assured Dr. Calabretta. Vivian hemmed and hawed, avoiding answering Ms. Kay's questions before she finally admitted what happened.

"He beat me up, Ms. Sandy," Vivian stammered.

"Who?" Ms. Kay started getting anxious as her breathing increased.

"My husband," Vivian revealed before a sigh of relief eased out. Ms. Kay heard Vivian's failed attempts to muffle her weeping.

"It's going to be OK. Tell me what happened," Ms. Kay encouraged Vivian while she texted Jean. She needed Jean to get word to Matthew, so he could locate and arrest Antonio.

Antonio's military unit deployed three months earlier, and Vivian wasn't expecting to see him for at least a year. Antonio neglected to inform Vivian about his impromptu leave from the military. Instead, he hid in the closet and waited for her to come home from work.

"I just got out the shower and was relaxing on the sofa when he pounced on me like a predator," Vivian confessed with an uneasy voice. She provided vague details explaining how he beat and raped her all day long. He tied her up with rope and a gag before he passed out. "He would wake up and rape me again," she said. Ms. Kay heard Vivian sniffling. The last time he fell asleep, he forgot to tie her up, and that's when she made her escape.

"I waited until he was snoring and slid down off the bed. I crawled to the front door, grabbing only my purse." Vivian retold her daring escape to Ms. Kay.

Vivian had no time to grab anything, so she purchased a new uniform from a store and came to work. "Good thing my boys were at the neighbor's house," she groaned. Her boys spent a lot of time at her neighbor's house because of Vivian's work schedule. Her neighbor's kids were around the same age as her boys and went to the same school, making it convenient for the neighbor to watch them.

Vivian and Antonio attended the same high school. He was jock with a reputation for being combative and belligerent. She was considered a nerd. They were vastly dissimilar. Once during a basketball game, a fan made a derogatory comment about his mom. A blind rage like a forest fire swept over him. He abandoned the court and bounded up the bleachers. He punched the fan in the face, and the referee ejected him from the game.

Vivian knew of Antonio, but he didn't notice Vivian until their junior year. Several times, he asked Vivian out on a date, she turned him down flat each time. Antonio enjoyed the chase and remained determined to conquer Vivian. She never gave in to his advances. Although Vivian dated other people in high school, Antonio never stopped asking her out. After graduation, Vivian went off the college and Antonio joined the military. He kept tabs on her through mutual friends.

"He really likes you," one of Vivian's friends confessed.

"Well, I hope the military is able to whip all that anger he has out of him," Vivian replied.

They reconnected one summer, and Vivian noticed a more mature and respectful Antonio than in high school. "The military changed you," she commented during their first official date. They dated her junior year in college and married once she graduated from nursing school with her master's. Antonio wanted children right away, but Vivian wanted to wait a few years. Vivian had her first son after two years of marriage. Her second son came a year later. Her third son was born a year after that.

Antonio masked his violent streak for years, but Vivian noticed a major shift in his behavior when their youngest turned three and she returned to work. A shove here. A slap there. Antonio demeaned her in front the children, but always apologized with sex. His aggressiveness became so intense; Vivian took a part-time job to avoid Antonio at the house. This incident marked the third or fourth time Antonio had beaten her up in the past six month.

"Why didn't you tell me?" Ms. Kay questioned Vivian.

"I was embarrassed. I didn't know how . . ." Vivian said as her voice trailed off and was replaced by sobs.

Vivian learned she was eight weeks' pregnant with twins. The news came weeks before Antonio's deployment. She dreamed of having a little girl and couldn't wait to share the news with her husband. Antonio's reaction was not how Vivian envisioned.

"I don't want no more children!" he screamed at her. He body-slammed Vivian to the ground. His boots collided with her stomach. Vivian curled up in a ball, trying desperately to protect her twins.

"Please, Antonio. Stop! You're hurting me," Vivian pleaded with him. Vivian said she lost count after fifteen kicks. She also lost the babies.

Matthew issued a warrant for Antonio. "We'll find him, Vivian. It won't take long," Matthew assured her when he called. Vivian's nerves cried the blues all night. Anna and Vivian both tossed and turned, searching for comfort and assurance. Neither had a restful slept in days. The chairs in the hospital were uncomfortable, and Vivian longed for a bed. The next morning the police escorted Vivian home to gather a few items before she absconded to a hotel.

Vivian drove in the direction of the hotel as she spotted the same black car she saw on her street when she left home. Once she made it to the interstate, the police escort left. She was convinced someone was trailing her. Vivian maneuvered her car in traffic with attempts to lose the car.

She parked her car at the hotel and scanned the parking lot with no signs of the car in sight. Vivian took a chance and darted to the room. Her room key dangled helpless in the door when, out of nowhere, Antonio descended on her, knocking her to the ground. The items she carried scattered all over the hotel floor. The force he used to open door shook the wall behind it. He snatched Vivian up off the floor and propelled her on the bed. Her legs and arms flailed, attempting to gain balance.

He straddled Vivian, pinning her arms and legs down. He spit on her. "Why did you get the police involved?" Antonio questioned. He smacked her face before she responded. She pleaded with him to stop, but he was in a zone. Antonio released his grip to smack Vivian again. She used that opportunity to push him off. She scrambled to the front door, but he grabbed her leg and her head hit the floor.

He stood over her kicking as she blocked his kicks with her forearms. She screamed and wailed like a snake struggling in a vulture's grasp. Another hotel guest saw Vivian's door slightly open and heard the commotion. He peeked in the room and called 911. The police were there in three minutes. Antonio was arrested and released in less than twenty-four hours.

By now, Vivian is beyond terrified. "The safest place for you to be is at the hospital," Matthew suggested. He followed Vivian home to gather some belongings. He escorted her to the hospital and walked her to Anna's room. Vivian hugged herself as she rocked backed and forth in her chair. She squeezed her arms whenever anyone walked past Anna's room. "Ouch," she winced, forgetting the bruises on her arms hurt at the slightest touch. Vivian flinched at the sight of her own shadow.

"I need to find a way for him not to find me," Vivian said when Ms. Kay called.

"Matthew said Antonio is still locked up so you have time. Why not start with trading in your car?" Ms. Kay recommended.

"That's a good idea. I will get a new car," Vivian sounded slightly relieved.

"I'll watch Anna. You don't have to be back to work until this evening," Nurse Miriam chimed in.

Vivian traded in her old car. She even booked a hotel room outside the city limits. Vivian thought she had a fail-safe plane; what she didn't know was that Antonio had placed a tracking app on her phone, locating her every move.

Vivian came back to work that evening, looking somewhat refreshed. "I got some rest at the hotel," she told Miriam. The next morning a police officer escorted her to the hospital parking lot. "I think I will be safe now," she told the police when they asked if she needed an escort to her hotel.

Vivian made it to the hotel but noticed her husband in a car parked on the opposite side of the parking lot. Antonio used the history on the tracking app to find out her moves in the last twenty-four hours. He didn't seem to be paying attention to her, so she decided to make a move.

Vivian bolted to her room like prey being hunted. She locked the door and informed Matthew of her predicament.

"We are on our way. Don't leave the room. You're safe," he assured her.

"Well, I don't feel safe," Vivian cried out.

She called Ms. Kay.

"How does he keep finding you?"

"I don't know, but I can't keep doing this," Vivian stated. There was silence on the phone.

"It's your phone." Ms. Kay had an aha moment. "He has to be tracking you on it. How else would he know to come to that hotel, which is way off the beaten trail?" Ms. Kay was sure if it.

"It must be." Vivian was convinced. "We do have a friend who works for the cell phone company." Vivian sat on the bed, scrolling through her apps, looking for the tracking one. "I found it." Vivian snorted. "Says it was installed over three years ago." Vivian shook her head in disgust as she deleted the app and downloaded a malware software program on her phone.

They were chatting on the phone when Vivian heard a bang on her door. "Open up the door, Vivy. I know you in there." Antonio yelled.

"He's at the door," Vivian whispered. She slid off the bed and crouched behind it.

"It's OK. Matthew will be there shortly," Ms. Kay reminded her.

"Yeah. Let us in." Another male voice said. "We just want to talk." He added. Antonio brought his best friend with him. They were in his car when Vivian arrived at the hotel.

"I thought that car looked familiar," Vivian whispered.

"Police! Freeze!" Vivian heard through the closed door. Her heart beat like a bass drum. She heard a scuffle, and a few minutes later, she heard Matthew asking her to open the door and assuring her safety. The police searched the car and found a loaded gun.

"That's his," Antonio snitched on his friend. They arrested the best friend for the illegal handgun. Officers arrested Antonio for violating the restraining order Matthew put out on him from the last time he attacked Vivian. This time Antonio stayed in jail until his trial date.

Antonio's supervisor used his pull and scheduled Antonio's court date a week after the last attack on Vivian. Antonio strutted into the courtroom with his head held high. He was dressed in full military regalia. His patches and service stripes stood at attention on the pressed uniform shirt. Civilians have a soft spot for military men, and that tends gets in the way of good judgment.

Vivian sat in the courtroom wistful and withdrawn. Her shoulders hunched, barely exposing her neck. Fresh bruises were visible on her face and arms. She flinched when Antonio looked in her direction and blew her a kiss.

The police charged Antonio with assault and rape. "Marital rape is difficult to prove. He is your husband. How can he legitimately rape you?" the judged questioned Vivian directly, refusing to hear her lawyer's pleas. "If your husband wants sex, you comply without back talk. You owe him sex for all his hard work in the military. You need to understand the male's psyche." The judge sneered as he turned his lip up, showing only his canine tooth. The judge's words struck Vivian like a blow to the gut.

"Unbelievable," she whispered to herself. He threw out the rape charge based on his own misogynistic opinions.

The judge refused to accept the submitted paperwork from the doctor explaining the brutal beating Vivian received from her husband. "You probably said something out of line," he suggested, glaring at a battered Vivian. "This man is protecting our country and bullets flying over him and you fussing about him not washing the dishes or whatever chore he didn't perform?" The judge used finger quotes when he said "chore." The judge gave him an insignificant punishment of a one-hundred-dollar fine for the assault charge. The judge winked his eye at Antonio as he warned him to watch his temper. Again, his used finger quotes for the word temper.

The judge thanked Antonio for his dedication and services to the military. Antonio's ego swelled like a sponge. His leave was shortened and was required to immediately fly back to his station overseas. Antonio was to remain in police custody from the courthouse to the airport. Vivian sat in disbelief how the verdict went down but also relieved he remained handcuffed and being shipped back overseas in a few hours.

After court, Vivian proceeded home to get some well-needed rest before work. She slept for three hours before waking up to Antonio choking her. Antonio managed to slip away from police custody. He used his keys and snuck back into the house. He raped Vivian one more time before his plane took off.

Vivian refused to enter her house until she had proof Antonio actually returned overseas. She contacted his supervisor every day for two weeks, asking about Antonio's whereabouts and if he requested any leave. "No, he is still overseas and hasn't asked for leave," his supervisor stated as a matter of fact. Vivian didn't trust his word.

For weeks, she posted up in various hotels, making sure she wasn't still be followed. Vivian hired a locksmith to change the locks at the house. She installed a high-tech security system. When Vivian felt the house was safe, she moved back in.

Two months later, Vivian's neighbor noticed a locksmith's van parked in front of Vivian's house. "I think Antonio is getting the locks changed at your house." The neighbor called and warned Vivian not to come home after work.

Antonio was back in the states and hired the locksmith to open the door so he could get in. "Here is my driver's license proving I live here," he showed the locksmith. The locksmith opened the front door, and it triggered a silent alarm. Within minutes, the police were at Vivian's front door. He informed the officers that he in fact lived at the house.

"I have been overseas, and I guess my wife either changed the code, or I can't remember what the code is," the quick-witted Antonio suggested as he gave the officers a sheepish laugh. The officers believed his story and left without incident. He contacted the security-system company and persuaded them into giving him the code to disarm the system. Vivian received a courtesy call, informing her that her husband had updated the security code.

Vivian called Antonio's supervisor and inquired why her husband was back in the States and why no one informed her.

"Ma'am, he requested leave for his son's birthday," his supervisor explained.

A confused Vivian hung the phone up. Vivian's boys turned seven, eight, and ten earlier in the year and Antonio attended their parties.

"He's back in the States, Ms. Sandy." Vivian's voiced sounded shaky. She relayed what his supervisor told her.

"Vivian, every lie has a little bit of the truth in it." Ms. Kay had a hunch Antonio had a child stashed somewhere in the city, unbeknown to Vivian. She asked Matthew to confirm her suspicions.

An investigation revealed Antonio fathered a child while engaged to Vivian. His oldest son was born two months after he married Vivian. Thirteen-year-old Antonio Jr. was the only child Veronica had.

"I couldn't get up with Veronica, but I spoke to some of her friends," Matthew told Ms. Kay.

Veronica and Antonio met at a bar and slept together the first night they met. Veronica wanted a child, so she planned her pregnancy within months of dating Antonio. Veronica resided on the other side of town in an apartment Antonio paid for. He paid all the bills, making it a love nest for the mother of his firstborn. Veronica was pleased with the arrangement, and her family didn't mind that Antonio was married either. Her mother called Antonio "son." While Vivian worked twelve-hour shifts along with her part-time job, Antonio spent time playing house with Veronica.

For over fourteen years, he lived this other life. Veronica was well aware of his marital status. She needed a sperm donor with benefits who would provide for her and her child. For years, Veronica enjoyed pretending she was his wife when they went to the pediatrician. When they went out to eat, she demanded the server address them as Mr. And Mrs.

"I have to tell you something," Ms. Kay told Vivian to brace herself. "Antonio has a thirteen-year-old son. He was the son Antonio came to see about," Ms. Kay blurted out.

Vivian's leg gave way, and she found herself on the floor still holding the phone. The hurt lingered like an unwanted guest.

"I know she is his mistress, but this woman needs to be warned about Antonio's erratic behavior," Ms. Kay continued, without knowing if Vivian was on the other line. "No need for anyone else to be put through the hell you went through," Ms. Kay cautiously explained to Vivian.

Vivian nodded in agreement even though she was on the phone. "I need a minute," Vivian told Ms. Kay as she hung up phone.

"I'll be right back, Anna," Vivian said as she went to the hospital bathroom and threw up.

Veronica and Antonio Jr. lay dead in their apartment for three days before the police found their bodies. The boy's body was found naked in the bathroom slumped over the tub half filled with water. Brutally beaten, raped, and choked with bear hands. Hand prints visible around his neck. The boy had defensive wounds on his hands. "He put up a good fight," one of the investigators suspected as they prepared the rape kit for Antonio Jr. His anus was penetrated by the toilet plunger, which lay bloody on the floor next to him.

"We will check for DNA too." As another investigator swabbed his butt and grimaced at the thought of a child being anally raped.

"It appears his head was forced under the water where he was being choked and eventually drowned." The coroner sized up the crime scene.

Veronica's face and body were so mangled she was barely recognizable. Her bloody hair matted to the side of her face and neck. An extension cord bound her ankles and wrists. A dirty kitchen dishrag shoved in her mouth. Her naked body crumpled on kitchen floor. Puddles of blood formed from her mouth and her butt. "They penetrated her using a foreign object." An investigator cringed as he placed a rape kit down beside the bloody broken broomstick.

Bruises already formed and covered over 75 percent of her body. Several of her teeth sprawled under the kitchen table, resembling broken ceramic tiles.

"Her two middle fingers are missing," someone noticed.

"I found them shoved in her butt," the investigator performing the rape test announced. He hummed to suppress his gag reflex. The autopsy determined repeated blows to the head and face caused her injuries, but strangulation was her ultimate cause of death. Antonio Jr. was an innocent victim. Veronica paid her karma debt.

Three months earlier, Vivian's best friend gave birth to a baby girl. Vivian visited Kimberly in the hospital the next day. "I have something to tell you," Kimberly refused to look Vivian in the face. Kimberly took a deep breath and closed her eyes.

"I have been sleeping with your husband for years, and this is his daughter," she said as she held up her newborn for Vivian to see. "The one you could never give him," Kimberly blurted out. She braced herself for a slap from Vivian. Vivian stood motionless.

"How could you? We have been friends for over twenty years," Vivian lamented.

"You always talked about how good he was in bed. I wanted to see for myself," Kimberly justified her reason and almost accused Vivian of taunting her.

"You got some nerve." Vivian chopped Kimberly in the throat and left. Kimberly gagged and coughed, attempting to get air back into her windpipe. The baby fell into her lap. Vivian covered her face as she walked unsteadily toward the parking lot, like a blind man feeling his way around without a cane.

———— ⚬⚬⚬ ————

Kimberly's words haunted Vivian. It was all she obsessed about the last time she was pregnant. Antonio wasn't the only one longing to have a daughter. Vivian sat in the car and clutched her stomach to relieve the sharp pain in her belly area. "I was able to give him girls," Vivian mumbled to herself as she sped out of the hospital parking lot. Antonio beat the last children she carried right out of her womb. The doctors informed her the babies she lost were twin girls.

Vivian contacted Matthew, so they could warn Kimberly. After she spoke to Matthew, Vivian shut her phone off. "I need to get my boys and leave town for a while," she grumbled to herself as tears blinded her way toward the babysitter's house.

———— ⚬⚬⚬ ————

The police discovered Kimberly unconscious on her bedroom floor covered in blood and bruises. Kimberly's legs were broken in three different places. Her head was partially scalped using dull scissors. Chunks of skin and hair were strewn over the kitchen floor. An attempt to remove the tattooed name "Antonio" off her lower back was beastly. A hot iron was applied to Kimberly's back causing third-degree burns. All that remained of the tattoo was half the letter A and a partial O. Pictures around the house captured the original tattoo that cops used later to identify her body.

Kimberly lay in agony on the floor for days. The real torture was being unable help her baby and having to listen to her hunger screams for three days. Kimberly cried herself to dehydration. She eventually passed out from blood loss. Antonio left the baby unharmed in her high chair to starve to death. "I didn't want you no way," he hissed at the baby before he slammed the front door closed.

A police officer pressed his ear to her chest and heard a faint heartbeat. "She's still breathing, but barely. Call for the paramedics." His voice cracked. They rushed Kimberly to the hospital, but her survival rate was less than 10 percent. The doctors were unsuccessful in saving Kimberly. A pediatrician treated the baby girl for malnutrition, and she made a full recovery.

People Who Create Their Own Drama, Cause Their Own Karma

Ms. Kay called Vivian several times to warn her about the two women, but no one answered. She called ten times back-to-back before Antonio eventually answered Vivian's cell phone.

"Whadda wah wif ma why? Whys you keeps calling?" His slurred words almost made it impossible for Ms. Kay to understand him. Ms. Kay attempted to explain they were friends.

"I need to know if Vivian was OK. Can I speak with her please?" Ms. Kay asked with a polite tone. As Antonio was refusing to put Vivian on the phone, she texted Jean, hoping Matthew could trace the call.

Matthew was in the precinct working on the trace, so Jean was the go-between.

Keep Antonio on the phone for as long as you can, Jean texted.

"Vivian and I are friends, and I need to know if she is OK," Ms. Kay explained herself again. "Please let me talk to her. I want to make sure she is OK," Ms. Kay begged.

Antonio refused. He shoved the barrel of the gun even further in Vivian's mouth, so she would not scream for help. Ms. Kay didn't hear Vivian's retching sound.

He yelled about wanting to spend time with his wife. "Ya knee ta stah callin!" He hung the phone up before Ms. Kay knew Vivian's whereabouts or the condition of her health. Ms. Kay called back, but Antonio wouldn't pick up the phone again. Ms. Kay phoned Matthew to let him know what she knew about the situation, which wasn't very much. In Ms. Kay's frustration, she threw the phone on the bed.

"Please, Lord, keep Vivian safe," Ms. Kay prayed aloud.

Ten minutes later, Vivian phoned Ms. Kay from her bedroom closet. She managed to grab the cordless phone and escape while Antonio pulled down his pants to pee on the floor. She gathered her knees to her chest, so she resembled a small ball in the closet. She sat behind the closed door, rocking back and forth and sobbing uncontrollably.

"Calm down, Vivian. You have to calm down," Ms. Kay pleaded with Vivian. She prayed another quick quiet prayer.

"What's your address, Vivian?" The phone trembled as Sandy texted Jean. It took several tries to text the right address. *Get it together, Sandy.* Ms. Kay fussed at herself.

The police will be there in ten minutes, Jean texted back. Vivian mentioned to Ms. Kay that the basement door always stayed open, so the police can get in that way if they were quiet. Ms. Kay kept talking to Vivian to calm her down while she texted the information to Jean. She needed to know how Antonio captured her.

"I was picking up the boys up from the neighbor's house. We was gonna stay in a hotel when I found out Antonio was back in town," Vivian whispered between sobs. "Before I left the car, I looked around at my surroundings," she recounted the story. "I swear I didn't see anything, Ms. Sandy," Vivian recalled, trying to hold back tears.

Vivian arrived halfway to the front door when Antonio ambushed her. He put her in a chokehold and shoved the gun in her mouth. He threatened to kill her if she screamed. Vivian's legs flailed wildly, and her heels left small divots in the yard as Antonio dragged her across the street to their house. The neighbor was unaware.

The tears fell like rain on Vivian's face. "Count to ten and breathe," Ms. Kay directed Vivian. "You can cry later," she instructed. "We have to get you out of there. Jean texted and said SWAT was five minutes away. You can hold on." Ms. Kay assured a discouraged Vivian. Ms. Kay heard Antonio in the background yelling for Vivian.

"He keeps saying he wanna talk, and he's not going to hurt me," she whispered. Vivian knew better than to believe him. She curled into a smaller ball and rocked even more profusely.

Ms. Kay directed her to stay in the closet and to keep quiet.

"I am," she whispered.

At one point, he came in the room where Vivian was hiding.

"Way are you, Vivvy? I juss wanna talk. Dat's all," Antonio announced.

Ms. Kay and Vivian both held their breath for two minutes while he walked the perimeter of the room. He determined she was not there and proceeded to another room in the house, giving the same speech.

When he left tears gushed down Vivian's face. A great pain welled up in her. Ms. Kay reminded her there was no time for crying right now.

"SWAT is coming through the basement." Vivian heard them.

"It's going to be OK. It's going to be OK," Ms. Kay consoled her.

In the background, Ms. Kay heard Antonio yelling and the cops trying to calm him down. She couldn't hear the exact dialog, but it seemed Antonio refused to surrender without a fight. She heard Vivian quietly sobbing and a faint "death before dishonor" quote from Antonio.

Ms. Kay assumed SWAT cut the phone lines when everything went dead on Vivian's end. Three knocks on the closet door broke the silence.

"Don't say anything," Ms. Kay warned Vivian. "Wait for the police to identify themselves," she stipulated.

"Ma'am." He knocked again. "I'm a police officer, you're safe now," the officer explained.

Vivian reached up and opened the door. She looked up and saw the police officer. He reached out his hand to help her up. Vivian's legs were jelly as she struggled to get her balance. She fell into the police officer's arms still holding the phone.

"You can cry now," Ms. Kay said.

Ms. Kay finally cried too.

Antonio's system was so drugged up, the police tased him twice before it took effect on him. They placed the cuffs on him and took him downtown. They searched his car and confiscated forty thousand dollars' worth of high-end cocaine, ten pounds of white widow weed, thirteen grams of meth, and thirty-two ecstacy pills. Product seemed to be missing from a few of the bags. Antonio started selling drugs years ago but couldn't control his habit once he started using. He owed many people a lot of money.

Without any prompting, Antonio confessed to killing Veronica and her son. He admitted him and his boys went to Kimberly's house to rape and beat her up. Antonio failed a random military drug test and went AWOL before the impending court-martial and jail time. He declared his life was over and determined his family's life was over as well. He wanted to kill everyone he loved before he killed himself. "If I can't be with my family, then nobody else can have them either," Antonio resolved.

"Vivvy and my boys were last on the list since she was officially my wife," Antonio went on. He decided to murder her and the boys, and then kill himself in his home. "Sorry I didn't get to see the boys," he disclosed before he passed out from all the drugs in his system. Antonio was charged with three counts of murder, felony drug possession, and rape and stalking.

A week later, Antonio's childhood home was riddled with over two hundred bullets. His parents resided in the home but were not present when the drive-by took place. The neighbors heard the multi-gunshots and called 911. Witnesses described a silver car and men with big machine guns aimed at the house. The police phone his parents to find their whereabouts. No one answered any of the phone numbers on file. They have yet to locate his parents. The dealers Antonio owed money to would stop at nothing to get their money back. His recent incarceration didn't settle his debt. They were determined that someone needed to pay.

Four callous and conscienceless brutes paid a visit to house where Vivian's mom and dad live. These burley men lay in wait for any activity from the house. Vivian's dad came home an hour after the brutes had parked their car on her parents' street. They ambushed her seventy-year-old dad as he was getting groceries out of the car. Vivian's dad put up a fight but was outnumbered. His wife heard a commotion and went to the window. She witnessed these husky men pounce on her 150-pound husband. She dialed 911, but when they arrived, the men had already done their damage and retreated. Her husband lay in a bloody pulp on the driveway. The doctors confirmed he suffered from three broken ribs, a broken jaw, and a concussion. He remained in the hospital for three months and made a full recovery.

The same ruffians ransacked Vivian's house, searching for money and drugs days after the attack on her dad. They were unable to collect any cash, but stole televisions, video game machines, and anything else that plugged into the wall. They appropriated two thousand dollars' worth of lawn equipment. Three months later, Vivian finally built up the nerve to go back to her house. She was elated to discover that the $7,000 she hid in her tampon box was untouched.

"Thanks for that idea," Vivian told Ms. Kay when she found her money safe.

"That's where I hide my money," Ms. Kay revealed. "Most thieves search under mattresses and in sock drawers. Vivian. Don't no thief want to touch some tampons." Ms. Kay and Vivian laughed.

A week after the attack on her dad, Vivian arrived at work, acting out of the ordinary. Ms. Kay spoke to Vivian after Dr. C texted about her peculiar behavior again.

"You need to tell me what is going on," Ms. Kay demanded.

Vivian was hesitant to inform Ms. Kay about the threatening phone calls she received all hours of the day and night.

"It's usually the same conversation," Vivian noted. The drug dealers threatened more violence toward her family if she didn't hand over the money.

"I don't have his money," Vivian attempted to point out their misunderstanding.

"Yeah you do and you gonna give it to us," they said menacingly.

"It's at the police station. I don't have the money," Vivian repeats before they hang the phone up.

"I think they tapped my phone, Ms. Sandy," Vivian said she heard people in the background whenever she made a phone call.

"Call me from your phone, so I can hear what's happening on the line," Ms. Kay directed Vivian. Vivian heard the clicking sounds as soon as Ms. Kay answered.

"Whoever you are, we're gonna get you. I promise you. I promise you, Ms. Kay spoke directly to them with hurried eagerness.

"I can hear them laughing, Ms. Sandy," Vivian reported.

"Ha-ha. Hell," Ms. Kay stated with a sarcastic tone. "I promise you. I promise you. We are going to get you," A confident Ms. Kay pledged. Vivian hung up when she heard them laughing again.

"These people don't know who they messing with. We are gonna get them," Ms. Kay assured Vivian, who remained nervous. After work, Vivian took her phone to Matthew, but he was unable to trace the calls. "Call me from Anna's phone. I have a plan," Ms. Kay announced when Vivian texted the bad news about the trace.

Later in the evening, Vivian was at the Logans when she called Ms. Kay from her cell phone. She mentioned a party she was attending at a hotel and wanted to invite Ms. Kay. Vivian heard the clicking sounds. She hesitated.

"Tell me where the party is," Ms. Kay prompted Vivian. She didn't want her to get nervous and clam up.

Vivian blurted out the hotel name and gave explicit directions on how to get there. Ms. Kay asked several times the name of the hotel to make sure whoever was listening heard.

"I already got a room just in case I decide to spend the night." Vivian felt a little more confident as she spoke. "My cousin is gonna have the boys, so it will be just me. It's room number 529. I'm going to be there by 9:00 p.m. So you gonna make it?" Vivian asked nervously.

Ms. Kay commented how she loved a party and needed Vivian to call her when she made it to her room, so she could meet her there. They hung up. The bait was set. Now they waited for the predators.

Matthew booked the room for Vivian, and other police officers were occupying all the adjacent rooms. Matthew met Vivian in the hotel lobby and reminded her she was safe. Vivian locked the hotel-room door and called Ms. Kay.

They talked like normal for a while.

Can you hear the clicking?

Yes.

"I'm about to take a shower and lay down before the party," Vivian said. "A night without the kids is what I need," she mentioned before she hung up the phone.

Moments later, Vivian called Ms. Kay. "Are you at the door? Because I hear someone knocking?" she asked.

Don't answer the door, Matthew texted her.

Vivian's heart was a jackhammer that rattled her ribcage. She took a deep breath. Her family's life as well as hers was on the line. She placed her hand on her chest and prayed.

"Someone's at the door, and I didn't order room service." Vivian attempted some humor. She looked out the peephole and saw two men toting guns in each hand. She leaped back from the door and locked herself in the bathroom. When they knocked for a third time, the police descended on them. There was nowhere for them to run. The men dropped the guns, threw their hands in the air, and surrendered without incident. Matthew patted them down while another officer handcuffed the assailants. The police charged the men with illegal gun possession, drug possession, wiretapping, and stalking.

Vivian and Ms. Kay remained on the phone while all the commotion took place in the hallway. "We got your punk friends like I promised, and we coming after you next," Ms. Kay announced to whoever was still listening to the conversation.

The clicking stopped. Karma took care of the promise.

One of the other thugs, who helped with the wiretapping, died in a horrific car accident a month later. The driver of the car he was in sped down the interstate, going over one hundred miles per hour and lost control. He hit a telephone pole. Everyone in the car died on impact. The car flipped then caught on fire. The coroner requested his dental records in order to identify the body. The last thug met his match at a nightclub five months after the arrest of his friends. He started flirting with a woman who was there with her husband. The thug refused to stop flirting. He found himself staring down the business end of a revolver. The husband shot him nine times in the face and chest. He died instantly.

In the midst of all this chaos and confusion, Vivian didn't miss one day of work. The universe took notice of Vivian's devotion and dedication. Weeks after everything calmed down and went back to normal, Vivian received a phone call.

"I need to tell you that Irene Lashley died," the voice on the other line said. Vivian's heart sank. She provided home health care for Irene years ago. Irene didn't have any children, and her husband died years ago.

"I thought she was getting better?" Vivian asked the voice on the other line.

"She did get better for a while, and she peacefully died in her sleep a few weeks ago," the person said. "I called because I am the attorney of her estate. She left you money in her will. I need for you to come down and claim it."

Vivian inherited almost a million dollars from Irene. A note attached to the will thanked Vivian for being a wonderful provider.

"If I had a daughter, I would have wanted her to be just like you. Thank you for always being there for me." Vivian laminated the note because her tears kept saturating it. Vivian always dreamed of building a rehabilitation center for seniors and now has the money to do so.

> **I believe in karma. If the good is sown, the good is collected. When positive things are made, that returns well.**
> **—Yannick Noah**

Chapter 18 —————————

The Logans

Jean and Matthew spent most of their childhood in church. Sundays were triathlons. Attend Sunday school then participate in morning service. They went home to eat and had to be back for afternoon programs, which could last until after nine at night. Some Sunday evenings they traveled to sister churches for programs and events.

Both their fathers were ministers in the same area, so their paths crossed at various revivals and church events. These preachers' kids officially met at a church convention when they were teenagers. The youth minister told the teens to find a partner. Matthew pushed two people over to make his way to Jean. Matthew knew Jean was the one. "It's your smile," he confessed. "It drew me right to you." Jean flashed her smile before she blushed. They exchanged numbers, and the courtship began.

After high school graduation, Matthew signed up for the police academy, and Jean became a pharmaceutical sales rep after years of schooling. On the weekends, they were inseparable. They married a month after Matthew graduated from the academy. "We are having children right away," Jean stated to her friends and family. She named her girls Elizabeth, Ruth, and Hannah. "Growing up, I read about these women in the Bible and how God showed them favor. I want you all to be as strong as they were," Jean told her girls when they asked for the origin of their names. There was no question that they would name their son Matthew Jr.

For years, they bounced from Jean's home church to Matthew's home church not wanting to slight either family. They eventually joined a church separate from their parents to get a fresh start. This move launched their ministry. The pastor requested Matthew take on the role of a deacon in the church. Jean and Matthew became church leaders who held classes on Wednesday evenings.

Jean's health declined rapidly several months after the incarceration of Anna's dad and sister. Her doctor diagnosed her with cancer during Reginald's trial. She kept it from her family because she didn't want them to worry about her. Matthew and the kids had just helped Jean cope with the death of her parents. They assumed that her sullen attitude was her still being in mourning. Depression hung around her neck like a noose. Every day it tightened, inhibiting her ability to breathe. She lost her mother to lung cancer seven months earlier. Her dad died a week later from a broken heart. Her parents would have celebrated forty-six years of marriage on July 4.

"You better go to the cancer center," Ms. Kay demanded when she found out about Jean's breast cancer.

"I don't want my family to worry."

"So you going to just go out like a punk. You gonna go to hell if God has offered you help and you refuse to accept it." Ms. Kay misquoted the Bible but needed Jean to understand the severity of this situation.

"We can't do anything for you. Your body is too far gone for treatment," Jean solemnly repeated the doctors' words to Ms. Kay. The cancer center diagnosed her cancer as stage 4B.

"I just wanted to call to tell you good-bye. Let my family know I love them," Jean said. She sat on the phone and cried her eyes out.

"Ummm. It's not time for you to go. Page the doctor," Ms. Kay demanded.

"Let me check her chart, Kay." Dr. C sounded astonished that no one knew of Jean's condition until now.

"This center I am sending you to have different treatments than we do. They are going to be able to get the cancer out." Dr. C made a few phone calls and pulled a few strings. Jean's heart couldn't rejoice. She blankly stared at Dr. C "What's wrong?" Dr. C asked.

"Nothing. I thought I was at the end of my rope and you tied a knot on it," Jean attempted to explain. "I'm at a loss of words." Jean shed tears of joys.

"Your husband is on his way here. Kay made sure I called him," Dr. C stated before she left Jean's room.

Within an hour, the helipad transported Jean and Matthew to a cancer center in the neighboring state. Matthew took extended leave from work and stayed by Jean's side the entire time.

"You don't have to be here, Matthew," Jean exclaimed.

"Our vows said in sickness and health. I am never leaving your side." Matthew squeezed her hand then lightly kissed it. Matthew was as supportive as a pair of orthopedic shoes. "There is no other place I would rather be. Plus, you're not gonna leave me without a fight." Matthew snickered. Jean's eyes told him she loved him. "The kids will be here this weekend to visit," Matthew said.

Jean didn't fight back her tears. Their children visited every weekend to give her moral support.

Ms. Kay strongly suggested Jean watch videos and read books about healing your life, healing your body, and shifting your focus. Jean meditated and prayed. Somewhere between the absence of her parents and acquiring cancer, she abandoned her faith.

She read about faith being a three-legged stool. Each leg stood for believing, doing, and trusting. These dimensions of faith must be equal and practiced daily. One cannot stand on faith if one of those is missing or short. Jean understood when the three legs are balanced they make it sturdy enough to lift you up to a higher dimension.

She shifted her focus and changed how her inner voice spoke to her. Jean found in her what had been missing for a long time, a love for herself. Love broke the chains around her heart. Jean participated in group therapy as well as intense physical therapy.

Five months later, Jean returned home free of cancer and all the other obstacles that weighed her spirit down. She no longer felt less than. Jean embraced her new attitude on life. "I love you," she told herself when she looked in the mirror every day. Her children noticed an immediate difference in Jean's personality.

"Mom, you're different," Ruth commented at dinner one evening.

"Is that a good thing or a bad thing?" Jean quipped back with a grin. "It's awesome, Mom," Matthew junior chimed in.

While Jean went away to receive treatment, Vivian insisted that Anna move in with her and the boys. Her home was finally safe. Vivian's husband was serving a ninety-nine-year prison term. He will be eligible for parole in eighty years.

Jean still reaches out to check in on Anna and her well-being. She also enjoys the holidays where she can spend time with her daughters who all live in different states. Her son followed his dad's example of service and became a full-time firefighter. Matthew and Jean helped saved Anna's life and Ms. Kay will always be eternally grateful.

Change your thoughts, and you change your world.

Norman Vincent Peale

Epilogue

Ms. Kay

Confession time. The author of this book, Robin Turner, is Ms. Sandy Kay in the story. This is my chapter, so I will be writing it as me. Are you surprised?

I was presented with the idea to write the book after conversations with friends about what was going on in Anna's life. They insisted no one would believe the story, so I needed to write it. They assured me the book would change people's lives.

As I sat to write this book, I had a difficult time figuring out the genre. It is based on a memoir, a true story written by a ghostwriter, who is also a main character in the book. It landed on the genre of creative nonfiction.

Anna suffered dementia for about three weeks in 2012. She relived and acted out her entire childhood, and I wrote down everything. I asked questions that enabled me to construct her life story based on her words. Everything that happened to Anna is true. Some details were added to fill in the blanks, but the essence of the book is her life story.

A doctor asked me once, "If you cared about Anna so much, why haven't you come to visit her?" I not so politely said, "I knew more about what was happening in the hospital than all those family members who visit their loved ones on a daily basis." Why? Because I not only love Anna, I care about her. Anyone can love you. It takes a lot for a person to care for you. I mean really care about your health and ask the important question especially when they are sick and are under someone else's care.

Anybody who knows me knows how hard I fight for Anna. Anna is my number one priority. When doctors wanted to give up, I encouraged them to find other alternatives to help "fix" Anna's illnesses. Sometimes doctors are not always right. Get a second opinion or even ask what other treatments are available before accepting their diagnosis as the only option.

If you didn't noticed while reading the book, I never officially met any of the people I wrote about. All the correspondences were through texts or phone calls. The last time I saw Anna was when I handed her the lamb before she flew to the cancer center. Our conversations were mostly texts. I stayed away mostly because I felt if she saw me, she would give up wanting to fight for her life. Like people on their deathbed waiting for loved ones to visit before they pass to the other side.

I learned to trust the people taking care of Anna sight unseen. I guess you call it blind faith and gut feelings. Also, Anna had this keen ability to bring out the true essence of people. Church folks call it the gift of discernment. These people can spot a phony before anyone else can. If you are genuine and caring, that intensifies around Anna. If you are evil and hurtful, that intensifies as well even if you tried to hide it. My mom always says, "What's done in the dark will eventually come to the light."

I hated when the evildoers caused harm to Anna. It was for the greater good of other patients but often at the expense of Anna's health. Plenty of doctors and nurses were fired and unable to continue their reign of terror on helpless patients. Anna's gift had a lot to do with it. I knew if Anna was getting poor treatment, the other patients under their care were as well. The difference was, I knew about the mistreatment because I asked the right question. (See the letter to family members at the end of the book for a list of questions to ask.)

I consistently complained about the horrible treatment and demanded the medical staff be held accountable for their actions.

Some accused me of wanting Anna to get "special privileges." I asked them, "When is getting your medicine on time a special privilege?" Everyone in the hospital should receive exceptional service, not just Anna.

One CEO of a hospital asked Anna to come in and "read" some of the medical staff after hearing about her ability. Within minutes, Anna was able to discern the staffers who were on the right path and who were up to no good. During the observation, Anna pointed at one doctor and said, "You being sneaky. You doing sneaky things." Anna's lead doctor pulled that particular doctor to the side and questioned him. He confessed he was billing patients for procedures they didn't have done. He planned on correcting the problem right away. It happens more often than you know.

People ask me all the time how Anna is doing. I tell them that if I wrote about all the drama that happens to Anna, I would never finish the book. Since writing this book, I have put two more nurses in prison. The one common thread with the bad nurses was the lamb. They sensed the lamb had "spiritual powers" and needed to distance themselves from it.

One was a molester who Nurse Miriam saw on television during a raid on a personal-care home. This nurse managed to elude the system somehow and assigned as Anna's home health nurse. Miriam called the police when she tried to fondle Anna when Miriam went to kitchen to fix lunch. The home care nurse threw the lamb in a bag and tossed the bag in a closet right before she molested Anna. They arrested her on the spot.

The second nurse was a drug addict. She carefully opened Anna's seizure capsules and replaced the medicine with flour. Anna started having seizures uncontrollably. Once at the hospital, they ran a test on her medicine and found the flour. They called the nurse in and her random drug test showed Anna's seizure medicine in her system. She was charged with theft, attempted murder, and drug possession once they raided her home. This nurse also took the lamb and threw it in the garage.

After all the trials and tribulations, Anna has learned to live again. Currently she has her own apartment and Miriam is still one of her nurses. Anna has physical therapy three times a week, with the best physical therapist, in my opinion. Anna's health is a roller coaster. She goes from cooking all her meals herself and walking to the train station to bedridden in intense pain for days. Like Jean, Anna is learning to love herself again.

Anna has also been in contact with her birth family and her siblings. She went to a family reunion and everyone welcomed her with open arms. They were so glad to be reconnected with her, but not as glad as Anna was. Many of her unanswered questions about Audrey were finally answered. I saw a picture of Anna with her aunt. I had never seen Anna smile like that. She finally was home with her real family who loved her. That was all Anna ever dreamed.

Now that you have read this book, you may wonder how can one person endure all this pain and strife and still have the will to go on. I can attribute that to Anna's faith. It never wavered, even when she wanted to give up and thought God had given up on her. She lived to fight another day. My faith was slowly renewed, seeing how strong Anna was. During the darkest hours, my mind flashed to a tiny mustard seed. "That is all the faith you need." I was reminded.

On one particular night, I called my mom almost in tears from the day's events. I was at a loss on how to proceed with Anna and her crazy family. I was starting to lose sleep. "Robin," she said. "When things go bad like this, give it to God and go to bed. He's going to be up anyway." She said it so matter-of-factly, I giggled. Her words brought me comfort. That night I gave it God and had the best night sleep I had in months. I encourage all believers to do the same. Others, try writing your problems in a journal and leaving them there while you sleep.

Faith is believing things will get better. "It's the unseen hand of God," like my daddy says. There will be points in time when you think about giving up. You want to quit and say forget it. Take a minute to stop and think of the reasons why you held on for so long. Help is on the way.

> **Go confidently in the direction of your dreams.**
> **Live the life you've imagined.**
> **—Henry David Thoreau**

Appendix

Dear family members, caregivers, medical power of attorneys, patient advocates, and friends,

The only time I have ever spent in the hospital was when I was born. I am fortunate enough to have maintained a healthy life and had relatively healthy parents, who never needed an extended hospital stay. So I was totally blindsided by the unprofessionalism running rampant in the medical field. Don't get me wrong, there are plenty of good nurses and doctors out there as you read in the book. Don't assume that everyone who takes care of your loved ones has their best interest at heart. Also don't assume everyone takes their job seriously and gives 100 percent. Remember, hurt people hurt people. It's always good to be on the side of caution than regret.

Most loved ones have daily or weekly visitors to check in on them, and they ask the same questions: How are you feeling? Do you need anything? Are you OK? The one-word responses they may possibly give don't provide any insight on what is going on in your absence. I know you may think that you don't have time, but you have to make time. Even if it's a ten-minute phone call when you physically can't be there. Love that person. Fight for them. You may be in their position one day and will want someone to fight for you. Remember karma.

Top Five Questions You *Should* Ask Your Loved One *Daily*.

1. Do you feel safe?
2. Did you get your meds on time?

3. Did you have any issues with any of the nurses or doctors today?
4. Did you sign any paperwork today? (If so, find out what it was and get a copy.)
5. Did anyone come in your room that you didn't recognize?

Make your voice heard. As you know from the book, some people are equal-opportunity offenders. You may find that other patients have the same complaints and may be too scared to say anything for fear of retaliation. You have to speak up, not only for your loved ones, but also for those who don't have anyone fighting for them.

Top Five Things to Do If Your Loved One Has a Complaint

1. If the complaint is with a nurse, ask to speak to the head of the nurses' department. Express your concern for not only your loved one but also for the other patients the nurse deals with. If you feel there may be some backlash, request another nurse to be assigned to your loved one.
2. If the nurse's violations are serious like being incompetent (giving wrong meds) neglect (making patient wait hours for meds) or unprofessionalism, ask the head of the nurses department to file a complaint with the State Nurses Registry.

   Find more information about your state registry look here
   http://www.ncdhhs.gov/dhsr/hcpr/links.html

   Family members can also file the complaint. The Nurses Registry takes all complaints seriously. So make sure you have specific details to provide in the complaint. Which you will have already written down on your calendar. (See list that follows.)

3. If the complaint is with a doctor, ask to speak to the head doctor. Get a second opinion. Just because a doctor recommends surgery, your loved one doesn't have to get the surgery. Ask the doctor for other alternatives to fix the medical issue. Doctors get money for each surgery they perform whether it was necessary or not. Do some legwork and look up the surgery they want to perform, and make sure it will solve the medical problem. Also, look for alternatives you can suggest they try.

4. The hospital social worker is also a good resource when you have a hospital complaint. They also organize medical services (therapy, dialysis, etc.) when your loved ones leaves the hospital.

5. If you have a complaint about a doctor, hospital, or provider you can visit http://empoweredpatientcoalition.org/. This organization was created by patient advocates devoted to helping the public improve the quality and the safety of their health care.

Encourage anyone else who had a problem to complain as well. There is strength in numbers. Make sure you do a follow-up if your loved one has any complaints.

Being actively involved with your loved ones' heath is a sure way to keep the nurses and doctors in check. Once they know you actually care about your loved one and are willing to fight for them, they tend to be more helpful and will provide you with the best care they can. Patients who don't have frequent visitors can sometimes be neglected or even abused.

Here is A Guide to Speaking Up When You Are Dissatisfied with A Health Care Experience http://www.assertivepatient.org/how.html

Top Five Things You Should Do Either in Person or Over the Phone

1. Ask the nurses to keep you posted of any changes in your loved ones' health (fevers, bruises, coughs, aches and pains not associated with the original illness, etc.). Sometimes these changes can be a result of neglect or from some other health issue they hadn't diagnosed. If you visit with them, do your own body check. Check for bruises or other abnormalities and report your findings to the nurse.

2. Find out the names of the nurses that are taking care of your loved ones. There are usually two nurses depending on the hospital shifts. Make sure you get to know each nurse. You can tell a lot from a person with a five-minute conversation.

3. Get a calendar. Jot down any information you get about their health, surgeries, medicines they are taking. You have a paper trail when you need to discuss any information concerning their condition or any changes in their health. It will also help if you need to file a complaint.

4. If they have an extended stay in the hospital or have been confined to a bed, make sure they are being turned daily. Bedsores can develop quickly and are often difficult to treat. They may often take months to heal with the medicine the doctors provide. If your loved one does get a bed sore, I suggest looking up natural remedies to help with them.

5. Make sure your loved ones are getting the correct medicine and the right dosages. Ask your loved ones to be aware of what medicines they are taking and when they are supposed to get it. Question any new medicine they are getting. Make sure it is compatible with the meds they are currently taking. Also, find out if there are any drugs your loved one cannot have because of allergic reactions or

health conditions. People with compromised livers cannot have Tylenol.

Visit http://www.patientadvocate.org/ The Patient Advocate Foundation's Patient Services provides patients with arbitration, mediation, and negotiation to settle issues with access to care, medical debt, and job retention related to their illness.

Last Two Important Things You Should Know

1. If your loved one dies in the hospital, get an autopsy, even if you believe you know the cause of death. They may have been given the wrong medicine and it stopped their heart. I have heard stories about that. Make sure the hospital doesn't use their own medical examiner. If the staff's incompetency was the cause of their death, they may try to cover it up to prevent being sued. Tell them you want another hospital to complete the autopsy.

   Here is an article that is a part of an ongoing investigation with this practice. This website has won a Pulitzer Prize for its investigation journalism. http://www.propublica.org/article/without-autopsies-hospitals-bury-their-mistakes

2. If your loved ones require home health care, get references from the nurses who come to the house. Call the family members of their previous client and ask questions. Ask if they came to work on time and why do they not work for them anymore. Treat them like you would if you were interviewing someone who was going to take care of your baby while you went to work. Sick people can be as helpless as babies and need someone who can be compassionate. Just don't trust the agency's word that the nurse they sent is

good. Ask the agency if the nurse has any complaints with the nursing registry.

Find out what nursing home problems are in your state: http://projects.propublica.org/nursing-homes/

Questions to ask when selecting the right home care provider: http://www.nahc.org/consumer-information/right-home-care-provider/

Some of these tips are from my experiences with Anna in the hospital. The rest were from doctors who have witnessed hospitals covering up accidental deaths and not reprimanding bad nurses, doctors, and other medical staff. Everyone should be held accountable. No one is above the law.

This letter is no way saying every single nurse and doctor are shady and out to harm your loved one. As I said before, I have met some outstanding people in the medical field. These tips are to make sure your loved one has the best possible care while they are in the hospital.

Kindness is the key. Fighting for your loved one doesn't require actual fights and arguments. Find a nurse or doctor you can confide in. Make them your ally. Once you do, they will also be willing to fight for your loved one as well.

I wish you the best. Remember dreams can come true and karma has no expiration date.

Robin Turner

Anna's letter to the judge

To whom it may Concern,

I need to tell my story. I would like for this to be read out loud in the court room please.

I was adopted by the Calloways when I was 5 years old. When I was in the 7th grade, Alisha found out our father and uncles had been sexually abusing me for years. She took me to the hospital twice to get treated because the beatings and rapes were brutal. The first time she told me to tell the hospital that a boy at school did it so "daddy" would not get in trouble. The second time I had an STD. She told me to blame the same boy from school. Alisha never told anyone. Not the nurses, not CPS, no one. Alisha never provided me help. She left me there to be abused for years. I never heard from her again.

When both my children died, she was not there either. She didn't call or try to reach out to me to offer any help or condolences. When I was diagnosed with cancer, she was not there either.

When our father finally went to court late last year for all the abuse and she was there in court. She found out I was sick with cancer again and had weeks to live, she decided to come visit me. I was a little happy at first because I missed my sister, but then she changed.

She wanted to take me to Germany to be with her and her husband. I didn't want to go. First I was sick in a Cancer Center. I had been in the hospital for months. She told the doctors she knew what was best for me. Second, I have someone taking care of me. The nurses told her several times. I can only assume she felt guilty about everything that had happened to me all those years ago.

I told her I didn't want to go and she quickly got upset and hostile. Nurses Vivian and Nurse Miriam had to get hospital security to escort her out of my room and off the premises on several occasions because of her temper. It reminded me of how my dad would speak to me right before he raped me. Even Dr. Calabretta had to speak to her about her tone in the hospital.

Then she started calling my phone. One day, the nurse told me she called 45 times in a row wanting to talk to me. I ended up getting a restraining order against her, but she is very aggressive like our father. That didn't stop her. It made her mad. She was asked not to come up to the hospital because of the restraining order and I told her I didn't want her in my life. She still didn't listen and spent almost a week in jail on harassment charges.

That didn't stop her either. She kept coming back to the hospital. The nurses and doctor told her that I died so she would leave me alone. They did it under the instructions of my Power of Attorney. They all felt it was the only way to get her to leave me alone. As a matter of fact, my step mother was in court on a harassment charge against me when she found out I had "died". I heard she cried. I know the tears were fake. She was upset because she didn't get to cash in on the fake life insurance policy she had on me.

Every time I try to get better, some family member comes and pushes me further back from recovery. I have back-to-back seizures when I know they are near me. The entire Calloway family has bullied me all my life. I have been sexually, mentally, physically and verbally abused and tortured by almost everyone in the family since I was 5 years old. Even my so-called stepmother, Janice Calloway came up to the hospital with a syringe full of bleach to kill me.

I have a restraining order against her as well. I know she is sitting in the court room. I sat for months in the hospital shaking and nervous because I thought at any time she or other family members would come in the room. Alisha thinks she knows what is best for me. The others wanted to kill me. I think Alisha does too. Why would anyone want to take a current cancer patient on a 24 hour plane ride out of the country with no health insurance? I would have died before the plane landed.

Just recently she called me 13 times in a row. The nurse finally told her she had to wrong number.

I do not want any dealings with Alisha. I don't want to be found. I don't want or need her help. I would like for the court to help put in place something for my safety. I have to have nurses 24 hours a day watching me because these people are like hunting dogs. They will keep going until they track me down. Then they will keep bothering me. Alisha even called every hospital in Atlanta area looking for me.

I would like if Alisha Jones or Janice Calloway or any other family member tries to contact me, call me, bother me, or harass me; they will face some sort of harsh prosecution. My father and sister are both serving 10-25 years plus life in prison for harassing me. Alisha is their blood. She is just like them.

My body cannot take the stress. I am recovering from cancer. I have someone taking care of me and I don't want Alisha in my life. I do not need anyone in my life has their own agenda and wants to stress me out.

Anna Calloway

Thank You's (in alphabetical order)

I want to give special thanks to a few people who didn't make it in the book but were integral in helping with Anna's recovery. Some came in after the drama and remained true to keeping Anna safe. Some were there from the beginning and helped maintain sanity throughout this process.

Brenda and John—What can I say? I thank God for you two every day. Thanks for helping us avoid plenty of heartache. You always stayed one step ahead and were able to guide me in the right direction with Anna and my other "patients." Thanks for your healing hands and words of wisdom. Also, thanks for pushing me to write this book.

Bri—Thank you for helping Anna with your visits and phone calls. You saved the day when you got her a new phone. Anna appreciated how sweet you were to her. You never changed. I appreciate you and your constant concern about how she is doing.

Cindy—Who is no longer with us. Thank you for caring about Anna and being an awesome nurse. I wish I had gotten a chance to meet you. She still has the back pillow you bought for her.

Jason—Thanks for being my sounding board. You offered great suggestions, which ultimately helped with the direction of the book. You told me to write from my heart and I did. Your encouragement and support will not soon be forgotten. You are a wonderful friend.

Mary—Oh Mary. My private investigator. You made sure nobody messed with Anna while she stayed with you. You kept me up to date with the events in the house. Thanks for all the times you drove Anna to the hospital and purchased things for her with your own money. Ummmmm . . . I wish you and the "La's" continued success.

My parents—What can I say. Thank you for the prayers. You taught me to help others who were less fortunate. Thanks for the Bible passages. Mommy, I never forgot from a long time ago when you said, "laugh or bust out crying." I remembered that on those frustrating days. Daddy, you always told me to maintain professionalism. I was not always successful (as you heard from the stories), but I tried. I love you both for choosing me.

Dr. Simms—I don't know what I would do without you. Your professionalism is amazing. Thanks for protecting Anna's well-being and safety. You came through when I needed you the most. You always managed to get us anything we needed. You never gave up on her. Look at my face. Thank you for always fighting for her and holding in your laughter when I was cutting up.

Dr. Turner—T. You know you're funny for real, right? Thanks for making Anna laugh during her therapy sessions. You are one of the few doctors Anna trusts. Also thanks for staying extra hours when we were in need of help. You went beyond your duties, and I want to thank you for that.

Whaudie—All the stories I told you were true. I was not making this up. Thanks for being my friend and listening to me ramble on about Anna and her crazy family. You always managed to find a way to make me laugh during this crazy time. I appreciate you.

Book Club Questions

1. The author didn't provide what Anna's race or nationality was. She didn't for any of the main characters in the book. There was no actual setting in the book, no city or state in where the story took place. Why do you think the author did that?

2. How was Sandy able to gain the hospital staff's trust? Why didn't they question why she didn't visit Anna?

3. If a family member raped and impregnated you, would you keep the baby? Why? If it happened to a friend of yours, what would you suggest they do?

4. It is not stated in the book, but Anna's best friend, Vickie, grew tired of Anna's health issues and neediness and ended the friendship right before Anna's family tried to kill her. Was that the best thing for her to do? If Vickie knew about the rapes, why didn't she report them herself?

5. What do you think contributed to Anna's survival? Was it Ms. Kay? Was it faith? Was it sheer determination? Was it luck?

6. How would Anna's life been different if Natalie lived? Do you think her family members would have ever gotten their karma? Remember, meeting the Logans was the reason they were all arrested.

7. What do you think Anna should do with her life now?

8. Have you or anyone you know ever had a bad experience with any doctor, dentist, podiatrist, etc.? Did you have a

procedure done that was not necessary? Did it cause more damage? What did you do? How did it change you?

9. Which character in the book could you relate to the most? Which most mirrored your life or someone's life you know?

10. The author struggled with a title for the book. Do you think the title fit? Can you think of a better title?

About the Author

Robin L. Turner earned a Master's degree in Reading and Literacy. She has been an educator for almost twenty years. Robin was encouraged by her parents to get in the classroom and make a difference. Growing up in Maryland, Robin spent her childhood Saturdays in the library reading books by Paula Danziger, Beverly Cleary, and other young adult authors. Robin believes good writers are good readers. Robin enjoys the writing styles of Amy Tan and David Sedaris. She likes humor, mysteries, and satire. Her favorite writers on television work for The Daily Show, Modern Family, and The Walking Dead.

CPSIA information can be obtained at www.ICGtesting.com
Printed in the USA
BVOW05s1758170615

405070BV00002B/110/P